The truth is some...

"I know you lied to the police a...

She crossed her arms over her chest. "Prove it."

I slid my chair closer to the table. "Why are you doing this?"

"Why do you care?" Cara hissed.

"You can't get lost in the grove at night—I could see the lights of the house the whole time we were looking for you. And a walk, really? Without a coat? In that cold?"

"It's none of your business why I was out there."

"You made it my business when you refused to tell the truth! My father thinks this is all part of some Rootless conspiracy to overthrow the gentry, and he's ready to crush them. You and I are the only ones who know that he's wrong."

"We don't know he's wrong," she said. "The Rootless could be plotting a revolt for all I know. If some conspiracy gets thwarted because of this, then no harm done. In fact, that means that I've done everyone a favor and helped unmask a threat to the gentry."

"Do you even have a conscience?"

"Do you have a *brain*?" She jabbed a finger at me. "If I wasn't attacked by a Rootless or some poor person or a servant—if I was attacked by someone in the gentry—do you think I could go around announcing it to the police? To your father? Do you think anyone would believe me if I accused one of us? Like it or not, Madeline, this is how our world works, and if you know what's good for us, you'll keep your head down and your mouth shut."

Other Books You May Enjoy

Champion	Marie Lu
Control	Lydia Kang
A Countess Below Stairs	Eva Ibbotson
Crossed	Ally Condie
Gilt	Katherine Longshore
Half Bad	Sally Green
Keeping the Castle	Patrice Kindl
Legend	Marie Lu
A Mad, Wicked Folly	Sharon Biggs Waller
Matched	Ally Condie
Prodigy	Marie Lu
Reached	Ally Condie
A Song for Summer	Eva Ibbotson

BETHANY HAGEN

speak

An Imprint of Penguin Group (USA)

SPEAK
Published by the Penguin Group
Penguin Group (USA) LLC
375 Hudson Street
New York, New York 10014

USA * Canada * UK * Ireland * Australia
New Zealand * India * South Africa * China

penguin.com
A Penguin Random House Company

First published in the United States of America by Dial Books,
an imprint of Penguin Group (USA) LLC, 2013
Published by Speak, an imprint of Penguin Group (USA) LLC, 2015

THE LIBRARY OF CONGRESS HAS CATALOGED THE DIAL BOOKS EDITION AS FOLLOWS:
Hagen, Bethany.
Landry Park / by Bethany Hagen.
pages cm.
Summary: In a futuristic, fractured United States where the oppressed Rootless handle the raw nuclear material that powers the Gentry's lavish lifestyle, seventeen-year-old Madeline Landry must choose between taking over her father's vast estate or rebelling against everything she has ever known, in the name of justice.
ISBN: 978-0-8037-3948-2 (hardcover)
[1. Science fiction. 2. Social classes—Fiction. 3. Justice—Fiction.
4. Nuclear energy—Fiction.] I. Title.
PZ7.H1233Lan 2013
[Fic]—dc23 2012045144

Speak ISBN 978-0-14-242548-0

Printed in the United States of America

3 5 7 9 10 8 6 4 2

To Anthony, Christina, Matt,
and Linda, my teachers

HOW WE GOT HERE

Two hundred years ago, America found itself at a crossroads. With sickness and famine came economic turmoil, and with economic turmoil came the looming threat from across the Pacific—China and her allies. The rich and the poor temporarily forgot their fight with each other and united to defend themselves. They failed.

The West Coast and all the land west of the Rockies fell to the Easterners, though the Americans were able to stop their advance in the mountains. Peace was restored, but a wary peace. America's arsenal of weapons was surrendered and destroyed, her access to most of the world's oil completely cut off. Fortunately, a forward-thinking scientist named Jacob Landry introduced the Cherenkov lantern that very year, which no less than changed the world.

In the coming years, Jacob Landry emerged as the voice of reason and stability, promising a new way of life whereby the wealthy could protect their own and gently spur the underclass into productivity. And then there was war. Rather than North against the South, it was each city against itself, each state against itself, all led by the Uprisen against the hastily cobbled

1

together but fierce resistance. After two years of destructive and bitter warfare, the Uprisen were victorious. The boundaries of race and gender and religion fell away as class became the most important delineator in society.

ONE

When I woke in the morning, it was spring. Spring came like that now, like a thief tiptoeing through the frost, saving its first warm breaths for early May mornings.

I'd fallen asleep under my silk canopy, my fingers wedged inside *The Once and Future King*, a dim blue lantern still unhooded beside my bed. Elinor, my lady's maid, came in to open the curtains and lay out my clothes.

"Good morning, Miss Madeline," she said.

"Good morning." My dreams had been wistful and restless and filled with the faraway hopes of people long since dead and returned to dust. I stood and walked to the window, where I could see the stark branches of the trees weeping with melting ice.

"Shall I prepare the ivory lace for the debut tomorrow night?" Elinor asked. "Your mother says you must dress to make a match."

She would. It was always about marriage with her. It was always about marriage with all the mothers; it was the gentry way. As late as last year, I'd been allowed to beg off dances and dinners, but since I'd turned seventeen last February my mother had stopped letting me neglect my social obligations. "The ivory will be fine, Elinor. Thank you."

After Elinor had buttoned up my day dress—a flowing gown the blue of glacial ice—I took my book downstairs to find a quiet place to finish it and then practice my speech to Father. I planned to avoid the morning room, where my mother was hosting a breakfast tea for her friends, but when I heard my name as I passed the doorway, I couldn't help stopping to listen.

"Does Madeline know?" a woman asked.

"Please," said a scornful voice that I recognized as belonging to Addison Westoff, one of the richest women in the city and my mother's childhood friend. "Why would any of our children care about scandals old enough to be in a museum?"

"But is it true?" the first woman asked. "Christine Dana is coming back to Kansas City?"

"What does it matter?" Addison asked. "Even if she is, she's a harmless widow. Olivia has done the one thing Christine could never do and that's give the Landry line an heir."

"Madeline," I heard someone whisper and then a low chuckle. My cheeks burned.

I crept away from the door and continued down the hall. Maybe I'd take a walk outside. The cold air would be bracing, and I would be well away from the gossiping women.

I traded my slippers for boots and slipped on my woolen coat. My steps echoed through the empty ballroom as I made my way to the windowed doors that led out to the patio and the grounds.

I crunched through the snow into the rose garden, where gardeners were wheeling out the solar-powered heaters to speed the melting that was already under way. Father was talking to one of them about laying a fresh layer of crushed gravel on the path as I approached.

The gardener doffed his hat. "Good morning, miss."

"Good morning," I said. "Preparing for the growing season?"

"That I am, miss, although I'm a bit worried about what we can grow with the winters lasting longer and longer," he replied. "Our plants need to be modified to grow faster."

Father was squinting at the ceiling of clouds, rolling and leaden and promising rain, but I knew his mind was on the various farms we owned. The crops on those farms, like the roses and ferns in our garden, had evolved to grow in the weather of the twenty-first century, not in our new world of snow and ice. Every year, the yields grew smaller and smaller.

"I'll be at it now, if you'll excuse me." The gardener replaced his hat and made to leave, but then stopped and turned. "And mind your pretty gray cat, if you will. There's a big brown tom that's taken a fancy to her whenever she steps out for a walk. I wouldn't want you to have a litter of brown kittens running about, spoiling that pretty thing's pedigree."

I smiled. "I don't believe any tomcat is a match for my Morgana. You should have seen my arms the last time I tried to give her a bath."

"If you say so, Miss Landry," he said, shaking his head. He excused himself and rejoined the other gardeners.

Father put his hands behind his back and regarded me.

"Well, Madeline?"

"Well, what?"

"You come forward so intently. I assume you have something to discuss?"

"Yes, Father." It was like him, to know just what I was thinking. He usually knew what people were thinking, which was what made him such a shrewd leader among the gentry. It was also what made him such an intimidating father.

He started walking and I stayed beside him, wondering how best to bring up the subject of my education.

"Have you finished reading John Locke?" he asked.

I nodded.

"And?"

"I find his argument for the ownership of property convincing enough, but he writes that it is only an individual's labor that gives him the right to own land. What does that mean for our land? I do no labor here, yet I'm to own it."

Father ran his gloved fingers along an icy bramble bush. "If we were not here to direct the labor, this estate and all of our forests and farms would be less productive. We're adding value by applying our wisdom."

I considered this, doubtful. I didn't know many people who'd equate "applying wisdom" with pulling up stumps or plowing or herding cows from pasture to pasture in the roiling summer heat.

He spoke again. "But I agree with you that Locke's argument can only be carried so far. Next, you must read Edmund Burke. Your six times great-grandfather Jacob Landry was a keen admirer of Burke."

Father had stopped and was examining one of the bushes, where rot had taken half the branches. I couldn't wait any longer. I had to speak before I lost my nerve, before Father went inside to his study and this private moment in the slushy beauty was lost.

"Father, my history teacher told us about the time before the Last War, when America was still the United States and the West Coast still belonged to us and not to the Eastern Empire." I'd prepared my speech with an appeal to history, since Father's own justifications were usually couched in terms of historical perspective. My father talked about the Last War and the birth of the gentry like it was more central to our being than the air we breathed. To him, the Last War was more important than the American Revolution or the Civil War. Referencing it would show that I'd done my research, thought about this carefully—even if I was technically citing the period before my ancestor had led America from chaos to order.

I glanced over at Father. He continued looking over the branches.

I continued. "When men and women dated whomever they wanted, whenever they wanted, regardless of money or class. Back then, everyone had been able to attend school, and everyone had an opportunity to study at the university, to choose their own way in life. I want to go to the university," I said this last part quickly, nervous but determined. "I graduated from the academy two weeks ago, and soon it will be time for me to submit my application if I want to go. And I do want to go."

"Indeed." Father's voice held nothing—no affirmation, no condemnation.

I pushed ahead, trying to hold onto the optimism I felt this morning. "I know it's unusual for an heir to spend any length of time studying, but I want a university education and I know I would be good at it."

"Is the education you receive here not sufficient?"

The coldness in his voice was a warning, but I chose to ignore it. "You know I value everything that you teach me, but I want to learn more. I want to learn more about history and philosophy and about land and business—I know it will make me a better owner of Landry Park, when the time comes." There. He could hardly argue against something that would help the estate.

"It's not possible." He straightened and brushed the ice from his gloves. "You know the rules. Eldest children inherit, marry, and carry on the family name. Younger gentry children may attend a college and take a degree, but the eldest child has a duty to her family. And you are not only my eldest child, Madeline, you are my only child. How do you expect to pursue your studies *and* fulfill your duty to this estate?"

The estate. Always the estate. Three stories of gray stone and large windows with a tower in the middle jutting up above it all, built by my ancestors after the Last War. The Palladian mansion sat on a sprawl of wide lawns and tumbledown gardens, scented by bobbing flowers and tossed with a breeze that whipped up from the Missouri River. From the copper-roofed observatory in the tower, one could take in the entire city by day, and at night, planets and stars and galaxies far overhead.

"But I don't want to marry," I told him, trying to keep my chin from quivering. "Not yet, at least. I could marry *after* the university. I know the Landry will says the heir must be married by their twenty-first birthday, and I wouldn't be finished with my studies by then, but if you could just change the will—"

He pulled my hands into his iron grip, the leather of his gloves cool and wet on my bare fingers. "That rule is in place for a reason, Madeline. The business of family must come first. You must be settled and ready to perpetuate the family name in the flush of your youth—when you have your health and energy to ensure a viable heir."

The sounds of the melting garden filled my wounded silence until he finally spoke again. "I didn't want to marry at your age either. But we have an obligation to the family and to the land. I married to help the estate, and so will you."

I ducked my head so that he wouldn't see my eyes shining with tears. I needed to be strong. Stoic. But despite my determination, a tear slipped down my cheek.

"I will not marry you to an ogre," he said gently. "But I will respect you by handing you the same expectations of honor and duty that my father handed to me. You are a Landry, Madeline. It's our obligation to uphold the standards of the gentry, to light the way as an example for our peers. Don't you remember our ancestor's words?"

How could I forget? They echoed down through history.

Order, elegance, prosperity.

The three ideals that governed our world.

"But wouldn't I be able to be ordered, elegant, and prosperous with a degree?"

He shook his head. "You're an heir, not a scholar."

I let go of a breath I hadn't known I'd been holding and tried to gather my composure.

But before I could say anything more, Father gave my hands a squeeze and left me standing in the frozen garden.

TWO

Wilder House was smaller than Landry Park, a simple brick affair with a courtyard in the middle and a modest grove of trees out back. The interior was clean and well-appointed—full of shining chandeliers and antique furniture, smelling of beeswax and lemon—but slightly cramped. The ballroom seethed with people, jostling one another for space, the older ladies fighting one another for the wooden-backed chairs that lined the room.

Twinkling lights glimmered in every corner, all powered by the small, silent nuclear charge in the basement. In addition to the nuclear electric lights, candles flickered in candelabras and chandeliers and on the tables, long white tapers in gleaming silver candlesticks. They were quite lovely, even if they did increase the risk of singed gowns in such a crowded room.

We were here for Marianne Wilder's debut, the ball that would ordain her entrance into the world of courtship and marriage, and yet another opportunity for gentry girls and boys to be put on display for one another. Another night wasted.

Jamie might be here, I comforted myself.

Jamie Campbell-Smith was one of the people who knew me

best in the world—a very distant cousin, brought over from England by my uncle Arthur Lawrence, who was sponsoring his education as a doctor. Since Jamie's family was middle class and without land, he would probably never marry within the gentry, even with his connection to the Lawrences.

Of course, there was another reason he'd never marry here: a young man back home, but only I knew about that.

I plucked at the skirt of my bisque-colored dress. It was silk like all of my gowns—like all of my mother's. Silk, along with plum wine, opium, and jade, were near to impossible to get from the Eastern Empire, since trading was practically nonexistent. But for a steep price, we wealthy could wriggle around these restrictions.

Mother sidled by, cradling a glass of champagne. "Smile, Madeline. You look so sullen just standing there."

"I'm waiting for Jamie." It wasn't entirely true—what I really wanted was to avoid the callow blandishments of the Lawrence boys, who were constantly sniffing around Landry Park, as if it was a dinner about to be served. But it wasn't entirely untrue either. Jamie was kind and genuine, which made him worth about ten of the gentry boys here tonight.

Not for the first time, Mother raised her eyebrows at the mention of his name. "You know you can't marry him, Madeline. Not as poor as he is. Landry Park needs money and lots of it."

"I don't want to marry him!" I protested too loudly. A group of men nearby turned in my direction. I lowered my voice. "We're just friends." And Jamie wasn't interested in marriage anyway. At least, not with me or any other girl.

Besides, we were related. With a small group like the gentry it was difficult to avoid *some* degree of intermarriage, but I could never regard Jamie as anything more than family.

Mother nodded. "Good. We do *not* need any rumors of marriage surrounding you when David Dana arrives."

"David who?" I asked.

"Christine Dana's son," Mother said, sipping her drink. "His father left him millions of dollars after his death, but their estate in Georgia reverted back to David's cousin. So he's rich *and* without any land to speak of. Plus, he's taking an officer's commission in a few months." Her eyes sparkled.

Another gentry bachelor. Wonderful.

"We need to meet him before anybody else," she continued, and I forced myself to pay attention. "Especially with Addison on the prowl. She wants David for her daughter, Cara, and mark my words, she'll do whatever it takes. She would not hesitate for a second to invent a romance between you and your cousin Jamie."

I sighed, but she didn't hear, since she was already waving and moving toward some of her friends, her small frame disappearing in the crush of people.

The Wilders may have had a small ballroom, but it certainly met the gentry standards for quality and opulence.

The floor and artwork had been flown in from a palace in France two hundred years ago, right after the Last War when the gentry and their estates were formed. All the Kansas City families were here, and the women wore their most splendid gowns—all low-cut bodices and seed pearls and filmy skirts that released the smell of jasmine when they moved.

Thankfully, Jane Osbourne arrived and came to stand beside me, offering a smile but no idle conversation. Jane was an eldest daughter, and therefore an heir like myself, and was well read and sensible and just as quietly reluctant to participate in the marketplace of privileged marriage. We frequently found ourselves together in these types of situations—wallflower heiresses. We shared a plate of strawberries in companionable silence while the other guests danced and chatted around us.

A group of laughing people came in from the patio outside. I craned my neck to try to see if Jamie was one of them but, at that moment, a booming voice announced Marianne's entry. Two heralds in green costumed livery blew into gleaming trumpets as the doors to the ballroom opened.

Preceded by her parents, Marianne Wilder and Mark Everly walked arm in arm, the skirt of her kelly green gown brushing against his legs. Her dark skin was striking against his white tuxedo, her long braids swept up behind a tiara set with emeralds. She was followed by another couple, the debut equivalent of a maid of honor and a best man, both of whom looked distinctly unhappy to be paired together.

Usually the rest of the family followed the debutante and her escort into the ballroom, but only Marianne's parents and grandparents trailed beaming behind her. Her older brother, Philip, was absent. I could hear a few disappointed girls murmuring behind me. Though the Wilder estate wasn't large, the family owned several lucrative orchards out west, and Philip still hadn't found a wife. For most of the single girls in the room, the math was easy.

"Let all men and women find a partner for the first dance!" a voice announced. People scrambled around—shuffling boys, giggling girls, hopeful young men and women trying to find the dance partner who would spark their own debuts—or if they had debuted already and not gotten engaged, hoping to win a proposal by the end of the ball. Jane—very pretty and too polite to refuse—was snatched up by one of the Lyons boys right away.

"Looking for a partner?" a gentle voice said next to me.

"Jamie!" I breathed a sigh of relief.

Smiling, he led me out onto the floor, where we lined up in rows facing one another. He bowed—glossy black curls bobbing—I curtsied, and we touched hands. I had to reach upward because he was so tall.

"See, how could you think of leaving all this fun behind?" Jamie said as we circled each other. "There is no dancing at the university. I should know."

"Dancing is only as fun as your partner," I pointed out as we stepped forward in the line, turned, and traded partners. My new partner was short, acne-riddled, and wasted no time in trying to squeeze my bottom when he slid his arm around my waist. He had terrible breath.

When I got back to Jamie, he conceded my point. "Maybe you *would* be happier cloistered in the university libraries. But how could you live without Landry Park? Even for just a few years?"

I didn't respond right away. To my parents, I'd offered up a defiant answer, but Father could see through my uncertainty, and I knew Jamie would, too. "I ask myself that question every day," I finally said.

"And?"

"Every day the answer is different."

The music ended, and I curtsied again. He offered an arm to lead me off the floor while the band struck up a reel, and as he did, a terrible noise, sharp and shrill like a rabbit about to be slaughtered, came through the open patio doors, piercing through the merry strings of the violins. The band stopped and people looked around, as if expecting the screamer to materialize underneath the chandelier or by the buffet.

"What was that?" I asked Jamie. "It sounded like a girl."

"Maybe it was an animal," he said.

But then there was another scream.

The room rippled in panic. People began to yell and shove

their way to the doors, and Arthur Lawrence rumbled for someone to call the police. I saw my father push his way outside, calling for a lantern. Marianne Wilder's father and our neighbor William Glaize followed him. Jamie gave me a look and made for the doors.

"I'm coming, too," I insisted.

A small set of doors opened onto a flagged patio. Our breath came out in steamy clouds in the chill air, and I immediately regretted not getting my pelisse from the coatroom before I came outside. Jamie shifted his weight from foot to foot as the cold damp from the stones crept through the thin cardboard on the bottom of his shoes. Seeing my shivers, he shrugged off his jacket and handed it to me.

"It came from the grove," Mr. Wilder said. His butler scurried out with two Cherenkov lanterns that emitted a vivid blue light. Leaded glass allowed the glow of the radioactive material to shine out steadily, while the rest of the water-filled case was made of a lightweight polymer that blocked radiation, which made the lantern completely safe to handle. It was these Cherenkov lanterns that built the Landry fortune over two centuries ago.

Father took a light and we walked toward the grove, the bobbing blue lights from the lanterns making swinging arcs along the path.

"It could just be an animal," Mr. Wilder suggested. "It must be. Nothing like this has ever happened on our property."

"Things are changing," Father said brusquely.

Mr. Glaize nodded. "I heard they've been having trouble with the Rootless in St. Louis. My cousin found his entire stable of horses dead the other week. Almost hundreds of thousands of gentry dollars, lost in a single day."

"But surely there is no evidence that the Rootless did that," Mr. Wilder huffed, trying to keep up with my father's long strides. "The horses could have taken ill?"

"And in Dallas, that terrible penthouse fire," Mr. Glaize added. "The old man who lived there almost lost his life. As it is, his hands are so badly burned that he'll never be able to feed himself again."

Father said nothing, but the tense set of his shoulders spoke volumes. Based on the amount of time he'd spent on his wall screen in his study recently, I guessed that none of this was news to him. He'd always been extremely attentive to the actions of the Rootless. As the caste in charge of handling the nuclear material that powered our lives, they were both vital to the gentry way of life and an ever-present liability.

The grove spanned no more than a half-acre, and the thick carpet of pine needles kept the undergrowth to a minimum. "It should be easy to find someone, if there's anyone out here." Father held his lantern high, the blue light turning his red hair purple. "Madeline, stay with me. Gentleman, shall we spread out?"

My slippers crunched on the frosted needles. A small brook ran midway through the grove, and I could hear its trickling ebullience from several yards away. Jamie and my father were both walking too quickly for me to keep pace easily. "Wait!" I said, but a high wind whistling through the trees and the noise of the stream drowned me out.

I suddenly felt uncomfortable in the dark, even with the lanterns bobbing in the distance and the Wilder House lit up like a festival behind me. I started jogging and then running to catch up, paying no attention to where I put my feet, just looking ahead to Father's bluish figure. My breath came in cloudy pants, and a sharp pain stitched itself in my side. Just before I reached the stream, my foot caught a tree root, black and invisible, and I fell hard. What little breath I had left was knocked from my chest.

I looked up, hoping that the men had heard me, but instead I saw a girl in a ball gown, her green eyes gleaming in the frozen darkness.

THREE

She was crouched on the ground behind a tree, as if she had been hiding. Her pink gown was ripped up to the thigh, exposing a long leg and a very swollen ankle. Blood clustered around her nose and lips, a dried streak trailing from the corner of her mouth down to her neck, and her hair was yanked and tangled out of its elaborate twist.

As I got closer, I could see that it was Addison's daughter, Cara Westoff, tormentor of my childhood and the most sought-after girl in Kansas City.

"Oh my God," I said when I could breathe again. "Are you okay?"

"Do I look okay?" she snapped.

"You look like you spent the night in a gibbet cage," I told her, and tried to brush a clump of hair away from a scrape on her cheek. She slapped my hand away. If we had been in any other situation, I would have walked away.

Cara and I were born days apart from each other to mothers who were best friends and rivals. We were both firstborn children and both destined to be heirs. But while Cara was born blond and plump and cooing, I was born red-faced and scrawny and stone-eyed. Cara was beautiful and vibrant, while I was quiet and racked with frequent bouts of the mysterious illness that plagued all the Landrys as children. She had everyone—parents, servants, strangers—convinced that she was the sweetest girl ever to twirl on the earth, and maybe even I believed it for a time.

However, it soon became clear she had a wild streak. As children, our games of hide-and-seek sometimes turned into vicious hunts that ended with hair pulling and Indian burns. She took my desserts at dinner and kicked my legs under the table. And any time I dared protest, she'd play sweet-voiced and contrite, probing whatever new bruise or scratch she'd left with long fingers.

"See? No harm done," she'd say, eyes flashing from my face to the corners of the room and back again.

When she was nine, she dared a servant boy to kiss her on the mouth and then watched without emotion when the boy and his family were removed to a distant farm. When she was twelve, she stole a pouch of her father's opium and smoked an entire pipe of the stuff, falling asleep right at the dinner table, then blaming her torpor on a late night spent studying. And the year after that—the year I became sickest of all—she tried to run away from home, but was caught after driving the family car into a ditch. She told her father that I'd convinced her to do it, had made her steal the car to come fetch me so that we could run away together.

I'll never forget Harry Westoff's face—ruddy and furious—looming over my sickbed like a malevolent moon.

"Daddy," Cara had said, her voice lilting up in that syrupy-sweet tone. "I'm sure Madeline didn't mean any harm." Even through my fever-racked haze, I could see her eyes darting around, just as they had when she tried to convince me that she hadn't hurt me.

"I'm sure it's a misunderstanding, Harry," Father said, his hand heavy on my burning forehead. "At any rate, I will not have you accosting my daughter while she's sick."

Father's word, as always, was law for other gentry. Harry glared at me before sweeping out of the room. Cara stayed to brush her lips against my cheek and whisper in my ear.

"See? No harm done."

We talked less after that. I remained housebound and frail for almost a year, and by the time we started the academy at fourteen, she'd quickly ascended the pyramid of popularity while my reserved nature and frequent absences kept me in relative obscurity. She chose dresses; I chose books.

We stopped writing to each other on our sleek white tablets, and even our mothers—the sole impetus for our infant companionship—stopped trying to bring us together.

As I stood next to Cara, our past flitting through my mind, I realized that this was the closest we'd been to each other in years. And she'd slapped me, as if I needed another reminder that we weren't friends—or even *friendly*—anymore.

"I'll go get my father," I told her. "My cousin Jamie is here, too. He can look at your ankle." The words came out softer than I expected; I realized that I did want to help, no matter how she'd treated me before. She looked so brittle and so uncertain with her shredded dress and bruised skin.

"No!" she said. "Just—just help me up and get me back to the house. No one needs to know I was out here."

"Cara, they're turning the house upside down to find out who screamed. How do you plan on blending in with blood on your face and an injured ankle?"

"I don't know! But they can't find me like this, they'll think—"

I never found out what she was worried they'd think because Father and Jamie finally noticed that I wasn't with them anymore. With a shout to the others, they came straight over to us, Jamie jogging and my father walking in long, brisk strides a few yards behind him, their lanterns casting strange shadows over Cara's face.

Jamie wasted no time in kneeling on the frozen needles and raising a hand to Cara's battered face. "May I?" he asked. She looked like she wanted to say no, but my father was standing next to her, his face cold and sharp, and Mr. Wilder and Mr. Glaize were approaching, so she simply rolled her eyes.

"Might as well," she said.

"Cara Westoff!" Mr. Wilder sputtered, his words labored from his hurry over to us. "What in the name of heaven are you doing out here?"

Cara tilted her head up to him. In the light, I could see the blood on her face more clearly, and bruises, too, running along her throat like a necklace. "I got lost." Her voice was surly, proud. Pure Cara. "And I don't need any help, thanks."

Father pressed his lips together, examining her with steel eyes. "You've been assaulted, Miss Westoff."

Mr. Wilder choked at the word *assaulted*, and Mr. Glaize started roaming the area around us, as if he expected the assailant to be skulking behind the nearby pines. I myself felt a twinge of fear. If someone could catch Cara, as athletic and tall as she was, by surprise, it wouldn't take much for them to overpower me, short and thin and with muscles just strong enough to pull a book from the shelf.

"We'll take it from here," Father said when Cara remained silent. "Did you see your assailant? Hear anything important?"

"Is he nearby?" Mr. Glaize asked, still tramping around the clearing. "Do you know if he fled?"

"Was he at the debut?" Mr. Wilder asked in a trembling voice. "Not a guest, surely, but maybe as a servant?"

Cara gave me a fierce glare, as if somehow this was my fault, but she didn't answer.

Father shook his head slightly. "I'm afraid the police will need to question you, and they'll want to do it promptly. It's best to get this taken care of quickly, for your sake and for ours."

Mr. Wilder pressed a hand against his chest, rubbing it as

if something was burning him from the inside. "Surely, Mr. Landry, we do not need to involve the police?"

"It's your property, Mr. Wilder. But a gentry girl's honor and health are at stake, and you can imagine Addison and Harry Westoff aren't going to rest until they've brought the assailant to justice. I assume you don't want to seem reticent to help the Westoffs?"

"Reticent? Of course not! Obviously, I'll do whatever it takes to help the Westoffs. But a brazen attack here at Wilder House, and on Marianne's debut night . . ."

Father ignored him and knelt in front of Cara. Jamie was still peering into her face, gently lifting her hair to probe the bruises along her jaw, but Father waved him away. "Miss Westoff, before the police get here, is there anything you'd like to tell us—about what you might have seen? Who you might have been out here with?"

Her lips parted as if she was about to speak, but she closed her mouth and shook her head. Her green eyes flicked to mine, then back to my father's.

She's hiding something, I thought, recognizing those darting eyes.

Just then, Mr. Glaize came crashing back to us, holding a battered leather satchel. Inside, one nuclear charge blinked red. Expired.

In order to be light enough to be carried and replaced easily, the charge boxes were made of a temporary polymer that only lasted for six months before they leaked radiation. It was a modified version of the same polymer that the Cherenkov lanterns were made of, except instead of casting off a small pool of light, these charges powered entire homes. And it was the job of the Rootless to remove these charges before they expired and began to leak radiation inside the houses of the gentry, and also their job to replace the expired boxes with new ones.

"A Rootless was here," Mr. Glaize said. "Maybe here to change Mr. Wilder's charges? Maybe he found Miss Westoff out here alone and took advantage?"

"It's just a bag," I pointed out. "It could have been there for weeks."

It was ridiculous how willing the gentry were to blame everything on the Rootless. Missing jewelry and mysterious pregnancies were never openly attributed to carelessness or forbidden trysts. Everything from a broken wall screen to a bad harvest could somehow be traced back to the Rootless.

Cara made a sound between a laugh and a sob. We looked at her, but she just looked down. Wetness glistened on her cheeks.

"No harm done," she whispered to herself.

I breathed in sharply. I'd heard that before.

"What was that?" Father pressed.

She looked up again, and all signs of defiance and shock where gone. "I said, I think maybe it was a Rootless," she answered. She could have been acting the part of a trapped princess, the pout and the trembling voice were all so staged. But the men leaned in closer. "I thought I saw dirty clothes and that leather bag. But it happened so fast." She buried her face in her hands. I thought I could see the glimpse of a bright green eye in between her fingers, as if gauging the reaction of her audience.

I'd seen this performance many times.

"All this talk is upsetting Miss Westoff," Jamie interjected. "Mr. Landry, may I take her back to the house? Surely, this kind of interrogation can wait until her injuries have been seen to and she's had a chance to compose herself."

Father looked around the grove, considering, and then nodded. "Madeline, go with them. Help tend to Miss Westoff, and for heaven's sake, don't let yourselves be seen. The last thing we need is an entire house full of panicked gentry."

"They will panic once they see the police," Mr. Glaize said. "It's hopeless to pretend this will stay quiet for long. If people don't figure it out tonight, gossip will certainly be circulating around the brunches and business meetings tomorrow."

Mr. Wilder looked miserable.

Father considered Mr. Glaize's words. "Perhaps you're right, Mr. Glaize. Perhaps we should explain the circumstances to the assembly and encourage their quiet cooperation with the investigation. Maybe they'll sleep more soundly knowing we already have a direction to take our inquiries."

Jamie stooped and lifted Cara into his arms. His thin frame struggled with her weight—slender as she was, she was tall and strong—but he gallantly walked toward Wilder House, the two of them silhouetted against the bright lights shining from the windows.

"Madeline, please go with them like I asked," Father said. "I want you safely inside the house until we can be certain the estate is secure."

I stepped toward the house, then stopped and turned. "Father, I don't think it was a Rootless who attacked Cara." My voice quavered a little at the end; Alexander Landry was not an easy man to disagree with.

His iron eyes turned their metal gaze to mine. "And what makes you so certain? In the midst of all the trouble the Rootless have been giving the gentry, the physical evidence that a Rootless was here in these woods, and the information Miss Westoff herself has revealed to us—"

"She hasn't revealed anything," I interrupted. "She said only that she thought she might have seen that bag. That's hardly proof, and you know how Cara can be." I couldn't explain to him the sense of responsibility I felt for Cara's testimony; I couldn't even really explain it to myself. I tried another tactic. "Why are you so eager to blame the Rootless?"

He stepped closer so that Mr. Wilder and Mr. Glaize couldn't hear. "Why are you so eager to defend them? If you knew how dangerous they've become and how ignorant and depraved their minds are, you would not be so quick to shelter them from justice. Must I remind you of your uncle Stephen?"

I paused. Stephen Landry—Father's older and only brother—had died shortly after graduating the academy. He'd been seen spending time with several rough working-class men—including some Rootless—and the rumor was that he'd gotten into some kind of trouble. They never found his body and they never tortured the truth out of the youths they arrested, but a pack of police dogs found his bloodstained jacket buried in the Rootless ghetto.

"Uncle Stephen died over twenty years ago."

"You feel the pain less keenly because you never knew him. But perhaps you'll understand now that your friend has been attacked."

I wanted to say something in reply, something to refute what he had said, but my mind stumbled under the weight of Father's gaze. So I remained silent. My best hope was that Cara would ultimately reveal whatever inscrutable reason she'd been out in the cold, without a chaperone, without a friend, without even a jacket.

FOUR

About half of the guests had stayed, talking together in clumps while servants gathered up the remains of the food and pushed brooms across the dance floor, now littered with fallen hairpins and crumbs. Some of the gentry left, fearful of another attack, but the remaining guests crowded around me as I tried to walk through.

"We saw Jamie Campbell-Smith carrying Cara. Is she all right?"

"Was she attacked?"

"Where is your father? Did he call the police?"

I just shook my head, mumbling that I didn't know. I needed to find Cara. I was the only one who knew that she wasn't being entirely truthful. Maybe I alone couldn't convince my father not to go after the Rootless, but if Cara would name her attacker—or at least confirm that he wasn't a Rootless—then Father would have to respect her word. And mine.

Mother came up to me, sliding easily between the clusters of people, keeping the train of her delicate gown from being trampled. "Darling, you must go see to Cara. Addison would, but she just learned of the whole thing after coming in from having a cigarette, and the shock made her faint. I volunteered to help her home to rest." Her voice was tender, but her eyes belied her concern. If she stayed by Addison's side, she'd be the first to hear of any news.

"Where is Cara?"

"Upstairs in the north end of the house. Miss Wilder kindly loaned her chambers."

I gave Mother a quick hug and set out for the staircase, pushing past a laughing Philip Wilder as I did. I pulled my skirts in close as I rushed down the hallway to the front foyer, hung with long banners displaying the Wilder crest: a bow and arrows set against a green forest. There I found a thin green carpet running down the shallow steps, with intricate balusters lining the sides of the banisters and a railing that gleamed with polish.

The chandelier in the foyer had been extinguished, leaving only the flickering wall sconces, which barely illuminated the stairs. The front doors were thrown open, and a small pool of lamplight from outside shone on the wooden floors.

I had started to climb up the steps when I heard the faint whisper of tires on the road. I stopped to see blue lights cresting the hill, mounted on sleek black cars. As they came closer, I could see the Cherenkov lanterns mounted on the tops of the cars. The gentry usually stored their lanterns in lead-lined cases when they weren't using them, but the police kept their Cherenkov lights unveiled at all times, letting the signature cerulean halo announce their presence.

The police cars pulled up to the house and stopped. The constables stepped out, then gestured to the back of the house while they pulled out notebooks and black bags. "They said she was attacked in the grove," one officer said, his voice carrying easily into the foyer. "Let's start there, assess the scene, and then interview the witnesses."

"When he called, Mr. Landry said it was possibly the Rootless," one said quietly.

"I wouldn't be surprised."

"Filthy beasts," a third one spat.

I flinched. It's not as if I were friendly with any of the Rootless—we'd learned in the academy that they'd inherited their lot due to inherent laziness and violent tendencies, and that mingling with them was dangerous—but the viciousness of the hatred toward them sometimes shocked me. They were people too. Human beings. And surely there was a basic level of respect that we afforded any and all human beings, no matter what caste they hailed from? And weren't we, as the gentry, supposed to be the leaders and examples for everybody else?

I stepped farther up on the staircase, wanting to watch but not be seen. Part of me wanted to run back to my father, to be there to temper his testimony, but I knew it wouldn't matter. Maybe when I was the owner of Landry Park—*if* I was ever the owner—my word would finally mean something.

I took another step, and someone spoke aloud. "Normally these debuts are terribly boring, so I make a point of arriving late, but I guess this time I missed all the excitement."

I turned to see a blond man, tuxedo-clad and completely unfamiliar, stepping into the lamplight from the shadows in the foyer. In the dark, I could tell nothing more than that he seemed about my age and had blond hair so light it looked almost translucent under the Cherenkov lights. A carefully tailored tuxedo revealed wide shoulders and a narrow waist— an athlete's body.

Had he been there this whole time watching the police? Watching me? I suddenly felt self-conscious of my hair— ruffled and slightly frizzy from the wind—and my dress, decorated with bits of leaves and pine needles from the grove. *It's dark,* I reminded myself.

Besides, who cares what a stranger skulking around the Wilder estate thinks?

He leaned against the doorframe and struck a match to light a cigarette. With the sudden flame, I caught a glimpse of sharp features and a wide mouth. Long eyelashes and eyes the same blue as the Cherenkov lights behind him.

"I almost didn't come," he said, after a long drag on his cigarette. "Really, I get bored to death at these things. But police! Drama! You people in Kansas City sure know how to throw a party."

Right there, I decided I knew his type, and we people in

Kansas City already had plenty. Rich, bored, and confident that the world hung on his every word, he thought that his disdain was somehow electrifyingly amusing to everyone around him.

"It's not funny," I snapped. "A girl was attacked. Hurt."

He cocked his head at me. "I suppose you're right. But the police said it was the Rootless—they'll find the animal soon enough, throw him in jail, and then everything will be as it was."

"It wasn't the Rootless," I said firmly. "My father and the other gentry, they just want the Rootless to be guilty." I stopped suddenly. "How long have you been here?" I asked.

"Excuse me?"

"I mean, here at the party. How long have you been here at the party?"

He shrugged. "A few minutes, I guess. Why—" His gaze sharpened. "I didn't have anything to do with that girl, if that's what you're implying."

I didn't respond.

He sighed and started digging in his coat pocket. He pulled out his tablet, pressed a few buttons, and held it out for me. From a few feet away, I could see the copy of an airplane ticket, putting his arrival time in Kansas City less than an hour ago. About the same time I heard Cara scream.

"I came straight here from the airport," he said. "Satisfied?"

"I'll be satisfied when I find out what really happened," I

informed him, although I was privately relieved that I wasn't standing alone in the near-darkness with a violent man.

We stared appraisingly at each other for a moment. "What's your name?" he finally asked.

I needed to be upstairs with Cara, not wasting time with a stranger in the dark. I turned to go, but he strode forward and caught my hand. I could smell tobacco and something else—something spicy and wintery. This close, I was shocked by the radioactive blueness of his eyes.

"Please," he said. "I would like to make your acquaintance."

There was a boyish earnestness to his request, as if once he decided that he wanted something, he wanted it with every atom of his being.

As I opened my mouth, a guest strode into the foyer, talking loudly into her tablet and relaying the details of the ruined party. So, instead of answering him, I abruptly withdrew my hand from his. Gentry boys and girls dated—and often did more than just that—before their debuts, but strictly speaking, both parties were expected to arrive at the marriage bed untainted and untouched, to ensure that the pedigrees remained carefully crafted and planned.

He stared at his outstretched hand for a moment and then looked back up at me with those alarming eyes. And then he smiled, a smile full of white teeth and mirth and charm. A curious pang caught in my chest, as if a hook somewhere above my navel was jerking upward, making it hard to breathe.

It was this pang—more than his question or the threat of gossip—that made me move my legs.

"Good night," I said, and climbed the stairs, my thoughts already turning back to Cara and her bruised face.

The upstairs hallway was better lit, with nuclear electric lights instead of candles, and the occasional window admitting moonlight from outside. I found Marianne's room with little trouble, but when I knocked, Jamie was already opening the door to come out.

He shook his head at me. "She needs to rest."

"The police are here. She won't be able to rest anyway."

He looked around the hallway almost guiltily. "She won't be able to wake up until morning. I gave her a couple of sedatives from the house medicine chest."

"You did what?"

"She asked me to," he said. "And she deserves to rest after all that she's been through. Thankfully, she assures me that nothing of a more prurient nature happened; she was spared that horror. Still, she needs to recover and process and sleep. The police are gentleman; they will respect that."

I felt a geyser of frustration threatening to erupt in my throat, but tried to keep my face calm. I had a lot of experience hiding my emotions, but Jamie could read me better than most.

"Madeline," he said, "why are you so preoccupied with this? Cara would never lie to the police, and the police would never go after an innocent person."

"Cara lies to her own parents constantly! And if you think our constables are so noble, then how do you explain the random arrests and releases without any charges? The beatings? The confiscation of rations?"

Jamie shook his head again, looking tired. "Those are in other cities, in the South," he replied. "I have more trust in the authorities here. Everything will work out."

"You sound like my father."

He gave me a short bow. "I'll see you tomorrow, Madeline."

I swallowed all the angry words and accusations that came to mind. Jamie was not the criminal or the liar; this was not his fault. And I couldn't deny that Cara deserved the oblivion unconsciousness would bring. But still, the frustration of being made to wait—of being forced to watch as these events unfolded in all the wrong ways—dug fiercely at me.

"Good night, Jamie," I said with a curtsy, but inside I was screaming.

FIVE

I could hear my father's voice echoing from his study, two doors down from the library. It had been three days since Cara's attack, but all I knew for sure was that she'd told the constables that it was a Rootless who'd attacked her. My father refused to tell me anything else about the case, even though I knew he'd been talking constantly to the other gentry and to the justices of the peace. Although the gentry had the privilege of governing minor disputes on their property, something as rare and barbaric as the attack of a gentry woman would have to involve the courts. But the outcome would most likely be the same. The judges and lawyers were merely gentry not fortunate enough to have been born heirs.

They would hardly be unbiased.

I closed another book—a biography of Jacob Landry—and put it on one of the several reading desks, not wanting to climb the ladder to shelve it again. The room was two stories tall, with ladders and spiral staircases leading to the upper floor where the least-used books were kept. Having such a large library was unnecessary when most people used their tablets to get information, but books—old and new—were expensive, and we Landrys had always loved showing off how we could afford expensive things. Of course, even our extensive collection was carefully curated; each book had been hand-chosen by Father or his ancestors, and there was nothing antithetical to gentry beliefs in any of the leather- or canvas-bound volumes. Even the data available for download on my tablet was limited, and I knew for a fact that Father kept tabs on what I read. It was something I had never thought to question, at least, not until a few days ago.

I followed the sound of Father's voice to the door of his study, but stayed well out of view. The wide marble floors of the ground-level hallway made for exceptional acoustics, so I could hear every variation in his pitch. He sounded uncharacteristically agitated.

"There has been an incident," he told somebody.

"Where?" The voice was male and digital sounding; Father was talking to his wall screen.

"An estate outside of Lake Chicago. A landowner was found dead. Strangled."

"And you believe it was the Rootless?"

"I do," Father replied with confidence.

"Just as you believe it was the Rootless who assaulted Cara Westoff earlier this week."

"I do."

"You know your father was equally eager to point a finger at the underclass."

I blinked at this. I'd heard before that my grandfather had been known for his sternness, but I'd never heard that he had been eager to go after the Rootless. Was that why Father was so intent on blaming the Rootless for Cara's attack?

"Lewis Landry wanted a secure life for his people. That's all I want."

I risked a look inside. Father's hands clenched and unclenched around his pen, always a sign of danger. As if aware that he was giving too much away, he set the pen down and casually rested his hands on a set of three books, thin leather volumes that were stained and battered.

"I am not suggesting that he was wrong or that you are now. It is simply interesting to see the Landry zeal once again."

"My father was nothing if not zealous," Father said, and his voice was impossible to read.

The man sighed, a heavy, theatrical sound meant to carry over the wall screen. "The Rootless have not tried to revolt once in two hundred years. What makes you think they're planning to do it now?"

"They're restless. The rash of trouble that started in the South is creeping closer to Kansas City. You know that Landry Park is the symbol of the gentry: Jacob Landry is buried here, and the Uprisen gather here to advise the government. Even the president makes an annual speech from my study. If they wanted to pick one place to start unraveling the gentry, they'll pick Landry Park."

I bit my lip at the mention of the Uprisen. After the Last War, America had retained vestiges of her governmental system—the Congress, the Supreme Court, and a President—but the real power lay in the hands of the gentry, and even more so in the shadowy circle of the Uprisen. Numbering only fifteen or twenty, they were the descendants of Jacob Landry's most loyal supporters during the Last War, and were now a quorum of powerful gentry families that influenced everything in America, from the military to Congress.

"Of course, the Landrys have always led the Uprisen and so the choice to assemble them is yours," the old man said. "If you are right, this is trouble like none we've ever seen."

Father considered this for a moment before answering. "I will wait for now, but I expect you and the others to be in touch. In the meantime, I intend to suppress any resistance in my city."

After the man signed off the screen, Father sat silently in his study. I remained near the door, pondering the idea of summoning the Uprisen from all corners of the country. I thought about the spate of rebellions cropping up in the South, of my father's fear that the Rootless were restless and losing their respect for the established order of things.

If Father was thinking about summoning the Uprisen, he must be worried indeed.

I tried to quell the wave of nervousness this realization

created. I wanted to trust Father. People like Father kept our world elegant and ordered. But the cost of elegance and order shouldn't be punishing someone for a crime they didn't commit.

And with that thought came the disorienting feeling of being unmoored, cut loose and cast off from the things and people I'd always thought of as certainties. Doubt was fractal, and no matter how many times I tried to stop it, uncertainty threaded through me in recursive loops, permeating everything.

The creak of Father's chair coupled with the rustling of paper reminded me that I needed to leave before I was discovered. I gathered the hem of my dress and crept away, hoping the soft padding of my flats would go unnoticed. I made it to the foyer and breathed a sigh of relief, ready to escape to my room and think over all I'd just heard.

But as I mounted the stairs, a large brass plaque caught my eye. Set into the wall next to a bust of Jacob Landry, it displayed a snippet of his most famous speech, delivered a few weeks after the end of the Last War. I leaned forward to read the words of the Nobel-winning scientist, even though its inscription was as familiar to me as a nightly prayer.

WE WILL CREATE ORDER, ELEGANCE, AND PROSPERITY IN OUR WORLD. HOWEVER, THERE IS ONE CLASS OF PEOPLE WE DENY THIS NEW ORDERED LIFE. THOSE WHO FOUGHT THE

MOST VICIOUSLY AGAINST US, WHO KILLED OUR WOMEN
AND CHILDREN, AND WHO DIDN'T SURRENDER AT THE END.
THEY SHALL NEVER OWN LAND OR A HOUSE, THEY SHALL
NOT BENEFIT FROM OUR SCHOOLS OR OUR DOCTORS. THEY
WILL BE LIKE BUGS ON THE GROUND, WITHOUT A FUTURE
AND FOREVER ROOTLESS. . . .

While Father contemplated suppression and control, Mother contemplated another type of combat altogether: courtship. That very next morning Mother informed us that she planned to host an emergency dinner party.

"Whatever for?" Father asked impatiently, setting down his tablet.

"Haven't you heard? Christine Dana and her son, David, arrived in town early—David himself was spotted at Marianne's debut. And to think, we haven't even introduced ourselves or invited him over! He must already be drowning in young women, and if he is to marry Madeline one day, we need to make her as visible to him as possible."

"I'm not marrying David Dana," I announced.

Father turned to me. "Don't be so certain about what the future will bring. But," he said, looking at Mother, "I'm not sure I see the necessity of a dinner party."

"Of course, it's necessary!" Mother said. "We've already missed a valuable opportunity at Marianne's debut. We need to display Landry Park and display Madeline and make a good first impression."

Father frowned, but his tablet began chiming. Excusing himself, he left to take the call.

The talk of marriage and good impressions made my head ache and my stomach churn.

But perhaps tonight wouldn't be a total loss. Addison would never miss an opportunity to flaunt her daughter in front of the city's newest bachelor, and if Cara came, I could finally talk to her. I finished my lavender tea and went back to my room, rehearsing my conversation with Cara as I walked.

Mother invited over twenty-four families for the impromptu dinner and sent Cook into the city center to purchase carloads of food and hire extra servants for the evening. I spent the day in my room being fussed over by a seamstress and watching servants and gardeners trot in and out of the house, filling every corner with fresh flowers. Smells of dinner began wafting into the upper stories by noon.

"This is ridiculous, going to all this trouble," I protested to Elinor, who shrugged as she handed the seamstress a tape measure.

"He is supposed to be very handsome, miss," she said.

"But Mother hates Christine! Why would she want to be related to her by marriage?"

"Maybe it would be some sort of victory for her. Christine may still hold some power over your father, but in the end, you will conquer her son."

I gazed out the window, where the tops of the budding apple trees rustled in a cool breeze. "Marriage is not supposed to be like war."

Elinor came over to help the seamstress pull my corset tighter. "With the gentry, everything is like war." She pulled the stays tight, leaving me breathless.

After another three hours of standing blue-lipped before the mirrors, my dress was complete enough for me to leave. "Don't forget to have Elinor do your hair," the seamstress reminded me, a needle held in the corner of her mouth. "Or your mother will have my head."

Elinor laughed. "And she'll have yours, too, Miss Madeline, frizzy waves and all."

She tied the wide silk sash of my lace gown and plucked at the princess sleeves to make them fuller. Her own slim figure was hidden under a long black dress and starched white apron, making her look older than her nineteen years. Every once in a while, a soft sigh would come from her mouth as she adjusted my dress.

"Do you think there will be lots of dancing tonight?" she asked wistfully.

"Probably," I said. "You know Mother would never miss a chance to turn a dinner into a full-blown party. And she invited practically everyone in town." I dreaded going down; with the academy finished for the year, the drinking and flirting would be much worse than usual.

Late spring and early summer traditionally marked a period of frenzied social activity for the young gentry. The heirs were free from any responsibility save for marrying, and the unluckier second and third children hadn't yet begun their toil at the university or at finding a mate who could support them. If they failed to find a good position or make a good match, they risked sinking into the middle class, albeit with a considerable amount of respectability.

Between the bottom rungs of the gentry and the upper levels of the middle class, there was some fluidity of movement, especially when large sums of cash or impoverished but ancient parcels of land were involved. Likewise, there was some movement between the middle and the working class. My own maid Elinor was born to a middle-class family, but her parents' early deaths meant that she had to seek employment at a young age. For a girl of six, it's either the textile mills or service, but luckily Elinor had been going to a school and learning to read. So her teacher found her a comfortable position, training as a lady's maid. As my lady's maid.

Money was the real determinant. With enough money, you could purchase the illusion of respectability and after a few generations, the origin of your fortune would be forgiven and your family could move within the highest circles. Without it, one slowly fell through the ranks to the working class—the people who labored in factories or farmed small chunks of land.

Only one class was a sentence for life—the Rootless.

If only Elinor and I could trade places—I'd happily hide upstairs while she danced with every bachelor in town. My fantasy evaporated the moment Elinor resumed the talk about fixing my hair. I made my escape when she went to search for the silver-handled brush and the hairpins—my mother's chosen instruments of torture.

Not for the first time, I wished I could talk to Mother seriously about going to the university, but every time I even mentioned the thought of delaying marriage, she would scold me into silence. I suppose that since she had devoted her life to marrying well and since it had paid such massive dividends, she wanted the same for me. But sometimes I felt like I could barely reach her through this wall between us, even when I wanted nothing more than to lay my head in her lap and sob in frustration that the house I loved was growing into a prison.

I wandered downstairs to wait for Mother to finish dressing. I let my fingers trail along the silk-covered wall as I made my way back to the darkened ballroom. A wall of windows and French doors overlooked a wide patio with shallow stairs leading down to a vast lawn, currently patchworked with unrelenting clumps of snow. The atomic symbol—our family crest—was rendered in platinum and inlaid into the marble of the patio. It gleamed dully in the low light.

Father stood at one of the doors looking out. The May twilight made his dark red hair look even darker, like wine or blood . . . redder than Mars, redder than the roses that grew in the English garden outside. He stood at least a head taller than me, but I knew we looked like a matched set standing so close, all gray eyes and pale skin.

"It's beautiful, isn't it?" Father said. And it was: the spring evening was blossoming into stars, while tendrils of faint orange light still reached over the lawn. To the north, the breeze tossed the slender branches of the apple and peach trees, sending storms of slush and ice crashing to the thawing ground. To the northeast, the skyline downtown lit the sky into a gentle lavender, and to the south and the west, the blazing lights of gentry estates looked like candles in the dusk.

I breathed in deeply. I could happily stand on this patio forever, surveying our land.

Mother came downstairs, slim and dark-haired like all Lawrences were, wearing a yellow silk gown embellished with crystals. It set off her deep brown eyes and dusky skin. "Are you two ready?"

Father extended an arm to me, and I took it. We both took a longing look back at the patio, with the gentle aspect fading into rapid darkness, and made our way to the front, where doors would be opened and the dinner guests admitted to Landry Park.

The band played a cheerful march while we greeted the guests. Nights like tonight were the reason the gentry relied so heavily on nuclear power. The powerful charges created enough energy for every bright light in every room and for the massive kitchen with its walk-in freezers and rows of stoves and ovens. Even when the winds turned bitter and icy, our houses stayed snug and warm. Solar power would never be able to sustain a proper winter season in a gentry house, nor would wind power. Only those little nuclear boxes could make an estate like Landry Park light up with glamour and music three to four times a week.

Strange to think that two or three hundred years ago, people still burned coal and gas for electricity, and that it took something as cataclysmic as the Eastern invasion and the ensuing treaty barring carbon emissions and oil trading to spark the new technology.

Power generation quickly became *the* delineator of class. Wind power, with its industrial nature, took root among the poor, with homemade turbines decorating every tiny house, factory, and small farm. The middle class favored solar power because it was easy to maintain, reliable, and more discreet than the noisy turbines. The nuclear charge—portable and immensely powerful—became the favorite of the rich, but the raw materials needed to produce it was rare, and by ten or fifteen years after the Last War, the gentry alone could afford to purchase the charges.

Mother and Father greeted the guests, and I was forced to stand in a dress I didn't want to wear, with flyaway hair and stray locks that blew in the chilly breeze coming from the open doors.

Addison and Cara glided into the open doors, arms linked like girlfriends walking around a ballroom, the candlelight glinting off their blond hair. They were the type of mother and daughter who were routinely mistaken for sisters. Only Cara's untamed nature set her apart; the feral streak that made her ride horses at a breakneck pace and dive naked into rivers and challenge the boys to fights, which she always won.

As they got closer, I could see that Addison's other hand gripped Cara tightly around the elbow, as if she was forcing her ahead. I thought I could just barely detect traces of greenish-purple along Cara's throat under heavy layers of makeup, and a slight limp hampered her normally confident gait.

Addison wouldn't want to miss a chance to have Cara meet David though, no matter how battered or in need of rest Cara might be. Jamie had once remarked that Addison lived through her daughter, and seeing Addison force her along like an injured horse, I couldn't help but agree. The Westoffs hardly needed the money from a marriage to the Danas, but that wouldn't make Addison's pursuit of David for Cara any less vicious. Especially when she was competing against my mother.

I felt a moment of intense kinship with Cara. We would both inherit fortunes, but those fortunes deprived of us of any agency we might have wanted in our lives, our loves, or our marriages. And I couldn't imagine being paraded in front of a potential suitor after what she had been through this week.

Despite the hidden bruises and scratches, however, Cara looked stunning, and no less haughty or regal than usual. She wore a very tight gold dress that showed off her back and arms, toned and sun-kissed, as if she existed in a world without winter

"What are you staring at?" she asked, noticing my gaze.

"Nothing." I looked away.

Addison gave my mother a warm hug and my father a kiss on the cheek that left a scarlet stain.

"Oh, Madeline!" Addison cooed. "I barely saw you there, you little imp!"

Ever since Cara and I were children, Addison had never missed a chance to point out how scrawny and short I was compared to her buxom daughter, as if we were puppies in a litter of hunting hounds. I suddenly recalled one of Jacob Landry's speeches about breeding healthy, intelligent children, children who themselves could bear more children, and thus the upper class would be able to stem the tide of the inferior and sickly children issuing from the poor. I wonder how he would feel now, knowing that almost all of the Landrys had been plagued with fevers and debilitating illnesses in their adolescence. That almost all of us had been born thin and pale, red-haired and flinty-eyed.

Addison came over to me and fingered the strap of my dress. "This gown is darling on you. It really shows off your . . ." she looked from my scant chest to my face " . . . eyes."

The dress was gray. This could be true.

"And your hair," she continued. "How *natural* of you to leave it down."

Her deconstruction of my flaws was interrupted by the guest of honor, Christine Dana, her red dress rustling as she walked in, looking like a fairy-tale queen. All that was missing was the crown. The men in the room turned, and even the footmen glanced away from the floor, their eyes tracing her slim waist and long neck. This was the first time I'd seen her, and I had to admit she was striking. Her face was all angles, with wide eyes, and hair black as onyx.

"Christine!" Addison simpered. "How wonderful to see you! I know Olivia and Alexander have missed you so much."

I was surprised Addison couldn't feel my mother's glare pierce through her skin.

"Where is David?" Cara asked casually.

Christine waved a hand. "On his way. He wanted to drive

himself and he left a little after me. I'm sure he'll be here any minute."

Father checked his watch. "Let's go inside and begin. No point in keeping everybody hungry over a teenage boy."

"Right as always, Alexander," Christine agreed. "Eighteen years, and you are still sharp as a knife."

My father gave her a fleeting smile. Mother looked livid. She let the others go ahead into the ballroom, then seized my arm. She looked me up and down, as if looking for something else to be angry about. "Why didn't you fix your hair?" she demanded.

"I—"

"Leave," she interrupted. "Go fix your hair. If you hurry, you could be back before David even arrives."

"I—"

"*Go*," she seethed, and off I went.

I never liked having Mother angry with me, but I was more than happy to leave the stuffy dinner before it began. My remarks as a younger girl had cost my father more than one business deal, and so he no longer allowed me to sit near his colleagues or potential business partners. "You think you're so clever," he'd said, after one particularly awkward meal. "But everything you say has a price. When the man next to you asks if you enjoy the orchards and you tell him that the harvest has been poor for three years running, or when you mention that half our livestock died from disease—these things all have a cost."

"I'm only telling the truth," I had protested. "You always say that the gentry are supposed to honest and dignified no matter what."

"There are matters more important than the truth. You do not want to get a reputation for being difficult, do you?"

"I don't care if people think I'm difficult."

"You will if it means you can't marry."

"But I don't want to marry," I'd objected. "I want to go to the university. Other gentry heirs have—why can't I?"

"Because they were not Landrys," he'd said simply. "Landry Park must have an heir dedicated to its survival. If you had an older brother or sister, it would be different."

That ever-wanted older sibling of mine. My whole life revolved around their absence.

I shook off these bad memories and went into my room to find Elinor, who was spreading a new bedspread across the bed. I saw a flash of silver thread—the Landry crest stitched into the silk.

I stared at the delicate cluster of the embroidered nucleus as Elinor quickly pinned up my hair. Several minutes later, I realized she had finished and was back to straightening my room, and I stood. In the mirror, I saw an antique hair comb nestled in my hair . . . the atomic symbol, wrought in platinum, diamonds sparkling from the nucleus. My house, my bed, my hair—it all belonged to my family. To my father.

I murmured a thank-you, and left my room. But something

kept me from returning downstairs. Mother would be angry, but I'd rather face a lecture tomorrow than the stifled conversation and blatant elbowing for David Dana's attention tonight.

Instead, I climbed a wide set of stairs that led to a third-story balcony. It hung above the doors to the ballroom, open for the party, and I could hear the delicate clink of china and silver, the low cultured murmur of the guests. Sweet music spilled out over the terrace and down the stairs to the garden where thousands of lights were strung.

It all looked so beautiful and effortless. It was easy to forget the days the gardeners had spent tending to the garden, the hours the servants spent hanging lights and dragging out solar heaters so that the paths would always be the perfect temperature for strolling.

I sat down on a bench and took off my uncomfortable shoes.

"Hello," someone said from behind me.

I jumped.

A young man stepped forward into the twinkling garden-lit balcony. The lights shined on his white-blond hair and sharp but pleasing face. I recognized him immediately from Marianne Wilder's foyer.

"You," I said.

He lit a cigarette. "Yes, me."

"Do you always hang around in the dark, smoking?" I asked, irritated that my hiding place had been claimed.

"Only when beautiful girls come visit me."

He emitted charm like a particle emitted light—I could feel it in the way he leaned toward me, the way he drew out his vowels in a slightly southern drawl. But I could feel something caustic underneath all that charisma, something trapped and restive.

"Would you care to dance with me later?" he asked. "I love to dance."

"Which would explain why you spend most dances hiding from everybody?"

"Maybe." A wide grin—I could see his teeth gleaming in the dark. "You are very opinionated, you know."

"And you are in my way." I indicated the doorway. "I'm leaving now."

He came closer. "Please stay."

I felt a tug somewhere in my stomach, begging me to linger on the balcony with him. *Stop being stupid,* I told myself. He wasn't different from any other guy I'd gone to the academy with.

"Despite all appearances to the contrary, I would like some company," he said. "You're the most interesting person I've met so far, and that includes the famously intimidating Alexander Landry. Now tell me again what you think about the Rootless?"

"What do you care?"

He leaned against the doorway and tapped his cigarette,

thinking. Then he changed the subject, looking down off the balcony to the trickle of guests wandering in the artificially heated garden with their glasses of champagne. "It's the superiority that's the worst," he said. "It was like this in Atlanta, too. And at the same time that they're congratulating themselves on being the happiest people in the world, they're either being manipulated or trying to manipulate someone else. It's wearing."

"You come from Georgia?"

"I just moved here with my mother. The name is David, by the way."

"David? *You* are David Dana?"

"What, you thought I was a leprechaun?"

I sat back down. "No," I said. "It's just the way people talked about you, I thought you would be . . . different."

He raised his eyebrows. "How so?"

I coughed a little. What I meant was that I had anticipated someone like the Lawrence brothers: spoiled, arrogant, handsome in the way that made you think of movie stars and clothing models. I hadn't expected David to be as bored as I am with dinner parties, and I hadn't expected him to be so quick and honest with his conversation.

It must have shown on my face, because he gave a little laugh. "I see. You were thinking I'd be more like those boys down there. Well, maybe I am." He took a step closer. "Would you still like me if I was?"

"Who said I liked you in the first place?" I said.

"You sat back down, didn't you?"

I brushed my fingers across the skirt of the dress Mother had commissioned for me to trap a husband. A leprechaun would be easier to deal with. "My feet hurt."

David grinned a self-satisfied grin, which nettled me into standing once more. He ignored me and walked over to the balcony, leaning over the railing. "I suppose the army will be the same way," he continued soliloquizing. "After all, it's just a place for gentry boys with no estates and middle-class boys without enough money. A chance to claw out a living and some influence." He tossed his cigarette onto the path below the balcony. It slowly winked out against the cold rocks. "My father was in charge of the Atlantic fleet when I was a boy, a navy man through and through. It's why I chose the army instead. That, and I get seasick."

At that moment, high-heeled footsteps echoed in the hallway to the balcony.

"David?" Cara called. "We've missed you. The dancing is about to begin."

I considered a moment. If Cara saw me alone with the man she was currently pursuing, there'd be no end to her anger, and I needed her amenable when I approached her for answers.

"David?" Cara called again.

I scrambled away from the bench and hid behind a large potted plant, tucking my dress behind me. David opened his mouth to answer, frowning in my direction. I held a finger up to my lips and shook my head.

"I was just having a smoke," he said smoothly.

Cara stepped onto the balcony, giving him a flirtatious smile. "I would have come with you if you'd asked," she remarked, sliding an arm around his.

"Well, if there's dancing, we should hurry back," David said. They headed inside, arm in arm, with him casting an intrigued look back at me before disappearing out of sight.

Strange. David Dana was certainly exasperating and self-indulgent. And there *was* something jarring about him. But it wasn't unpleasant. Not unpleasant at all.

I couldn't help wishing I could have spent more time on the balcony with him.

I passed the rest of the evening lingering at the edges of the party, avoiding my mother and trying to catch Cara alone. But she was in full coquet mode, clinging to David's arm, claiming every dance and doing everything she could to monopolize his time.

I went to bed vowing I would find her later this week. If she was well enough to attend a dinner, then she was well enough to have me over for tea and tell me what had really happened the night of Marianne's debut.

SIX

"It's me again."

I startled out of a doze, a book sliding off my stomach and onto the now snowless lawn. The blanket I was lying on was bunched and twisted underneath me, and it was slightly damp from the wet grass.

David Dana stood above me, squinting in the sun. In the long light of the afternoon, I could see his face in full detail. He wasn't as handsome as the pictures that had been circulating on the wall screens made him out to be, or even as good looking as I'd thought him last night. His nose had too much of a curve to it, and his smile was too wide, showing too many teeth—like a wolf. His blond hair was too pale and too fine, and his skin was almost swarthy from a winter spent surfing and drinking on tropical beaches. He looked like an overgrown boy.

"Hello," I said.

David cast himself on the ground next to me, ignoring the grass on his white shirt and pressed cream slacks—both Italian judging from their style. "Now, I have been thinking since last night, and I've come to the conclusion that a girl smart enough to hide from Cara is a girl I'd like to know.

Even if she is constantly skulking in dark corners."

"I just don't like balls," I said. "Or people, really."

He was close enough that I could see the individual lashes that framed his eyes and the long shadows they cast on his cheeks.

"You don't like parties or people. So what *do* you like?"

"I was in the school choir before I graduated," I offered. The breeze blew and I could smell that spicy smell again, the scent I smelled the first night I met him.

"Did you like it?"

Cloves maybe. Or coriander.

"I didn't *not* like it."

"Your enthusiasm is palpable. Surely there is something else that you enjoy? I will wager a guess . . . it's books, isn't it? You look like the scholarly type."

"What an astute guess, given that I have a book with me right now."

But I smiled.

His face lit up. "So she does smile! Now tell me about these books. Hobby? Hopeful career?"

Maybe cardamom and cinnamon. The scent wasn't overwhelming . . . but it was impossible to ignore.

I gave a small nod. "I want to study history and literature at the university."

"I could tell you were a reader when I first saw you," David said. "You have that dreamy look in your eye, like you're wishing yourself onto a page." He took my chin in his hands and looked deeply into my eyes. Even in the dazzling afternoon light, his eyes were bluer than any lantern. "It's easy to see in the way you hesitate before answering my questions, before asking any of your own. You're not used to talking to us flesh-and-blood types."

I knew he was flirting, that I shouldn't let him touch me, but his hand was so warm, like sunlight lived inside his skin.

"Can I hazard another guess?"

I nodded.

"I think I know what your favorite stories are." He pretended to close his eyes, but I could see him eyeing the book in the grass.

"You're just reading the spine of my book."

"Okay," he conceded. "But I would have guessed the tales of King Arthur and his knights anyway."

"Because you know so much about them?"

"Sure. Young boy with a warrior-king father is left to find his own fate, and when he does, he becomes the king of Britain. He founds an equal partnership of knights to bring justice to his wildlands. Tintagel is his birthplace, Camelot is his home, and Guinevere is his wife. You wouldn't like Lancelot—you believe in happy endings, and he complicates things too much. You like Merlin, not for his magic, but for his wisdom. Bedivere for his loyalty and Galahad for his purity."

"You forgot Mordred and Morgause," I said.

"Mordred the Ambitious, Morgause the Power Hungry. You wouldn't like them very much, would you?" His voice was quieter now.

"I'm impressed," I conceded. "And why would you have guessed this before you saw my book?"

"Because we are alike," he said, dropping his hand.

And there was that weird tug in my stomach again.

"I hate Lancelot for being weak enough to betray his best friend, and as soon as Mordred is born, I almost want to stop reading. Which is a shame, because it's a beautiful example of people struggling to be their best selves, even when it would be easier to abandon the Grail, or leave the damsel in the tower, or leave the sword in the stone."

"It's not true though," I said, almost hating myself for breaking the spell of the moment. "There were no knights errant, and there is no such thing as an ideal or humane form of feudalism."

"Not even now, when Madeline Landry is at the top of the feudalism food chain?"

I'd guessed that he knew who I was, since he found me lying in the grass at Landry Park, but I didn't like the way he said my name. As if he was mocking me.

I didn't answer.

"Imagine my surprise when I learned that my mysterious skulker-at-balls was none other than the heir to the Landry Estate. Jacob Landry's direct descendant."

The tug in my stomach went away.

"You know, they say his ashes are interred somewhere on the grounds."

"They've never been found. And they can stay that way, for all I care."

He squinted at me. "So you don't revere him like everyone else?"

I sat up. The fractal doubt was there again, impossible to ignore. I decided I didn't really want to talk about this right now. "What a pointless question. What does it matter if I revere him? He's been dead almost two hundred years."

"That sounds like a no."

"This house and this park and the farms outside the city all belong to us, and I'm thankful. Thankful to him for building it. I was born here, and ever since I was a girl, my father told me I was part of the house and it was part of me."

David opened his mouth to answer and shut it, as if not sure what he wanted to say.

"I think about Jacob Landry inventing the Cherenkov lantern to give light to people in countries with no infrastructure, and then the nuclear charge, which saved our world from a climate disaster."

"But his charges were a little late, weren't they?" David pointed out. "We lost the coasts to the rising sea levels, our Gulf cities to massive hurricanes."

"That's like arguing that the discovery of penicillin is less important because it was discovered thousands of years too late for Neanderthals."

"What about all the misery that comes from those tiny boxes?"

"You mean the Rootless?"

He nodded.

"They shouldn't be enslaved. But it's not my family's fault." I remembered my father, and his diatribe about the Rootless. "Not entirely our fault," I amended. "And, wait—just the other night, you were all for the police arresting the Rootless. Did you agree with me then? That it's wrong for us to blame them?"

"Do you agree with me that nuclear charges are not a gift to humanity?"

"I can be proud of my family and still perceive unfairness in my world," I said defensively.

David hastily changed the subject. "So what is it like to be the offshoot of the founder of the gentry? To have the oldest and most enviable estate in the country?"

I snorted. "Right now it's surviving on money from Canadian banks because our credit here is so poor. What would everyone think if they knew the cornerstone of the gentry empire was hollow and riddled with debt?"

David laughed. "Do you know that you're the only person I've ever met who has been honest about her family's finances? If I have to hear one more whispered suggestion that someone's family is worth untold millions of gentry dollars . . ."

Suddenly, I remembered that he probably had scores of girls trying to entice him with their dowries and land and family ski chalets. The thought of all that posturing surrounding him at parties, the ballroom math of annual income and acreage, made me tired.

"I should probably go," I said.

David put a hand on my arm. "My mother is having tea with your mother and I don't want to go back in there. I'm begging you, give me an excuse to escape the stories of secondhand ball gowns and who copied whose hairstyle."

Well, it *was* rare to meet someone who hated tea with those women as much as I did.

"Do you want to see the grounds?" I heard myself ask. In answer, David pulled me to my feet, his hands tight and strong around mine.

In the faintly warm and slowly fading afternoon, I showed him the rose garden, the herb garden, and the long terraced lawns. We toured the gatehouse, the guesthouse, the carriage house, and the lily pond. And still he seemed anxious to see more. We walked down a thin gravel path to the western edge of the estate, where a wooden door was set into the thick hedge. The neglected door had red paint curling off in long strips and a broken handle coated in rust. I opened it, and David and I walked through.

David looked around in wonder. "A maze."

"It's very old," I said. "It was built before the Last War, when the Uprisen were still meeting secretly."

"The people who reshaped their world and the lives of everyone in it," David said. "They still meet secretly, don't they?"

I thought of my father's conversation yesterday morning, about his decision to gather the Uprisen. "The descendants of the original Uprisen still communicate, yes."

Even though I'd been open about my family's money earlier, I felt less inclined to tell a stranger about our connection with the Uprisen. For Father, it was a point of pride, and he never wasted an opportunity to remind me that blood, legacy, and land were intertwined. That one day I would be among the circle to carry on the tradition.

It did make me fiercely proud to know a Landry had been involved with all of our nation's major decisions since the gentry's inception. On the other hand, the Uprisen also scared me. Especially now that they might align themselves against the Rootless on the word of a lying girl.

David and I moved slowly, even though I could walk the path in my sleep. He examined every statue and every bench along the way, marveling at the relics of a world lost to two centuries. We finally arrived at the center of the maze, greeted by a marble building covered in moss and grime.

"A mausoleum?" he asked. "Am I about to see the mortal remains of Jacob Landry?"

"Hardly. It's mostly empty inside." I pulled an old key out from the pocket of my yellow poplin dress and turned the lock. "This is where the Uprisen met to plan without arousing suspicion."

The door jerked open to a windowless room. Prewar electric lights were mounted on the walls, but they didn't work since no one had bothered to retrofit the system with nuclear charges. I uncovered the Cherenkov lantern I kept inside, illuminating walls still covered in crumbling maps and a chalkboard still drawn with intricate battle plans—so faded after the two hundred years that only the faintest of lines were visible. The maps still showed the pre-2100 coastlines, the ones without New-New York City and the expanded Lake Michigan, renamed Lake Chicago since the rusted spires of buildings could still be seen from the shore.

"This is where it all happened," David said, running his fingers over a moldering map. "Where they met and decided to fight. The end of democracy. The start of a new world."

David picked up an old handgun from the table and pulled back on the empty slide. "Whosoever pulls this sword from this stone . . ."

". . . is right wise born king of all the land," I finished.

While he gazed at the dusty and forgotten room, I gazed at him. I had been right last night, there was something jarring about him. He didn't fit into our world as he should. Underneath the good looks and the glamour, there was a changeling; a boy by turns serious and bitter and playful.

From outside the musty world of the maze, the ringing of the university bell disturbed the ivy-covered ghosts of war. "It's four o'clock," I said, looking away from him. "Tea will be over."

"Yes," David answered absently, still looking around the room. "Yes."

We quietly wound our way back through the maze until we reached the door. I pulled it shut and turned to find David standing just behind me. Away from the freshly cut grass, the smell of him was overpowering. "I enjoyed this afternoon. Believe it or not, my days are usually tediously empty."

We were barely a body's width apart.

"Given what I have seen on the wall screens since your arrival, I thought you spent most of your time partying or kissing debutantes."

David moved away with a quick laugh. "A bachelor must keep up appearances."

We were on the lawn now, with the sun streaming down and the soothing hum of the gardeners trimming the grass. The university bell rung again, but I felt reluctant to move closer to the house. "Mother will be wondering where I am," I said, stalling.

"Let's not keep her waiting then." To my surprise, David seized my hand and started running, pulling me along behind him. I could feel my curls pulling loose from the comb that kept them back. He looked back at me and said something, but the words were snatched away by the wind and the mowers.

Whatever wall I had been holding against him fell away, but I steeled myself against that smile, against that warm hand, against the flight of fancy on the velvet grass. I refused to be the kind of star-crossed girl who falls in love with the eager knight.

But then I found myself smiling back.

SEVEN

Uncle Stephen regarded me with solemn gray eyes while I paced in the gallery, waiting for Jamie to finish a tablet call in our drawing room. Since he'd started as a resident physician at the public hospital last week, he'd been subject to a barrage of calls from the understaffed medical ward. Predictably enough, his tablet buzzed as soon as we were about to leave for tea at Cara's house, and I couldn't leave without him since she'd refused to see me.

But she'd granted Jamie an audience, and I was determined to tag along.

My uncle looked a little disapproving. "It's the only way," I told the painting. "I have to see her." I wiped some dust from the bottom of his gilded frame. "I'm the only one who knows she's lying."

My grandmother's portrait looked at me with an eternally sad face. Never had there been a depiction of someone with such despairing eyes, a mouth so incapable of smiling.

"You'll see," I told both paintings. "I know I'm right."

Jamie came out of the library, and I tried to pretend I hadn't been talking to pictures. "Sorry. They've found a pair of interns to come in, so hopefully we can continue on to our tea unbothered. Trouble is that we're low on most of our supplies at the moment—donated blood being the most crucial—and they're in the uncomfortable position of having to choose who to care for and who to send away. Luckily, it seems to be a slow morning so far."

"You work too hard for them."

He offered his arm, and I took it, bidding a silent good-bye to my uncle, perpetually seventeen and brooding in the last portrait painted of him before his death.

"It's a public hospital, and <u>all</u> of the patients are working class or even Rootless. They can't pay so they can't get treatment anywhere else. If I don't help, who will?"

"There's always somebody else."

Jamie shot me look. "Maybe for the gentry, but not for them."

I felt a little ashamed. He was right.

We climbed into the silent car, and it took us a mile south to the modestly named Westoff Castle. It was the second largest estate in the city, and while not actually a castle, the house could almost pass for one with its spiked turrets and crenellations at the top.

If the size and ambitious architecture failed to impress, the overdone landscaping might make up for it. A long reflecting pond stretched out from the front of the mansion, and bright swaths of flowers and statues led up to the front terrace, which was made of slabs of pink marble. I looked up at the gold clock ticking four stories above, then stepped into the wide doorway, ushered in by Jamie.

I'd been inside the Westoff house countless times, but I never stopped feeling overwhelmed by its opulence. Mirrors and pastel paintings lined the walls, some stretching from floor to ceiling, others concealing hidden doors. Statues and ornate pedestals held gilt candelabras, while glittering chandeliers hung from the painted ceiling. Hand-carved chairs lined the hallways like soldiers, immaculately crafted but painfully uncomfortable. The floors were pink-and-black checked marble, and the curtains were a pale rose and gold. An artificial floral perfume pervaded the air, and a heavy silence hung in the empty castle, the still air of hundreds of rooms and lush carpets and thick drapes. The creeping quiet of unused excess.

The butler greeted us at the door and ushered us into a well-lit parlor, telling us that Cara had just come back from the stables. Cuddles, an old Yorkshire terrier, snored on the sofa. I remembered him being a threat to little fingers years ago, so I kept my distance. Cara came in the room with a smile for Jamie.

"Oh, God," she said, seeing me. "Not you."

I gave a curtsy. "Good afternoon, Cara."

She threw herself gracelessly into a nearby chair. The light caught the faded bruises on her neck and forehead; she hadn't bothered to put any makeup over them. She still wore her riding boots but had changed into a proper afternoon dress, a light silk with an empire waistline and knee-length skirt, which was downright chaste by Cara's standards. I noticed that the dress puckered slightly around her chest and waist, and wondered if she'd lost weight in the last week.

"Cara, it's wonderful to see you," Jamie said, inclining his head. "How are you feeling?" he asked as he sat.

"Like shit," she answered. Jamie looked taken aback by her rudeness, but I just smiled. This was the Cara I knew.

A maid slipped in with a tea tray, and Cara deigned to pour us each a cup, though she pushed mine so roughly across the table that umber drops splattered on the tablecloth.

"Let's get it over with," she said to me.

"Cara—" Jamie said, shocked, but I ignored him and leaned forward.

"I know you lied to the police about who attacked you," I told her.

"Madeline!" Jamie protested, but this time Cara and I both ignored him.

She crossed her arms over her chest. "Prove it."

"I don't want to have to," I said, knowing it was an empty threat. "I'm hoping that you'll do what you know is right. What if an innocent person goes to jail because you wouldn't tell the truth?"

"I *did* tell the truth."

"Did you?"

She regarded me for a moment, and I could tell she was deciding how much to tell me. "I stepped out for a walk and got a little turned around in the grove. I couldn't find my way out, and then I heard footsteps. It was dark and I couldn't see who attacked me at first, but I could see the red light of the nuclear charge nearby. When he ran away, I could see his clothes. Tattered, filthy rags."

She was doing it again. That thing where her eyes flicked almost imperceptibly around the room, and her voice raised half an octave.

"You're still lying."

Jamie reached out to touch my shoulder, but his tablet buzzed again. "Excuse me," he sighed, and exited the room, activating the video screen on his tablet as he walked out.

I slid my chair closer to the table. "Why are you doing this?"

"Why do you care?" Cara hissed.

"You can't get lost in the grove at night—I could see the lights of the house the whole time we were looking for you. And a walk, really? Without a coat? In that cold?"

Cara glanced at the door, but Jamie was nowhere near it. "It's none of your business why I was out there."

"You made it my business when you refused to tell the truth! My father thinks this is all part of some Rootless conspiracy to overthrow the gentry, and he's ready to crush them. You and I are the only ones who know that he's wrong."

"We don't know he's wrong," she said. "The Rootless could

be plotting a revolt for all I know. If some conspiracy gets thwarted because of this, then no harm done. In fact, that means that I've done everyone a favor and helped unmask a threat to the gentry."

"Do you even have a conscience?"

"Do you have a *brain*?" She jabbed a finger at me. "If I wasn't attacked by a Rootless or some poor person or a servant—if I was attacked by someone in the gentry—do you think I could go around announcing it to the police? To your father? Do you think anyone would believe me if I accused one of us? The gentry are supposed to defend each other at all costs. If I claimed one of our own attacked me, it would only hurt my reputation and any chance I have at a good marriage. Like it or not, Madeline, this is how our world works, and if you know what's good for us, you'll keep your head down and your mouth shut."

"I kept my mouth shut when you condemned that servant boy and his family. I kept my mouth shut when you lied to your father and told him that I convinced you to run away. But I'm done keeping my head down. All your life, you've gotten away with everything! Everything! And it's not fair!" I clapped my hand over my mouth, realizing how loud—and petulant—I'd sounded.

Cara smirked. "That's it, isn't it? You are jealous of me. Well, darling Madeline, no one is stopping you from stirring up some trouble yourself."

"Is that what this is to you? Stirring up some trouble?"

Her eyes flashed. "I'm saving the people I care about, not to mention myself, from trouble."

"And what about the Rootless? Are you saving them from trouble?"

"They'll be fine," she insisted. "If they haven't done anything wrong, then they won't be punished." Her rising voice told me all I needed to know; the lie was there in plain sight, like a crooked chemise under a dress. She didn't believe it was a Rootless who had hurt her, but she knew that they would suffer for it anyway.

"How?" I whispered. "How can you just sit there and not care?"

She pressed her lips together and looked away.

Jamie hurried through the door, pocketing his tablet and helping me to my feet. "My apologies, Cara, but I must leave. There's been a police raid on the Rootless ghetto, and several men and women were badly beaten. At the moment, there are only a couple of frightened interns trying to manage by themselves."

"They were probably looking for the person who hurt me," Cara said woodenly.

Jamie reached for her hand and gave it a kiss. "Don't be anxious. Soon your assailant will be arrested and you'll be able to feel safe once more."

At least Cara had the grace to look uncomfortable.

"We will talk again soon," I promised her.

She tossed her hair over her shoulder, but didn't reply.

Jamie took my arm and led me out the door. As we left, I heard the sudden crash of china, as if someone had thrown a cup against the wall.

EIGHT

The Public Hospital was a building of stone and stained glass, a relic from the 1800s perched on the bluffs overlooking the flat river bottoms. A gold-covered cupola rose above the nearby brownstones and millinery shops, with a bell inside that still rang across the city once an hour. It used to be a cathedral, back when people used such things, but had since been converted into a free hospital for the poor and for the Rootless, paid for by gentry donations garnered at elaborate fund-raisers and auctions. Arthur Lawrence himself paid the salaries for three physicians to run the hospital.

Not everyone felt so paternalistic, however. Some muttered that it was a waste to provide care for a people who were all dead by forty, tantamount to throwing medicine into the river.

Still, the donations paid for the ovaries and testes of the women and men of childbearing age to be routinely treated to protect against mutation, ensuring that any offspring they produced would be viable enough to carry on the work of managing the charges. Additionally, each fetus was inoculated against the radiation shortly after conception. After the vaccine did its work, making sure the child wasn't born with any crippling deformities, it wore off quickly, usually around the third or fourth year. From there, every Rootless child grew steadily more ill until they finally erupted in sores and started coughing blood.

Some grew sicker than others, depending on what kind of work they did. The changers only changed the charges in the houses and carried the charges back to the Rootless ghetto. The strippers and sorters had to strip the cases from the fuel and sort them into piles according to size, but at least they had some slim protection to wear while they did so. But the packers not only had to load the charges on the train to Cape Canaveral for extraction, but they had to ride along with the charges, too, to make sure there were no accidents or spills along the way. They handled the fuel the most and they were around it the longest. Most of them didn't make it past thirty.

But it was the only job out of all the work the Rootless did that paid money. Most Rootless were only given a ration card and were allowed to pick up food staples and limited household items, like nails and fabric, once a month. But the packers got paid, almost as much as a factory worker or a small shopkeeper, and the Rootless needed every penny of that money to make up for the rotten food the Rootless Bureau handed out and for the random taxes the gentry-ruled government levied whenever they felt the Rootless were growing too comfortable. Too lazy.

But as Jamie disembarked from the car, I didn't think the building looked like a grudging concession to keeping a caste viable and alive. With its roof gleaming golden in the afternoon light and its wooden doors thrown open as if in welcome, the hospital looked downright friendly.

"I'm sorry to interrupt your tea," Jamie apologized one more time. "I know you wanted to talk to Cara." Behind him, two Rootless women sat crying on the steps, their dirty and tangled hair caked with blood. I thought of my callous words earlier. *There's always someone else . . .*

Not for them, there isn't.

"You said you were low on blood earlier," I said, sliding over in the seat. "Can I help?"

Jamie blinked. "You want to donate blood?"

"Is my blood not good enough?"

"No," Jamie said quickly. "It is very good. Rather too good, if you understand me. The gentry don't usually donate blood here. In fact, they never do."

I climbed out of the car and shut the door. "Please, Jamie. Let me help."

With a baffled expression, Jamie led me inside, up the shallow steps and past the weeping women, and through thick wooden doors. Inside the marble-floored narthex, gold basins on pedestals dispensed bandages and packets of antibiotics instead of holy water. Bleeding, groaning Rootless leaned against the walls and slumped on the floor. More than one set of eyes locked on my bloodred hair and thin gold necklace.

"Landry," one of them hissed. Jamie steered me away.

Inside the sanctuary, the curtained clinic rooms and boxes of cheap medical supplies were dwarfed by a high ceiling, deep blue and set with twinkling lights, like a summer sky full of stars. White pillars marched grandly down the center of the room, while ancient stained glass threw triangles of color across the curtains, the faces of the wounded, the feet of the shuffling patients in line.

At the front, something more permanent than a curtained room was constructed: a sleek white cube made of gleaming metal with a single door. A few of the Rootless men and women stood in line before it, and they were among those few in the old sanctuary who were not injured.

"Where the altar used to be—that is the fertility treatment room," Jamie explained as we walked past it. "The serum is injected directly into the reproductive organs and is effective for three or four years. Each fetus is also inoculated, as a precaution."

"All so they can watch their children suffer later?"

Jamie rounded on me. "And what should I do? Order them to stop the treatments? So they can then grieve over stillbirths instead of enjoying a few short years with their children? It is a step, Madeline. A step toward humanity for them. No matter what the reasons are for doing it, it's still a good thing."

He was right. And I realized that as much as he had defended my father and the other gentry the night of Cara's attack, he did genuinely care for these people, his new charges.

I nodded and we moved on, behind the dais. I caught only a glimpse of Jamie's office: a small room covered in books and paintings of his home in London, a two-story house on a narrow street. A picture of his mother and sisters, some of them with brown hair and some with black, but all with glossy curls, hung above his desk.

Just down the hall, a cramped and sterile-looking room contained piles of laboratory supplies. Jamie gestured to a chair.

I sat.

He rustled around for a moment then came over with a tray full of equipment. He tied a tourniquet around my arm, clucking when I winced, and prepared a hollow needle.

"Clench your fist, and I will count to three."

I breathed in, nervous. The fevered illness of my thirteenth year had left me with a severe dislike of needles.

"One, two, three."

"Ouch!"

"You should've done it on two," someone said from the doorway.

It was a handsome young man, my age or a little older, with bright ginger hair and thick bands of muscle that swelled through his worn clothes. A scrape on his cheekbone and a dried trickle of blood along his jaw made me suspect that he'd been a victim of the recent raid. "She tensed as you said the word *three*, making it more painful."

I had never heard a Rootless so well spoken. Father always talked about them like they were brutes, barely above the level of animal communication. Something about his height and vivid hair seemed familiar. With a flush, I realized that he changed the charges at Landry Park. He'd been on my estate several times a year, and I'd never thought to say hello or even to ask him his name.

Jamie finished hooking an IV line to a bag that would collect my blood. "It is my experience that ladies are uncomfortable with needles. I try to be accommodating of this."

The man snorted. "Ladies don't need special treatment."

Jamie bristled a little at this. "Gentlemen believe otherwise, sir."

"Gentlemen do, but real men don't." The man settled in a nearby chair and started rolling up his sleeves. "Take this girl over here. She's here giving blood, even though she's clearly gentry and clearly doesn't belong here. But she's brave enough to do it anyway. Would you call that weak?"

"That is not what I was implying."

"And the women in my part of town—they work alongside of us carrying charges or sorting them. Some of the strongest are even packers. And today, when your police came and burned our houses and beat us, claiming to look for Cara

Westoff's attacker, our women fought alongside us. Would you call them weak?"

Jamie sighed. "No."

The man flexed his arm. "I'm ready, doctor."

Jamie moved over with another needle and bag.

The man turned and looked at me. "In my part of town, women are equals. We don't put them on pedestals, and we don't make them do our laundry or wash our dishes. We think of them as partners. Not princesses."

His gaze was intense, a wash of heat and conviction. Goose bumps prickled on my arms as I realized that I wanted someone in my life to think of me that way. To think that I was strong.

"Madeline is not a princess," Jamie defended me as he tied a tourniquet. "But she will run her family's estate someday."

"Maybe," I mumbled, thinking of the university.

"Maybe," Jamie conceded, and hung a bag from a pole. The man's blood dripped in.

"What does that mean?"

"It means my father won't let me inherit if I go to the university," I explained. "I don't know what will happen."

The man rolled his eyes. "Such problems."

"Be respectful, Ewan, or I'll have to ask you to leave," Jamie warned.

"I'm not being disrespectful," Ewan said. "Look, all I'm saying is that she doesn't need her father's approval to live her life." He looked at me again. "Be strong. Go do what needs to be done."

"But without my estate . . ."

He shrugged. "I don't have an estate and I'm still alive. And what about this gentlemanly doctor before us? He doesn't have one either, and he seems happy enough chastising fellows like me."

The funny thing was, I could almost believe it. Right now, talking with Ewan, I could believe in a life without an estate, without money, without gold necklaces and corsets. Life without the orchards, filled with fluttering petals in the breeze, without the white marble floors that were cold even in the summer.

"Will you come with me to tell my father, then?" I asked, only half joking.

Ewan laughed a deep laugh that could fill a tavern. "Wouldn't that be a sight?"

My bag was full. I stood—too quickly—and felt faint.

"Steady now," Ewan said. "You should probably eat something first."

Jamie looked around the room. "I'll see if I can find something," he said, and hurried out.

Ewan pulled a wrapped package out of his pocket and handed it to me.

"I can't take that."

"It's not radioactive, I promise. Just got it from the ration station before the raid."

"No, not that. I meant I can't take it because it's yours. Your food." I stopped. It seemed rude to imply directly to a Rootless that I knew they were starving. Especially when he had seen where I lived.

He held it out to me insistently. "Eat it. Your blood sugar is low, and I doubt the gentleman will find anything of better quality here. It's all gelatin desserts and oatmeal."

"Are you sure?" I did feel faint tingling waves at the base of my skull. My voice sounded further and further away.

"Just take it already."

I took the package and opened the plastic wrapping. Inside was a bar of compressed fruit, meat, and fat.

"Pemmican," Ewan said, and leaned back. "It's softer if you stew it. But somehow I think the doctor might get a little cranky if we use his Bunsen burner to make a hot meal."

I chewed and chewed, trying to break the bar into smaller pieces. "Thank you," I said through a mouth full of crumbled pemmican.

"If you're really nice to me, I'll let you have some sawdust bread and dehydrated potatoes, too."

"Thank you. I'm sorry," I said awkwardly, not exactly sure what I wanted to convey. Regret? Pity? General distaste for their deplorable food?

"For what? Your family enslaving mine?"

Enslaving. The word felt like a strike or a slap—an indictment. "Don't you think enslaving is a little strong? This isn't the Antebellum South."

Ewan leaned forward. "History repeats itself, princess. And you know what? My life feels an awful lot like slavery to me."

"Don't be unfair," Jamie said, walking into the room with a tray of anemic-looking broth and prepackaged crackers. "Society now is completely different than it was during the Civil War. Race is not a factor any longer; the Wilders and Osbournes are African American, the Lawrences are Hispanic, the Thorpes came from India, and they are all gentry and have been since the Last War. Your ancestors fought against the Uprisen in that war and that's why you now serve the gentry. This is about class, not race."

"Are you justifying our bondage with the fact that we happen to be different colors? Just because this isn't exactly like what happened back then doesn't mean that it isn't wrong. We toil, we sicken, and we die while you all play dress-up in your fancy houses, and we have no choice. If that's not close enough to slavery for you, then you need to return to your history books."

I didn't respond. Ewan had a way of being direct and challenging without being aggressive. A few moments of quiet pervaded the room as Ewan's blood filled the bag, and as I pondered thin soup and finished the pemmican instead.

An idea occurred to me as my steadiness returned, and I decided to seize the thought and act on it, like Ewan had encouraged me to do earlier.

"Ewan," I said, "do you know much about Cara Westoff's attack?"

A storm clouded his face. "I could hardly not know about it, given that I just had several police officers screaming her name in my face."

"I think she's lying," I rushed. "I'm not sure why she refuses to say who really attacked her, but I don't think it was a Rootless, and I want to prove it. I just don't know where to start."

"So you're asking me?" His voice was as clouded as his face.

"I'm sorry. I thought maybe you might have heard something."

"All I can say is that it was certainly not a Rootless who hurt her." He leaned back and looked up at the ceiling. "I've kept a close eye on Cara Westoff and the issue of her assault, and I can guarantee that no one from my camp was involved."

"How can you be sure?"

"I'm sure."

I didn't know if I should trust a man I barely knew—and a Rootless man at that—but Ewan was so open and approachable. And he'd shared his food with me, when he had impossibly little to share.

I decided to believe him.

NINE

Mother was screaming.

We were in the car, coming from a dinner at the Osbourne estate, and I was too preoccupied to notice when she got out of the car. I started in my seat when she began shrieking in terror.

Father put a hand on her shoulder to steady her when she swayed, but as soon as he saw the front of the house, he gestured for the driver to come support her. After easing her into the arms of the servant, he walked forward, a dark silhouette against the front of the house. I got out of the car last, and therefore saw it last, the dripping red paint scarring the light gray stone of our house.

WE ARE RISING.

The words were scrawled across the front, stretching over two windows and the antique, hand-carved double doors of the entrance. In my mind, I could think of only one "we," one group of people who hoped for upward movement and flight from pain. One group that would so daringly play on the term Uprisen, the name that all the gentry guarded with pride. One group that had been attacked yesterday, that had watched their women and children beaten for no reason other than a reckless lie.

"How could they?" Mother whimpered, now kneeling on the ground. I knelt beside her to comfort her, but to my surprise, she was the one who drew me in her arms. "Our lovely house."

It was lovely, in fact. Jacob Landry had selected the stone himself from a quarry in England. It looked dove gray in the daylight—almost like marble—but at night, the stone took on a distinguished silver color.

Like our eyes, our Landry eyes.

And at that moment, I felt a stab of anger at the Rootless. Yes, they'd been attacked, and yes, my father was partially responsible, but . . . our house? My house? Historic and strong and graceful, and now scarred with this angry graffiti. The paint was as red as the lights on the nuclear charges, and for a moment, I had a terrible vision of the house bathed in red lights, poisoned with radiation, uninhabitable and empty.

And then I realized why my father truly feared them. In forcing them into nuclear slavery, the gentry had also handed the Rootless a weapon.

"I will have to call the other landowners, and the Uprisen, too," Father said, moving toward the door. "We must find whoever did this, and after we do, we need to remind these criminals who takes care of them. Their livelihood is dependent on our charity, and if they lose that, they will starve.

They must respect us, and if they will not, then we will force respect on them."

God help them, I thought, at the same time as I wondered *How could they? To my beautiful house?*

Father stalked off, and I watched as the driver helped Mother into the house. I wandered inside, feeling in a daze.

The next night, the spicy and expensive smell of opium smoke curled from under the study doors, where Father held court with the other landowners in the city, no doubt discussing the vandalism to our house. It had been on every wall screen, the subject of every tablet call and tea-party conversation that day; dinner had been a fierce affair, full of frightened speculation and loud polemic. After my father and his friends cloistered themselves in the study, the rest of our dinner party had quickly devolved, with everyone eager for a break in the tension, and conversation bubbled on the humid patio as the remainder of the guests flirted and drank their way through our family's supply of plum wine and whiskey.

David and Cara were dancing to the slow, sultry music the band was playing, his hand caressing the small of her back. That night she'd come looking for him on the balcony . . . it hadn't been a one-time thing.

It had been a beginning.

It's not that I cared whom he dated, I just thought there was more to him than that—depth and curiosity and agitation at being trapped in our lovely and lifeless world. I thought he would want more than a girl like Cara, who was as selfish as she was beautiful.

I wondered how she could dance after seeing the front of our house scalded with invective, after hearing the panicked fretting of her neighbors, and all because she refused to tell the truth. I decided to go talk to her, but at that moment, David lowered his mouth to her ear and whispered something that made her toss her head back and laugh. It was a practiced move, designed to send her blond hair tumbling over her shoulders and expose her long throat. But even though I'd seen her do the same thing with countless other boys, it bothered me tonight. I remembered the feel of David's hand in mine as we ran across the lawn, the way he'd said *we're alike, you and I.*

Our eyes met across the room, and I shivered, because suddenly not caring about David Dana seemed unimportant . . . impossible. I wanted to go talk to him. I wanted to touch him. I wanted to dance with him in the cloud of smoke and music.

I excused myself from the noise and retired to the library. As soon as I shut the door, the echoing sounds of revelry vanished, replaced with the hush of thick carpet and untouched paper. A fire licked quietly at massive logs. Almost on autopilot, I grabbed a book from a stack on the table and sat, opening the book to read but thinking a million scattered thoughts instead.

The door opened, and the sounds and lights of the party spilled into my solitude. David appeared in the doorway and came inside, closing the door with a *click*. His jacket was off and his bow tie undone, the white shirt setting off his bronze skin.

He dropped into the chair across from me. "Leaving the party so soon?"

"I wanted to read."

"Ah. Of course you did." David reached over and plucked the book out of my hands. "*A History of the Last War*," he read aloud. "Sounds riveting."

"I like history," I said.

He tossed the book carelessly on a nearby table, then leaned forward. "What else do you like?" he asked.

"What?"

He sat back and ran his fingers through his hair. "What other things interest you? What do you do when you're not reading? What's your favorite food? Your favorite season?"

"Why do you want to know?" I asked. "Why don't you go ask Cara what her favorite things are?" I'd meant it playfully, but it came out sounding jealous. Which it wasn't. Because I wasn't jealous.

Was I?

"I want to ask you," he said, his voice low. "I want to know what Madeline Landry thinks. How she feels."

The intensity of his interest unsettled me. This was far

beyond my usual conversations with the opposite sex: ballroom observations and comments about the weather. This was something else altogether—something bewildering and irresistible. Something like that afternoon in the maze. My heart began to beat loudly, as if I was dancing a fast reel.

"How I feel about what?" I asked cautiously.

David looked around the library, as if casting about for a subject. "What about what happened to your house? It's all anyone has talked about today."

I stiffened, the red words flashing in my mind, the horrible premonition of Landry Park submerged in radiation and decay. "I can't believe you would ask about that, of all things." My voice sounded strange. Brittle.

He stood, rapping his knuckles against his leg. "I am sorry. I've offended you."

I realized I didn't want him to leave, not yet. "Wait—"

He stopped. "Yes?"

"I didn't mean to be rude. But you can understand why it's a sensitive subject for me."

"I understand." His kept his eyes on me. "I can see that you love this house."

I nodded, trying to steady my voice. "I think it's the most beautiful house in the world. It took Jacob Landry several years to build it after the gentry won the Last War and cleared the city to make room for the estates. He wanted it to be perfect."

He stepped forward, looking down at me. "Is there a but?"

There was, and I hadn't even realized it until he asked. "But," I admitted, "sometimes I feel trapped. By the inheritance, by my family. I may not be able to go to the university; the will stipulates that all Landry heirs are to be married by the age of twenty-one."

"Maybe you could marry after you take a degree? It would only be the difference of a year or two."

I examined my hands. "I've already asked. Father said no."

He considered. "Do you want to get married at all?"

I blushed and immediately felt ridiculous for blushing. "Someday, perhaps," I said quickly, hoping he wouldn't notice my discomfiture. "After I go to the university and if I meet the right person." I cleared my throat. "What about you?"

"If I meet the right person," he echoed.

We stared at each other for a moment. I wanted to ask if Cara was the right person, if he could see himself as the co-owner of Westoff Castle someday, but the idea of him saying yes was too upsetting. *I don't care*, I reminded myself. He was only another bachelor, interested in parties and women, while I was bound for the university and something different and exciting.

The fire popped loudly and he started. "I have taken up enough of your time," he said slowly. He crossed the rest of the distance between us in two long strides and gave my hand a swift and warm kiss, before turning and heading toward the door. I froze, barely daring to breathe, wanting to call him back.

But he was gone, walking back to the ballroom where Cara waited among the music and laughter.

Liberty Park perched on a high hill overlooking the skyline and river bottoms. Set in the exact center of town, it was a war memorial from the twentieth century that the gentry mostly ignored because it was close to the rougher edge of town. It was mostly frequented by the shopkeepers, factory owners, and others who made up the small but steady population of middle class in Kansas City, along with a handful of working-class factory types and visiting farmers with their families.

I liked the park because it was free of hairpins and waltzes and awkward conversation. I liked the wide leafy trees that rustled in the wind and the velvet grass that stretched out like a blanket down to the road below. Close to the top of the hill stood my favorite tree. It had a wide, smooth trunk, perfect for sitting against, and a view of the skyline that was unrivaled anywhere else in the city, save for the view from Landry Park's observatory.

I snuck out the servants' door early on Saturday morning, knowing full well my mother wanted to take me shopping for new dresses to impress David. I didn't know what I thought about this, but I could still feel his energy from last night, that sudden surge of interest in me that fled as quickly as it came. Why did he always seek me out when I was alone? Was he embarrassed to talk to me in public?

He certainly wasn't embarrassed to talk to Cara.

I'd brought my tablet to finish slogging through the Burke essays, but instead found myself engrossed in *La Morte D'Arthur*, trying not to think about David and the way his lips had felt on my hand the other night.

I was so caught up in my world of Arthurian knights that I didn't even notice the Rootless girl trudging past me until she fell down and cried out. Her lead-lined bag landed with a thud and several spent nuclear charges tumbled onto the grass, their red lights flickering.

What is she doing here?

The Rootless weren't allowed in any of the parks or public spaces in the city. They could only walk on the roads to the various discreet back doors leading to gentry basements where they collected the charges, and then take those same roads to their part of the city, where the charges were taken by train to be disposed of.

She must have been at least my age, but she was as small as a child. A sickly green tinged her skin, which was mottled with bruises, and her hair was falling out in clumps. I set down my tablet to help, but hesitated a moment. She was still on all fours on the ground, crying softly, bloody mucus dripping from her nose. I could see the sores caked on her hands.

I slid back behind the tree trunk so that she couldn't see me.

With a wave of shame, I realized that I was afraid to touch her. I was afraid of her sores and her blood and her crusted eyes. Even though I knew the right thing was to help her up, I couldn't bring myself to stand and walk over to her.

"Do you need help?" I heard someone ask kindly.

David Dana was kneeling next to her, taking her by the elbows and gently raising her up. He must have come from the other side of my tree, because I hadn't seen him. He put a steadying hand on the small of her back, the motion more warm and tender than when he had danced with Cara last night. There was no hesitation in his touch, no revulsion in his eyes.

My heart pounded and I felt heat rise to my face. Why was he in the park? Had he seen me? All I'd wanted to do today was avoid thinking about David, and here he was ten feet away, touching the bare skin of a Rootless girl, without a second thought, something even I, for all my progressive views, couldn't manage.

She sniffled, clutching his arms for support. "Sorry, sir, clumsy of me." She let go, but she swayed where she stood.

"Where are you walking to?" David asked. "Let me order you a taxi."

"A city taxi won't take me, sir. On account of the radiation." I could see dried blood on her neck from where it had run out of her ears.

"Then you must take my private car to your home."

"No, no. I'll be fine. Please, take no trouble."

David made sure she could stand, then he bent over. "It is no trouble." He started to collect the charges and put them back into her bag.

"Please, don't handle the charges!" She tried to reach for the bag, but stumbled and almost fell.

David finished putting them in the bag. "I'm sure it's fine."

He was either brave or stupid. If the charges hadn't been collected on time, the boxes could already be leaking radiation.

"Can you walk down to the street?" he asked, shouldering the bag. I could see the weight of it drag his shoulder down.

She nodded and took a step, then fell. Without hesitation, he picked her up in his arms and carried her like a child, the bag thumping heavily against his leg as he sidestepped down the hill.

And then they were gone.

I rested my head against the tree. Despite our strange encounters, David still struck me as someone primarily concerned with his own interests and his own image. And yet, when nobody was watching, he'd actually touched a Rootless person. Touched her and carried her and helped her, without hesitation, without thought. No wonder he'd scoffed at my jaded pronouncement that there were no knights errant.

He was one.

TEN

The swelling of summer had brought no evidence of who'd vandalized our house, although the reports of arrests and raids on the Rootless grew more frequent. Servants scoured the front of the house, but the paint had eaten into the old stone, and a disturbing shadow still darkened the places where the words had been. Life went on almost as normal, except that my mother now shuddered away from the sight of Rootless charge collectors trudging along the road, and my father spent all his time meeting with the other landowners in the area. Security measures were taken around the house: cameras, motion detectors, guards in gray uniforms, the atomic symbol stitched in red on their backs. The thought of more damage to my home twisted my stomach. I found myself pressing fingertips to paneled walls and rubbing drapes idly, as if reassuring the house.

About a week after I saw David in Liberty Park, Mother and I were invited to a brunch at the Lawrences. The weather was lovely, consistently warm and only occasionally rainy now that we were in June, turning the grass green and forcing slender shoots of the genetically modified crops out of the soil. It was the perfect day to read the chapter in *The History of the Last War* about the changing weather patterns, and how the rise in temperatures in the twenty-first century had affected the flora and fauna of the Midwest.

Kansas used to be a state of dry plains, ideal for the grazing of livestock and the cultivation of wheat, the book explained. *Precipitation was less than half of what it is today, only 26 inches a year. . . .*

The adults were strolling in the vast Lawrence pleasure garden, while the teenagers had opted to stay on the patio and drink plum wine. Cara was using her tablet to talk to her friends, and Mark Everly was staring dreamily at the back of Marianne Wilder's head while she loaded her plate with more crisp spring rolls. One of the Lawrence boys reached over to snap at Cara's bra strap, and she turned to give him a look of such venom that even I was startled.

"Don't touch me," she hissed. "Don't you *ever* touch me."

"Oh, now look who is all too good to be touched," Stuart Lawrence mocked.

Philip Wilder snorted nearby. Cara's fingers twitched, but so did her chin, as if she was holding back tears. She abruptly stood, sweeping her tablet and stylus into a crocodile-skin purse, and left the patio without a word. Stuart giggled while Philip grinned and stretched his long legs under the wrought-iron patio table.

Despite summers warm enough to breed thunderstorms and

microbursts, the average temperature has been dropping steadily over the past two hundred years while snowfall increases.

Still pretending to read, I narrowed my eyes at the thought of the boys across the patio, trying to remember everything I could about the night of Cara's attack. I thought I remembered the Lawrence boys laughing in the ballroom after we found Cara, but Philip Wilder hadn't been there, unless perhaps he was hiding from the constables and my father after committing his crime.

I mentally added Philip and the Lawrence boys to the list of people I needed to talk to, right after Cara and David Dana, the strange and unexpected savior of fallen Rootless. He stayed on my mind for the rest of the brunch and for the rest of the afternoon, even while I wandered the dusty stacks of the university library. It was like the thought of him had leached the color out of everything else, him and how unflinchingly he'd helped that girl while I cowered behind a tree. It didn't escape my attention, however, that he'd believed himself unseen. I doubted he would have helped her if Cara or I had been standing next to him.

I gave up on the books after an hour of mostly unproductive browsing at the university library. I started the two-mile walk home from the campus, ignoring the clouds dragging their soggy bellies across the sky. Heavy raindrops splattered the stone walk, here and there, with increasing frequency. Soon the downpour would begin in earnest. I dug out an old book from my bag and held it over my head, but the rain was falling in sheets and curtains, drenching everything. The thin white dress I wore quickly became heavy and dripping, soaking me to the skin. A car pulled next to me and David leaned out the back window. "Get in!" he called over the noise of the rain.

It was too wet to argue. I climbed in the car.

For a moment, my leg was pressed against his. He nonchalantly slid over to give me more room in the seat. Goose bumps raised along my arms, and not only from the sudden chill of being wet in an air-conditioned car.

He pressed a button. "Back to Landry Park, please," he told the driver. He caught my look. "I was just over at your house to call on you, but then your mother told me you sometimes go to the university in the afternoon."

"Yes." I ducked my head, worried he'd see the thousands of questions I had for him written on my face.

"But clearly you are not there, you are here in my car."

"Yes."

He settled into the seat and folded his arms, giving me an amused stare. "Don't just say yes to everything I say. That is not how a conversation works."

"Sorry," I said, and looked out the window. So many strange thoughts and ideas burned at my throat, but I didn't know how to give voice to them, how to ask a person I barely knew—but shared such intimate moments with—about his real motivations. Was he privately kind and publicly cavalier? Or just as subject to his own sudden whims as I was?

He threw up his hands. "Madeline! It is impossible to get anything out of you!"

"Sorry," I said again.

"You're shivering," he observed. "How rude of me not to notice." He slid closer again, so that his knee was nudged against the wet skirt of my dress. He shrugged off the cardigan he wore over his button-down shirt and tie and draped it over my shoulders. I could feel the warmth of his fingers through the wet fabric of the dress, branding my skin. He smoothed the thin sweater against my neck and shoulders.

"Warmer?" he asked quietly.

His hands still rested on the sweater, on my collarbone. "Yes."

"Good."

He was still so close, so close to me. Dancing in crowded ballrooms being the exception, I had never been this near to a man I wasn't related to, and certainly not in a wet and clinging dress. I wished I could name what effect David had on me, what it was that both made me nervous and vaguely irritated and made me think strange and bold thoughts about the way his lips were shaped and the way his waist narrowed into his hips.

His fingers trailed from the sweater to the hollow of my neck, where he took my necklace between his fingers. He lifted the heavy cameo away from my chest, studying the black and white silhouette of Genevieve Landry, the atomic symbol rendered in pearl at the bottom. "This is beautiful."

"It was my grandmother's."

"She looks so sad."

I thought of her portrait in the gallery and of the forlorn expression both she and my uncle shared. Someone told me once that my grandfather never let her leave the house, not even to visit family. After a while, she'd faded away, like a rose left too long in a vase.

I coughed and looked out the window. He—reluctantly it seemed—pulled his hand back and reached for a tumbler of gin sitting near his seat.

"How are you enjoying Kansas City so far?" I asked politely, pretending that my neck wasn't still tingling from his fingers.

"Oh, it's fine." He waved a hand at the window. "Lovely houses, birthplace of the gentry, et cetera, et cetera."

"You don't sound very enthusiastic."

"About the city? I am not. But the people—there are some that I will truly regret leaving when I take up my post in the Rockies." His words were relaxed, but his fingers betrayed him, tapping quickly against his glass.

Who was he talking about? There was no doubt that I wanted him to be talking about me, if the hammering in my chest was any indication, but he could also be talking about Cara or even some other girl I knew nothing about.

Or maybe he was simply being polite, and I was behaving very stupidly right now.

He took a drink and then offered his glass to me, as if he was used to such casually intimate gestures. As if *we* were.

I shook my head. He resumed gazing out the window, his head braced on his hand. "Yes, I will miss the people here quite a bit. I hope to see much more of them before I leave. I hope to see much more of you, Madeline."

I felt like I had been plunged in ice water. I searched desperately for something to say—anything—that would demonstrate, to him and to myself, how completely unaffected I was by this.

"And Cara?" I knew as soon as I said it that no answer he could rejoin with would give me any pleasure, but it was as if every unhappy thought about David and Cara had crowded into my brain, making it impossible to think about anything else. He wasn't allowed to make offhand comments that made me fight for composure when he spent his evenings brushing cheeks with Cara on the dance floor.

He glanced over at me without moving his head.

I gazed back without answering. I had significant practice at being silent.

"Yes, I will be sad to leave Cara, too," he finally said. "Tell me, have they found her attacker or does your father just plan on arresting all the Rootless in Kansas City until there are none left?"

I tensed. Yes, I had criticized my father's actions, had witnessed their direct result at the Public Hospital, but having a stranger disparage my family was completely different and it made me defensive. "You know about the vandals at Landry Park. It's hardly surprising that it would further my father's desire to find the attacker at any cost."

"At any cost," he repeated softly. "Spoken like a true Landry."

"Well, I am a Landry first and foremost—"

"And what, a Madeline second? Don't you ever want to be something other than a vessel for your family's legacy? I thought you felt trapped by that place, by all the stupid rules set down by your father. What changed?"

"You wouldn't understand," I told him, my voice cold. "You aren't going to inherit an estate and the responsibility that comes with it. My father has a duty to his fellow landowners and to this city to keep the people safe—"

"But no duty to the Rootless," David interrupted. "Right? They do not need safekeeping because they are not really people."

"You know that I don't believe that."

"No, Madeline, I don't know what you believe. Apparently, I don't know anything about you except that you care about your house and your family more than anything else. We are here, by the way."

And with that, he reached across me to open the door, his entire torso in my lap. I breathed in sharply at the contact, and

David jerked upright. "Keep the sweater," he said. "I'm sick of it anyway."

I stepped into the rain and the car sped away, the tires hissing on the wet drive.

A week passed. I kept waiting for David to seek me out, like he had before, to gallantly apologize or even to bait me into another fight—I would have welcomed either. What I couldn't stand was this vacuum of contact, this week without a single dinner party or dance or *anything*. David preoccupied me more than finding out the truth about Cara's attack or convincing my father to allow me to study—and it infuriated me to no end that he had infected my mind in such a way.

One of the servants poured me another glass of tea, while another mimosa arrived for Mother on a silver tray. I realized she had been speaking to me.

"Pardon?" I asked.

Mother tilted her face up to the sun, the light catching hints of silver in her dark hair. "I just love lunch out on the terrace. Don't you?"

I did normally. Solar-powered coolers pushed away the worst of the crushing pressure of the storm on the horizon, so I could enjoy the wild colors of the flower garden and the rustling of the nearby apple orchard in peace. A light fruit smell drifted toward us. And in the dead space between my graduation and the deadline for applying for the university, I could devote more time to reading whatever I chose, though I kept coming back to Arthurian legends, wondering what David was reading. Which, of course, invariably led to agonizing meditations on our disastrous car ride last week.

"I saw Christine Dana yesterday," Mother said after a long drink, beginning her weekly rundown of the best gossip. "Do you know she was at a luncheon with your father and several of his business associates? She said they were just discussing the possibility of her investing in some of the Landry lumber industries, but it galls me that Alexander allows *her* at business luncheons. Whenever I want to come, he insists on my staying away. As if he's embarrassed by me."

I'd opened a book and was reading while picking at a plate of fried dumplings and coconut sweets, but I paused. I was reminded of my own thoughts about David and Cara.

"Nasty bit of business about Philip Wilder losing his temper during a boxing match. Why they claim it is a gentleman's sport is beyond me."

"Who was he fighting?" I asked idly, still trying to read and not to think about David.

"Your cousin Tarleton. Philip is taller, but Tarleton is quicker. All of us Lawrences are."

"Tarleton probably cheated."

Mother agreed and closed her eyes. "How my young cousins can be so wild when my uncle is so genteel, I will never know. Could be Aunt Lacey. She's a Lyons, and they made their money smuggling from the East. They are natural thieves."

I rolled my eyes. "Half the families in America make money from smuggling or from investing in smuggling."

"Well, you just know everything, don't you?" Mother adjusted herself to get more sun, then continued. "The constables are out in force after the Rootless ration station was robbed last night. Our driver could hardly see the road for all the Cherenkov lights. And now that the mayor is sick . . ."

"The mayor is sick?"

"Madeline," Mother chided. "Don't you read your wall screens or your tablet? He has been sick for over a week. Everyone says cancer, but I do not know how his doctor wouldn't have caught it before now if it was. I would say food poisoning. He was visiting Lake Chicago, you know, and they have all sorts of strange food there. . . ."

I didn't see how his doctor wouldn't have caught it either, but before I could probe it further, I saw a black car pull to the front of the house. The Danas' car. Had David come to visit?

I quickly finger-combed the loose waves that tangled over my shoulders and tried to adjust my dress so that it looked less like I'd been crumpled up in a chair all day. I set down the book and then picked it up again. A servant walked out onto the terrace with another silver platter—this time with an envelope—and then I heard the car start and drive away. I slumped back in my chair.

The servant approached me. "Mr. Dana came by to hand deliver this to Miss Landry."

My mother's mouth hung open. I took the envelope off the tray and politely excused myself, not wanting her to see whatever was inside, a knot weaving itself in my chest as I walked across the terrace and into the house. I ran up the stairs to the fourth floor, trying to convince myself it wasn't anything important and trying not to dwell on the fact that David didn't come find me to give it to me himself. Was he still angry about what I'd said last week?

I opened the envelope with trembling fingers in the privacy of the observatory, surrounded by glass and sunshine. It was an invitation to a ball. A ball in his honor.

Because, in less than six weeks, he was leaving.

In all my ruminating about his strange act of kindness, in all my obsessing over his strange questions and mood swings, I hadn't given much thought to him leaving. Even though he had referenced it in the car, even though I had known since he arrived that his visit was a temporary stop on his way to the mountain forts, it had just seemed inconceivable that he could really, actually leave before I had a chance to untangle my impressions of him.

ELEVEN

The next day did nothing to alleviate the confusion that pulled at me.

"David has asked Cara to be his partner at the ball," Mother said over breakfast.

My stomach tensed, and I had the sudden, stupid urge to cry.

"I have heard they are combining his going-away ball with Cara's debut." The bitterness in her voice was unmistakable.

"Maybe he's just taken pity on her because her prospects are slimmer since her attack," Father suggested.

"Oh, I do not think her prospects are dimmed at all," my great-aunt Lacey said in a chirping voice as she used silver tongs to load more toast on her plate. She was a rare breakfast guest, but she was planning on going shopping with Mother later, and so she'd invited herself over for food and gossip. She talked and ate as much as three great-aunts. "I hear all sorts of boys are asking her to dances, and Addison says that she expects Cara will have an offer within a month of her debut."

"Well, I heard Addison saying that come hell or high water, Cara would make a good match, and if you knew Addison like I do, you would not doubt it," Mother said.

"My dear niece, I do know Addison like you do, and believe me, I do not doubt it!"

My father took a drink of coffee. "That is unfortunate about David," he said, looking at me.

I shrugged. "I don't care," I told them. "He and Cara deserve each other."

"Unfortunate," Father repeated. "Because David could have brought a considerable sum to the estate."

I bit my lip. When I was little, my father had often twirled me out on the lawn. I wondered if now all he could see in me was a way to ransom his land. To carry on the Landry line.

"At any rate, he will be in town a couple weeks after the ball." Mother pointed a finger at me. "A debut isn't necessarily a proposal. You will still have time to make an impression before he leaves."

"I don't care," I said again.

Father, having clearly decided that the conversation was over, picked up his tablet and stylus. Outside, another laborer was at work on the stone, trying to bleach the vandalized portion back to its original smoky gray.

The Westoffs emptied their coffers for Cara's debut. Invitations edged with gold lace and hand-penned in gold ink were sent out to every family in the city, regardless of whether they had received David's first invitation or not. Rumors of smuggled cherry trees, aged wine, and European seamstresses began to float around at tea parties and dinners. In just a few short weeks, Kansas City would see the most lavish debut in its history.

And in just a few short weeks, David Dana would leave.

I hid from the usual summer parties—barge trips atop the muddy Missouri and picnics on the surrounding river bluffs. I wouldn't have been able to bear watching David and Cara together, laughing and kissing, the couple that the city had its eyes on. No matter how many times I told myself I didn't care, that I only cared about his connection to the Rootless, and that it was inevitable that he singled out Cara from the very beginning, it still stung. I still had to force myself to remember to breathe when I thought of his blue eyes and his quick laugh.

Addison taxed my mother with her gloating, making sure to anguish over every minute detail of the party, fawning over the idea of David as her future son-in-law. After two days of this, servants packed several suitcases and Mother went on an impromptu retreat to some mineral springs north of the city.

This meant that I no longer had to spend my meals listening to her grieved denouncements of the selfish Westoffs, or long and venomous outbursts where she ranted about Christine and her whorehound son. But even her grating rants couldn't penetrate my misery. My thoughts chased themselves in constant circles.

I want him to go.

I want him to stay.

I don't care about him.

I can't stop thinking about him.

Before she'd left, Mother had commissioned a seamstress for me and had taken the liberty of choosing the fabric and style of dress that I would wear to Cara's debut. Silver to match my eyes and set off my pale skin. The seamstress pinned the pieces on me in silence, needles pressed between her lips.

I looked in the mirror. On my pale frame, the silver was drab and gray with no shimmer or depth. Rather than highlighting my hair, it simply forced the dark circles under my eyes and my pale lips into prominence.

A sharp clicking sound brought me out of my daze. Christine Dana stepped into the room, looking light and fresh in a suit and heels. Married women occasionally wore pantsuits or skirted suits since they weren't worried about snagging a husband. But far from looking like a woman on the shelf, Christine managed to make the tailored lines look sensual and chic.

"Madeline, darling," she greeted, taking my elbows into her hands and kissing me on the cheek. "I was hoping I would catch your mother. Is she here?"

She had eyes identical to David's. I couldn't find my voice to greet her back.

She waved a hand. "No matter. I am sure your father will entertain me. He is so accommodating that way." Then she caught sight of my face. "Are you quite all right, Madeline? You look so pale."

I nodded.

She paused, then took a seat on the seamstress's stool, earning a mordant glare from the woman, who was about to sit down. Christine paid her no attention, and pulled a cigarette from her purse. She offered me one, but I declined. The spicy scent told me it was opium laced, like the kind my father preferred.

She sat for a moment, wreathed in smoke, and then asked, "When do you think you will debut, darling? Soon?"

"No," I said. My voice was rough from not talking. I cleared my throat. "No, I do not think anyone will ask me soon."

She gazed at her cigarette. "When I was your age, I was in love with the man I was sure I would marry." Her voice was distant. "But he asked another girl to debut and eventually proposed to her, and I ended up in Virginia with my aunt. But if I had not gone there, desperate and heartbroken, then I never would have met Admiral Dana, David's father. We were very happy for many years, until he died." Her bright eyes pierced mine through the smoke. "Do you see what I am saying?"

"Am I that obvious?" I whispered. I don't know why I

asked, or why I felt like I wanted to hear her answer, but she had taken more interest in my feelings in the past ten minutes than my mother had all spring and summer, and I wanted to believe that underneath the glamour, underneath the sharp face and equally sharp self-assurance, was someone compassionate. Empathetic.

She stood and snapped her clutch closed. "If I had my way, Madeline, we would be putting my grandmother's tiara in your hair tomorrow and supervising flower arrangements downstairs. After the way David has spoken of you . . . well, I was surprised that he chose Cara, is all. Take heart, dear," she said, and kissed me on the cheek. I watched her leave, fiddling with the pins on my dress and trying not to think of David. Her cigarette still smoldered in the ashtray.

"We're here," the driver announced.

The car rolled to a stop, and the Westoffs' footman stepped forward to open the door. He helped my mother out of the limo and caught her as she stumbled, tripping over her dress. She'd been sipping sake mixed with plum wine since we woke at dawn to get ready.

My father sighed impatiently and climbed out. "Compose yourself, Olivia."

Her eyes flashed but she said nothing. The footman's face stayed studiously blank.

Father held out a hand to me as I tried to pull myself and the expansive rustling dress out of the car. After twelve or more hours of mineral soaks, lotion treatments, hair, and makeup—all so I could hold my own with the radiant Cara—my body felt too weak and drained to even walk. I wobbled a little on the smooth flagstones of the entry walk, knees like jelly.

Father examined my face. "Are you anxious about the ball?"

"I just want tonight to be over," I told him.

"You and me both." He touched my cheek, his face softening. "Sometimes I forget how much my daughter you are."

I smiled at him. At least I would have one pleasant moment from tonight to tuck away.

The gold clock clanged grandly above his head, the chimes echoing across the grounds, and two footmen appeared from the shadows to open the doors for us. Father ushered us in.

Tonight, as was tradition, the debutante's favorite flowers were in abundance. Pink roses hung in garlands above doorways, nestled in bunches on the dinner tables, and made halos and wreaths around every statue, pillar, and banister. The smell permeated the air, making an almost palpable miasma. I felt the fingers of a headache begin to creep over my temples.

Addison and her husband stood in the foyer greeting guests. I merely shuffled by, uttering the barest of hellos, before squeezing into the front hall, packed with guests waiting to enter the ballroom. I craned my neck, trying to peer around the people crowding the hall, wanting both to see David and to be reassured he was nowhere in sight.

"David is upstairs waiting with Cara," Mother mentioned. She was holding a fresh glass of plum wine. "That is the tradition, you know, to come down together. Your father stayed in my room with me for the entire night and day before."

"He spent the night with you?" I asked, before I could help it.

"Yes," she answered, looking past me at something else.

I turned to see what she saw—Father and Christine Dana talking together, laughing. He leaned over to say something in her ear and she put a hand to her chest, blue eyes cast to the floor.

My mind went back to David and Cara. "You don't think David and Cara spent the night together, do you?"

"Of course," Mother snapped. "Cara knows what she's doing, and she—"

Christine's laugh carried across the room. I looked over to see my father's hand lingering on her waist as they strolled toward the ballroom. "Excuse me," Mother whispered, and pushed past to catch up with them.

I felt so sick. All those flowers. I needed some fresh air.

I pushed past everyone to a door hidden behind a painting of a water nymph. Checking to make sure no one would witness my escape, I opened the door and slid into the space behind the painting, having to wrestle with the skirt and train of my dress to close the door again.

Faint lights lined the dark hallway of the south wing, shut down for the summer season. I stepped forward quickly, silk slippers silent on the marble, grateful to leave the din of the ball behind me. I used to hide from Cara in this wing when we were little girls, and I knew every closet, trapdoor, and ground-level window. I opened the seventh door on the right to get to the winter library.

Expecting it to be dark and abandoned, I started when I saw a man sitting on the wicker divan, reading. Evening light slanted through the windows and reflected off his silky curls.

"Jamie! You scared me!"

He came over and kissed my cheek. "Apologies. I've been at the hospital all day, and I needed some peace before I spent the evening telling everyone for the hundredth time how grateful I am to Arthur Lawrence."

"No need to apologize." I sat in one of the low chairs, trying to breathe in my punishing corset. The stiff layers of tulle under my dress made a wall around me. I pushed fruitlessly down at them. "I needed to get away, too."

Jamie cocked his head at me. "Jealous of Cara?"

"No," I said automatically, then remembered I was talking to a friend. I put my hands over my face. "Yes," I said through my fingers.

Jamie came and sat next to me, skinny legs crossed, his too-short pants exposing his socks. "And this doesn't have anything to do with David Dana?"

I lowered my hands. "I'm just as ridiculous as all the girls we used to make fun of," I mumbled.

"You are not ridiculous," Jamie said, patting my hand. "We made fun of the people who were chasing after marriage and money for marriage and money's sake. You genuinely like David. That's different."

"Is it? Not that it makes any difference now," I said bitterly. "I should have realized how I felt earlier, not after he asked another girl to debut. I kept telling myself I didn't care about him, that I thought he was arrogant and fake."

"He certainly acts that way, doesn't he?" Jamie mused. "They could not have built a better gentry boy in a laboratory."

"It doesn't matter. I can't compete with Cara. I couldn't when we were little and I can't even after she is covered in bruises and scratches."

Jamie tensed.

"What?"

"Nothing. It's . . . nothing."

I turned to look at him. "What is it? Is it about Cara's attack?" When he didn't answer right away, I knew I was right. "Jamie, please tell me. I've been trying to figure this out for almost six weeks, and I have nothing to go on."

He fidgeted. "I overheard Philip Wilder at the country club the other day. Something about putting Cara in her place."

"What?" I got to my feet, mind racing, replaying his mocking behavior at the Lawrences' last month. "He wasn't with

Marianne when her family escorted her into the ballroom . . . he must have been out in the grove with Cara."

Jamie raised his hands. "I didn't hear much, and hearsay is not proof. I just heard him laughing to his friends about meeting Cara the night of the debut. He said, 'she deserved it, and I'd do it again.' Then he and his friends called her names a gentleman should not repeat."

"It makes sense," I said. "He attacked her, but Cara knew she couldn't accuse him, not when she would have to admit to agreeing to meet him privately at the Wilders' and risk creating a new scandal. So she accused the Rootless, knowing the police wouldn't bother to prove otherwise."

"Even if Philip did attack her—which we can't prove—how do you explain the abandoned Rootless bag on the scene? It's not worth one of the Rootless's lives to leave an expired charge on gentry property. The punishment for willingly exposing a non-Rootless to radiation is torture and death, and then imprisonment of one's family."

"I don't know," I admitted. "But I'm going to find Philip and force the truth out of him."

Jamie looked worried. "Don't get yourself into trouble. Especially now that the Rootless have marked your house. Do you think that anything you do will change your father's mind and stop his campaign of discipline?"

"Do you really think it's that pointless?" I asked.

"Will it even make a difference to the Rootless?" Jamie

asked. "If you manage to prove that they didn't attack Cara, but the gentry still punish them for the vandalism and for the minor arsons and for the robberies at the ration station— do you think they'll stand up and thank you?" He shook his head. "I work with them every day, and while I genuinely pity their suffering, I also see that your father has made them too angry and too desperate to react in a civilized manner."

I nodded to be polite and to stave off another argument, but I wasn't convinced. Not in the least.

TWELVE

The brassy blare of horns interrupted our conversation. Jamie offered an arm, and we left the library and the winter wing, closing the door behind us and entering the rose-strewn hall.

Now that everyone had moved to the ballroom for the grand entrance, the hall was mostly devoid of life. A few harried-looking servants tended to the buffet tables and to the marble floor, littered with crushed pink petals and fallen beads. No one noticed us creeping into the ballroom—their eyes were ahead on the staircase, where David and Cara were making their first appearance of the night.

I scanned the room for Philip Wilder, but as soon as I saw the debut couple, I could focus on nothing else.

I saw Cara first, the deep pink of her silk dress catching every ray of light, making her shimmer and glow. Fresh pink roses were set in her hair, and she carried a small nosegay in a silver holder. Murmurs rumbled through the crowd—look at her dress, look at *her*—but after glancing at Cara once, I only had eyes for David.

He walked easily down the stairs, one arm supporting Cara,

the other swinging at his side. Amusement lit the corners of his mouth and eyes. He was happy. He wanted to be here. He wasn't just after Cara for her family's influence or her non-debt-ridden estate.

I felt like I might be sick.

Servants began to circle the room, handing out glasses of champagne for the toast. David and Cara paused at the foot of the stairs, waiting for the requisite speech. Addison climbed a low dais at the side of the room. "We are here tonight to celebrate my beautiful daughter's debut into society," she said proudly. "Cara has worked so hard . . ."

As she continued with her speech, I stared at David, drowning out everything except the sound of my memories.

We are alike, you and I, he'd said. But then he'd flung *spoken like a true Landry* at me, like an insult, like a knife.

Though one hand was in his pocket and there was a relaxed set to his shoulders, his eyes flicked around the room ceaselessly and his left foot tapped against the marble stair. He was possessed by the same nervous intensity I'd noticed a few weeks ago in the library, when he'd badgered me into confessing my turmoil over my future.

". . . So please join me in raising a glass to my daughter, Cara, and to her escort, David Dana."

David looked surprised when he was handed a glass—clearly he hadn't been listening to a word of Addison's speech. The guests raised their glasses and murmured their individual benedictions, then drank. I held my flute with trembling hands, unable to bring myself to take a sip.

The band started playing, and David led Cara to the middle of the ballroom floor, where the crowd parted to give them room to dance. The onlookers sighed and clapped at intervals, taken with the couple, with Cara's beauty and David's charm, but I could barely watch. My stomach churned every time he pulled her closer, his hand so low on her waist that his fingertips brushed her bustle. Once, a slender lock of hair fell into her face and he reached to tuck it behind her ear. I found myself remembering what it felt like, his fingers on my skin.

One moment caught my attention. David leaned in to kiss Cara, and instead of welcoming him, she turned her head ever so slightly so that his lips landed on the corner of her mouth. It looked simply like she had turned her head to make her next step in the dance, but from where I stood, I could see a brief flash of distaste flit across her face, as if enduring his kiss was some sort of chore. I had seen that expression many times in our childhood, in etiquette lessons, in school, in our beds late at night when I insisted on reading passages from books aloud.

But as soon as I noticed it, it was gone. I suspected that I had probably imagined it in the first place.

The dance ended and the crowd erupted with applause. Now everyone could dance and the debutante and her escort would partner with as many guests as time would allow.

I took a seat in the back of the room and watched the parade of hopefuls approach Cara and David. Their dancing cards would no doubt be filled within the next few minutes. To my surprise and the surprise of the girls surrounding David, he broke off and started walking toward me. People moved out of his way as he strode across the room, staring at him and then at me. Equal parts mischief and desire were in his face, and I had no idea if he was David the bachelor or David the boy who could guess my favorite stories or even David from the car—barbed and full of uncomfortable questions I didn't have the answers to.

"Would you like to dance with me?" he asked, extending a hand.

I was frozen to the chair. "I—"

All eyes in the room, including Cara's, were on me. I knew without looking the expression on her face: livid, territorial. Every ounce of logic in me begged me to say no to David, yet, this close, I couldn't ignore the message he was telegraphing. He genuinely wanted to dance with me.

He took my hands and pulled me to my feet. "Luckily for you, I have learned how to interpret your silences. This silence means, 'Yes, David, I would love to dance with you.'" He led me to the center of the floor. The band raised their instruments, David placed my hand on his shoulder, and suddenly, I was in his arms.

He danced lightly, but the heat from his hand at my waist burned through my dress.

"You don't look like you are enjoying yourself, Madeline," David reproached. "It is a debut. You are supposed to be drunk on plum wine by this point, and why not? The Westoffs imported crates of the stuff."

We spun in a circle, and I could see the curious gazes of onlookers, wondering why David had picked me, and why I'd consented, when I'd made a career out of only begrudgingly dancing with people, unless they were Jamie.

David pulled me closer as we spun. "I want to know," he said, his mouth very near my ear. "Why does my Madeline look so forlorn?"

"I am not forlorn," I said. "And I am not your Madeline."

"And the gray eyes flash. You're mad at me, then?"

"Yes." I didn't risk saying more—he didn't need to know how confused I felt.

His gleaming shoes slid against my slippers, our steps completely synchronized, his leg pushing against my skirts. "Are you sad that I am leaving?" he asked. "I am quite sad myself."

I felt suddenly tired of his act—and of playing along with it.

"You are not fooling me," I said, keeping my eyes on the band, on the other dancers, anywhere but on his face.

"I assure you that I am indeed sad—"

"I know you are," I interrupted. "I don't mean that. I mean

this act you're putting on for everybody. All charm and no substance."

He grinned a quick canine grin. "It's not an act, I promise." He lifted me up, his hands dangerously close to my breasts, flattened by the corset.

The girls nearby giggled while being lifted by their own partners. Once my feet touched the floor, I moved David's hands back to my waist.

"Why can't you just accept that I am really this charming?" he asked.

"Because I know better." As part of the dance, he drew me close, so that my mouth was next to his ear. I took the opportunity to press my point. "I saw you help that Rootless girl."

For a moment, his grip on my arm grew so tight, I thought he'd bruise me.

Finally he let go. "You saw nothing," he said, stepping back and bumping into a dancing couple. The clockwork of the dance jammed. The dancers stopped to stare and the band stopped playing mid-tune. Gone was the casual air, the expression that suggested David thought the whole evening was a grand joke. He looked pale.

And furious.

"You should go," he said, his voice choked.

"Why? Because I know that you helped her?"

He glanced around the room. The murmurs and rustles stilled to nothing as everybody leaned forward to listen. "I think you are mistaken. I was not in the park that day. Maybe you were just daydreaming about me."

My face burned. "You're lying," I told him.

"And you're delusional."

We were both breathing heavily by this point, inches away from each other. "You should go," he said.

"You can't make me leave. This is not your house."

Cara swished up, eyes narrowed. "But it is my house, and you're making a scene."

"I won't forget what I saw," I told David. And with the eyes of the city boring into my back, I left the ballroom, forcing myself to walk as slowly as dignity would allow.

THIRTEEN

I woke up the next morning feeling exhausted and listless. I'd spent the night stirring and sighing in the silvery moonlight, vacillating between anger at David and anger with myself, between feeling hurt and feeling confused. In the darkest hours, I let a sharp needle of remorse dig at my stomach as I went over everything that had gone wrong since Marianne Wilder's debut.

I hadn't found Cara's attacker. I hadn't obeyed or pleased my father. I hadn't discovered why David helped that girl in the park, why he seemed so interested in me, or why he flitted around the edge of my thoughts constantly when all I wanted to do was forget him.

And the look on his face when he told me to go . . .

I curled up on my bed and let that needle of shame grow hotter and hotter until I thought it would burn a hole inside me, falling asleep only after I'd numbed my mind with programs on my wall screen.

The morning was no better. As Elinor brought a breakfast tray to my room, I put my head in my hands.

"Are you all right, miss?" Elinor asked, leaving the tray and helping me sit. "You look like you're about to be sick."

I caught sight of myself in the mirror. My sleepless night had left dark circles under my eyes and an ashen cast to my skin. I looked terrible.

"I'm okay," I said. "I just—I feel a little lost right now is all."

"Why don't you take a walk to the university and stroll around the grounds?" Elinor asked, walking over to the wardrobe and pulling out a floral organza dress with flouncing sleeves and a wide green sash. "You could even take lunch at the country club, since it's so close."

The country club. Philip Wilder might be there.

"You know, Elinor, I think that is an excellent idea."

I skipped the university altogether. I didn't know if Philip would be at the club or not, but he and his friends usually spent most of their days playing golf or tennis while working their way through hundreds of dollars of whiskey and opium. I also didn't know what I really hoped to accomplish; it wasn't as if I expected him to admit to assault and battery in the middle of one of the oldest gentry institutions in the city, but I did know that I couldn't stand this nagging feeling that I wasn't doing enough, that I was standing by as uselessly as those people in the old video files from the academy, who simply watched as victim after victim was forced into the gibbet cage.

The country club had been founded a century or so before the Last War, by a man named Nichols who'd developed much of Kansas City. Though he'd died before many of the Uprisen had even been born, he was revered as a man ahead of his time, pioneering the idea of an engineered society, of a leisurely and protected life for the upper class. A statue of him gazing gravely toward the world he'd helped inspire stood outside the country club.

I steeled up my courage and walked past the statue, into the dimly lit lobby, all heavy wood and stone and blank-faced servants. Inside, the shouting from the pool and the zipping sound of the hydrogen golf carts vanished, and was replaced by the sound of murmuring voices and clinking glasses.

I ordered lunch and waited for Philip Wilder to appear.

After I'd finished a light meal of roasted pheasant and jasmine rice, he finally walked in with Mark Everly and Stuart Lawrence, Tarleton's brother. I stood, smoothed out my dress, and strode over to him before I could lose my nerve.

"Hello, Philip," I said, trying to steady my voice. "Would you like a drink?"

Stuart barked out a short, mocking laugh, but Philip looked genuinely surprised. I never talked to him—or to any of them—unless forced to while dancing or by an unfortunate seating arrangement. Mark Everly gave me a small but friendly smile. I tried to smile back, but found myself struggling with the effort.

Philip nodded to Stuart and Mark, then took my elbow and steered me to the bar. He looked a lot like Marianne—he shared the same wide eyes and high cheekbones—although he was much taller and broader. Strange to think that in the twentieth century the Wilders wouldn't have been let into the country club with their dark skin, or the Lawrences with their ancient roots in Mexico, or even the Thorpes, who'd come from India two centuries ago. In fact, most of us wouldn't have been let in back in those days. Our tradition of marrying only other gentry had given many of us mixed ethnicities, and so most of the gentry were now dark-haired and olive-skinned, like my mother, which made my own pale skin and eyes all the more unusual.

We sat at the bar and Philip ordered us each a glass of plum wine. Philip kept glancing between the glass and me, as if he wasn't sure if he was supposed to start the conversation.

"I heard you and Tarleton Lawrence got in a fight a couple weeks ago," I said after a few awkward minutes.

He shrugged. "We were boxing, and he cheated. He always cheats. And sometimes, I let my temper get the best of me."

"Would you say you get angry often? Angry enough to hit someone?"

"What kind of question is that?" he asked, the irritation plain in his voice.

I gripped my glass tighter, fighting the urge to run away.

"Only if they deserve it," he finally answered. "I hit people if they deserve it. And believe me, Tarleton deserved it."

"Did Cara Westoff deserve it?"

His mouth dropped open, and I felt stunned myself. I couldn't believe I'd just blurted that out.

"What are you suggesting?" he asked heatedly. "That I hurt Cara?"

I cleared my throat. "Maybe."

"What the—" he stopped and, looking around, lowered his voice. "Why the hell do you think I would do something like that? Cara is one of my friends. Why would I hurt her?"

"I don't know. Why would you? Did she refuse you or something? Did she turn you down?"

He gave a quick angry laugh. "Cara refuse *me*? Hardly."

"Then what happened? Why would you say that you put Cara in her place and you'd do it again?"

"How do you know I said that?" He frowned. "Are you spying on me or something?"

"I am not spying on you." I took a drink to hide the shaking in my voice. I wasn't used to confronting people. "I want to know what happened. I think it's a mistake to go after the Rootless; I think that they're innocent. I know Cara's lying about something to protect the gentry or to protect her reputation. I intend to find the truth and to tell everyone when I do." I took a deep breath. It was getting easier, bit by painful bit, to push past my quiet nature.

Philip didn't say anything for a moment. He just swirled

the remaining wine in his glass. "I was going to meet Cara at Marianne's debut that night," he admitted. "She had seemed interested for a while, like she wanted to date, and then she asked me to meet her in the gallery, which would have been empty during the party. But I've got my eye on someone else and didn't want to meet her. The Lawrence boys thought it would be a great prank to stand her up—you know, embarrass the great Cara who has humiliated pretty much every boy in this city.

"But at the last minute, I lost my nerve. I didn't want to fool around with her, but I also hated the thought of her waiting alone. So I went up to the gallery to tell her that it wasn't going to happen, that I wasn't interested. But she wasn't there and that's when I heard the scream." He drained the last of the wine. "I haven't told any of the guys that I went to the gallery. I let them think that I had really tried to stand her up. Stuart and Tarleton and Frank, well, you know how nasty they can get. I guess I just got carried away joking around with them."

A bleak smile. "The ironic thing is that if Cara was in the grove, then she was planning on standing me up, too. Guess it is a good thing I decided not to meet her."

"Philip, I'm sorry," I said. "That I thought . . ."

He shrugged a powerful shoulder. "I suppose that's my fault. If people think I could be capable of something like that, then I must have done something to deserve it."

I left him alone then, trying to sort through my thoughts.

I had to readjust my impression of Philip. I'd always assumed he was cut from the same cloth as the Lawrence boys, but he wasn't. He'd been honest and polite, much more like his sister, Marianne, than his friends.

And most importantly, if Philip was innocent, then the perpetrator could still be anyone and I was back to knowing nothing.

That evening, I paced the length of the observatory, watching the coming dusk through the glass roof and walls. Usually I would have been reading or preparing the telescope for the coming night, but at the moment I was unable to focus on a single task and was possessed by a need to move. The sunlight was glinting off the modern skyscrapers downtown near the river, but I turned my eyes south and west, where I could see the windows of Glasshawke, the Glaize estate, reflecting the orange and pinks of the sun.

I stopped at one of the north windows and leaned my head against the glass. There was nothing I could do about Cara's attack at the moment, but knowing that didn't make me any less restless. I wanted to be out of the house, out of the endless churn of dances and dinners, away from the tedium that had followed the conclusion of my academy studies. And then I knew exactly what to do.

I walked downstairs and found Father reading in his study.

The dusk filtered into the room, the orange light revealing galaxies of dust motes sparkling and swirling the air.

He set his book—an old one, judging by the worn leather cover—on a stack of similarly aged books and stood. "Care for a walk?" he asked, as I'd hoped he would.

"Yes," I assented with a smile.

After leaving the house, we walked arm in arm down the wide stone steps to the gardens, Father quizzing me about Edmund Burke and different species of plants as we went.

"We have just received several black irises from Israel this morning," he was saying. "I ordered them to be put in the greenhouse, but our gardener thinks perhaps next year we could attempt to grow them outdoors."

I nodded, wondering how to phrase my question without seeming abrupt and overeager.

"I really find them quite striking. Jacob Landry is said to have bred black roses using some of the genes from the black iris, but unfortunately, those roses no longer grow on the estate. I wish that we still had some experts in genetics in the city who I could commission to breed them again, but as you know, there are none." He sighed. "Of course, physics and astronomy are nobler sciences than biology, and so I don't begrudge the fact that gentlemen limit their studies to these. But what is a man to do when he would like some black roses for his garden?"

"The vaccines and treatments require biology," I murmured.

He waved away an oncoming lightning bug. "I did not say that biology wasn't necessary. Only that it wasn't noble. Physics is the gateway to understanding our very existence—our beginnings and ends. Those who study it are contemplating the largest questions in the universe. Biologists today are nothing more than laboratory technicians, replicating vaccine recipes created centuries ago."

Seeing my chance, I pounced. "Perhaps I could contemplate those questions, too. Have you reconsidered my going to the university?"

Father stopped, his mouth twisted in amusement. "Are you seriously still preoccupied with this business of going to the university? After I told you expressly that it was not possible and that you must marry?"

I raised my chin. "I won't change my mind. I want to go and I think it's best for the estate—and for me—if I have an education."

"How could it be best for the estate if you were celibate and shut away for four or five or eight years, when you should be marrying and providing the family with another heir?"

I pulled away from him. "I can't waste my days in utter boredom while I wait to be bred like a horse. I hate feeling like my life is not really my own."

"Your life is not your own," Father said calmly. "And it never was. Just as mine was never my own, and your uncle Stephen's and your grandfather's were never their own. We are Landrys.

And without Landry Park—which cannot be safe without an heir—and without our history of contributing to this great way of life, we are nothing. We are servants to our dynasty."

"I can't believe that," I whispered. "Or I shall go mad."

His face softened. "You are not a broodmare or dog or even a Hapsburg princess to be married off to shore up alliances." He took me gently by the shoulders. "Do you not see that you will be the mistress of this house and of your marriage? That whoever you marry will be eternally grateful to you for your condescension in letting him live in your house? *You* will join the ranks of the Uprisen, Madeline, and your children will bear the Landry look, not that of your husband's. I am not condemning you to a life of vassalage, but a life of leadership."

"Can't this life wait until after I have attended the university?" I asked one last time. "Please?"

"It cannot." He kissed my forehead. "It's my fondest wish that you will see the wisdom of all I have asked of you. And please, for the sake of our amity, do not trouble me with this conversation again."

FOURTEEN

David Dana was walking the wrong way.

It was three days after Cara's debut, and I was browsing in a dusty bookstore in the middle-class part of town. I'd found a battered copy of *The Faerie Queen* and pulled it off the shelf. We had a four-hundred-year-old copy under glass at home, but this one was newer, with annotations.

My lips murmuring the verses, I had looked up to see David, dressed in a shirt and vest like a servant, with a gardening cap pulled low over his face and his shoulders hunched. He glanced backward every now and then to make sure he wasn't being watched.

He was walking east, into the poorest part of town. Soon he would be among the scullery maids and laborers and factory workers. If he kept walking after that, he'd reach the rusted chain-link fence and tumble-down gate leading to the miserable slums of the Rootless.

He's probably just going for a walk, I told myself. *Stop being so suspicious.*

I couldn't help it, though. I had to know what he was up to, walking so quickly and so furtively. If he was going to the

Rootless ghetto, it could have something to do with the girl he'd helped in the park. I entertained the fantasy of running up alongside him, asking him where he was going and why. But the harsh words uttered in Cara's ballroom still hurt. My pride refused me asking him plainly.

Mind made up, I set down the book and slipped out of the shop, careful to stay several feet behind as I trailed him. Enough people roamed the sidewalk with fresh loaves of bread and bottles of milk in hand that I could easily weave in and out behind David without being seen.

"What are you doing?" someone to my left demanded.

I turned to see Cara—of all people—looking radiant and sunny in a tennis uniform and sneakers. She frowned at me. It was another opportunity to pester her for answers, but the thread connecting me to David was too compelling, too strong to break.

"Nothing," I told her. "Just out for a walk."

I turned back to David, relieved to see the gardener's cap still bobbing in the distance. I scrambled to follow, forcing my short legs into long strides.

Cara easily matched my pace. "Madeline, what are you doing?" she asked curiously. "Why are you going east?"

"Why are *you*?" I asked.

"I am hiding from my mother," she said, and for a minute, the imperiousness in her voice faded. "I told her I'd meet her after tennis at the country club, but I decided to leave instead."

"Why?"

"It's none of your business." Her voice was clipped. I looked over and was surprised to see something like unhappiness on her face. She glanced at me. "You didn't used to be so nosy. I wish you would stop."

"All right then." I turned my eyes to the back of David's head.

"So why are you heading toward the bad part of town?"

"Well, that is none of *your* business."

"Is that—" she squinted up ahead. "Is that David? Where on earth is he going?"

I didn't answer, but wondered—not a little sulkily—why she didn't know, since she had debuted with him three days earlier, since they were the couple constantly being photographed holding hands and cuddling. I wished I had the willpower to turn off my tablet and my wall screen, and shut out the stream of gentry gossip. But the lure of his face, of even a glimpse of his bright eyes and big smile—it weakened me. Paralyzed me. I bit my lip, resisting the urge to look at him again, at the way his back and shoulders stretched his shirt and at the way the sunlight caught the ends of his hair under his cap.

"Oh," she breathed, after I kept my face averted from hers, trying to hide my thoughts. "I get it. You're *following* him. Does this have something to do with your fight at my party?"

"No," I answered quickly.

She smiled a sharp smile. "Of course not."

"I am curious about where he's going, is all. Most gentry avoid this part of the town like the plague."

"And so should we. Who cares what he's doing?"

"I care," I said, redoubling my pace. "And I would have thought you would, too."

She cut in front of me, making me stop short. "No, really. It's one thing for a man to stroll into the eastern part of town, but we're two girls and we're not exactly dressed to blend in. Let's go back."

"This doesn't involve you," I said.

She gave an exasperated sigh. "But it will if the constables find your body stuffed in an alley somewhere and I have to spend the rest of my life feeling guilty that I didn't stop you."

I narrowed my eyes at her. It wasn't like Cara to care about what I was doing or where I was going. I sincerely doubted that she was trying to stop me out of fear for my safety.

"I want to see where David is going," I told her firmly, and pushed past her.

She stood there for a moment then skipped up beside me.

"I'm coming along," she announced. "I want to see what he's up to as well."

"Shouldn't you already know what he's up to?" I asked, "Since you're together and all?"

"I'm not his secretary," she replied. "Just his girlfriend."

I tasted bitterness like bile in my mouth. "You sound like you are really in love. Congratulations."

"And you know so much about love?" Cara scoffed. "I know for a fact that you've never even kissed a boy, much less dated one."

"What do you know about it? Have you ever actually cared for someone? Not just what they could do for you or how they could make you feel—but cared about them as a person? Put their thoughts and wishes above yours?"

"*Yes,*" she said, and I was shocked by the intensity in her voice. "And if I were you, I would shut up now."

Well, at least that threat led us back to normal Cara behavior. The sound of cars and fountains and people murmuring filled the space where our conversation had been.

We passed a series of small but respectable row houses with their neat window boxes of yellow flowers. We walked past tall apartment buildings with children playing outside, past homes with patchy yards and auto garages with rusted wind turbines on top. We walked for almost an hour, the hot concrete of the sidewalk burning through my slippers.

"Are you ever going to tell me what happened the night you were attacked?" I asked finally, the worst of my vexation with Cara draining into my legs, into my feet, into the sidewalk.

"No," she said.

"I talked with Philip Wilder, you know. A few days ago."

She threw up her hands. "Why on earth would you do that?"

"Because I thought he might have been the one to hurt you."

"Philip?" she scoffed. "Please. He couldn't hurt a fly."

"He hurts his boxing partners."

"Because he has zero training as a boxer and can't control his own strength. I could fight him off easily if I wanted."

"Why did you stand him up?" I asked. "He said you were supposed to meet him in the gallery, but when he went, you weren't there. Why were you in the Grove instead?"

"It's really none of your business." Her jaw was clenched.

I watched her face carefully. "Were you going to meet the Lawrence boys instead?"

"It's none of your business!" she exploded. "Who touched me, who touches me, who wants to touch me—it's over, it's done with, and it's none of your concern."

I thought of the Rootless raids, of the red paint on my house. Of my father pushing the Rootless and the Rootless pushing back. "You're wrong," I said softly. "You've made it my business now."

She focused her green eyes on me. "I am sorry about your house," she said after a minute.

"Are you?"

"Listen, it's not my fault that your father is some kind of dictator when it comes to the Rootless. But I *am* sorry about your house. I know how much you love it."

I examined her face for any sign of sarcasm. There was none. For some reason, this unsettled me. Cara being selfish and haughty was one of the most consistent facts of my life.

That she had genuinely noticed my feelings and expressed some form of pity—it bothered me.

Four or five miles out from the bookstore, I could make out the twisted metal and crumbling stone that separated this ghetto from the ghetto beyond. David was walking straight toward it.

The neighborhood by the Rootless fence was rough; the roads were potholed and weedy, and there were few people out and about, though the sound of barking dogs and blaring wall screens filled the open air.

Those people who were outside stared at us hard, taking in my long flowing dress and Cara's sparkling bracelets. They knew we didn't belong here. They knew we had no business heading east. But whereas someone from the middle-class part of town might have stopped us, might have begged to escort us away from those twisted pointless gates, no one here seemed interested in helping us.

Cara, for one, seemed entirely unconcerned, which was curious, given her earlier insistence that I avoid the dangers of this area.

It's not that dangerous, I reassured myself. *The Rootless are always polite and quiet when they collect the charges.* But then I remembered the red words scrawled across the front of my house. It was possible that they wouldn't take too kindly to two gentry girls waltzing into their neighborhood, no matter how much one of them theoretically sympathized with their cause. I knew the constables patrolled the Rootless part of town, but how frequently and with what degree of diligence was a mystery. No one knew where I was—I could be missing for days before anyone thought to look here.

FIFTEEN

The Rootless lived in a vast enclosed space that had once been a massive park. Before the Last War, people came here to visit the zoo and the large outdoor theater. Children played soccer or baseball on the expansive fields. The zoo and the theater were gone now, but the crumbling stone pillars of the entrance remained, as did the occasional stone park shelter—isolated, ancient things out of place among the shacks and ration stations and wind turbines spinning nearby. Stone and steel, side by side.

At first, the town on the other side of the Rootless gate looked much the same as the neighborhood before it. The road was rough and potholed. A corrugated metal ration station displayed shriveled and bruised fruit, while a carpentry shop next door smelled of sawdust and metal.

Disconcertingly, the bread station nearby smelled of the same thing.

The farther I crept past the gates, the more differences I noticed between the two neighborhoods. There were no weeds growing up in the streets here. Delicate charcoal and chalk murals ebbed and flowed from one building to the next, sometimes spilling onto the sidewalk below, sometimes flowing across the street in black-and-white rivulets. Concrete statues and shining steel sculptures guarded doorways and intersections, and hand-carved benches lined the roads, set in the shade. Trees and wildflowers filled the spaces between buildings and houses, and the sidewalks were meticulously paved with white stone. Farther in, the not-quite-houses here were infinitesimal, barely there specks of shelter, but despite the mismatched shingles and plastic for windows, all the houses were repaired and clean and had well-trimmed lawns.

There were no gardens here. No vegetables or herbs, or anything of the like. Even wild onions were not allowed to grow in the Rootless ghetto. Growing your own food was punishable by arrest and possibly worse, depending on the gentry's mood.

And the gentry's mood was evident everywhere in the otherwise peaceful neighborhood. I counted five or six burned houses, with only charred metal and broken concrete remaining among the ashes. The plastic that many used in lieu of glass for their windows was puckered and tattered, as if batons and rocks had ripped it apart, and everywhere, on walls and doors and signs, the authorities had pasted a large, colorful poster: a gentry man from the waist up with his arms spread wide. In the foreground were smiling families holding nuclear charges with sacks of food piled at their feet. Behind the gentry man's head was the familiar atomic energy symbol, the orbits of the electrons painted in silver and the nucleus a ball of shining gold resting on top of his head. The electrons were painted emerald and ruby and sapphire, making the symbol look like a crown studded with jewels. Like a halo.

◂We are all family, read a banner at the bottom.

A few older men and women sat on the shaded benches, their eyes on me. I nodded to them and attempted a half-hearted sort of wave, hoping the gesture seemed friendly and not pretentious.

Their expressions didn't change, but I could feel the dark hostility hovering around them. I picked up the skirt of my soft cotton dress and hurried past them with my head ducked. I felt embarrassed by my long pale arms, smooth and still smelling of ivy soap and chamomile from my bath this morning. Of the wide silk sash just under my chest, of the silk slippers on my feet. Cara just gave the people we passed a jaunty smile.

"Stop it," I hissed.

"What? I'm being friendly."

"You are being supercilious."

David took a left, and we hugged the shadows of the buildings, ducking behind a statue when he looked back. There were only a few people out and about—most were probably out collecting charges, or sorting them onto the trains at the very eastern edge of the old park. I fervently hoped that we wouldn't go anywhere near the sorting yards; my only knowledge of them was gleaned from whispered conversations of the servants, and those conversations were always riddled with fear and horror. I knew they were underground, in a concrete and lead-lined cave, the same as the train tracks and the hundreds of miles of tunnels that led the trains to Florida where the charges were shot into space.

David stopped and scanned the street. I yanked Cara behind a nearby statue and held my breath.

"This is so stupid," I heard her say, but she stayed still and I got the feeling she was actually enjoying this, in some weird way.

After a minute like this, David turned around and continued on his way. I scurried to catch up, with Cara following close behind.

We came upon a low brick building with darkened windows. A sign with a picture of an overflowing stein swung above the door. David walked in. I crept up to the door, thinking hard. Perhaps if I snuck in quickly, no one would see me. Or maybe if I followed someone in, I could hide.

But there were two of us, and in our fresh clothes and with our long, gleaming hair—so different from the Rootless women with their lank strands tucked underneath kerchiefs and caps—we'd never be able to walk in unnoticed.

The roar of greetings and clunking mugs diverted my thoughts. There was an open window at the side of the building. I slipped into the narrow alley and sat beneath the open window, fighting the temptation to take a peek at the men inside. Cara arranged herself beside me, wrinkling her nose at the damp stone currently ruining her tennis skirt.

"Now that the pretty boy is here, can we finally begin?" a gruff voice asked from inside the tavern.

"Good to see you, too, Smith," David said pleasantly. Some chairs scraped against the floor, as if people were pulling up to the table. Given how clearly I could hear everything, I surmised that the group was very near the window.

"What news from the other side of town, David? Will they stop the arrests?"

"How could they?" David answered. "With the mayor sick with radiation-induced cancer? With Smith's stunt at Landry Park last month? The gentry are all paranoid, but Alexander Landry is more paranoid than most, and with him convinced that one of you attacked the Westoff girl and ruined his house, he is hell-bent on punishing the persons responsible. You're lucky that no one has been killed."

"He's afraid of us," someone said.

"He has reason to be afraid," Smith growled. "Soon everything he loves will be gone."

"You have to be careful. The landowners are beginning to meet in secret, and Alexander is likely ready to summon the Uprisen from around the country. If they go after you, your revolution will be over before it even begins."

"Of course you want us to be cautious. You're one of them."

"I support your cause, Smith."

"You support our cause, eh?" Smith said. "For an entire month?"

"Two, actually," David replied calmly. "Not to mention my involvement with the Rootless in Atlanta. Since I was a boy I brought them food and money."

"You've brought enough money to fund a small country—"

"And we're grateful," someone interrupted.

"—But action is what we need to see. Revolution. We may be eating better because of you, but we're still enslaved. Still sick and dying."

David sighed. "I know you're anxious to see change. We all are. But we have to *strategize*. Rushing headlong into violence will get us nowhere."

Smith made a noise like he was going to interrupt, but someone else spoke instead.

"David has a point," a measured voice said. Hoping no one was facing my direction, I dared a look, raising my eyes just above the sill and squinted into the gloom. Ten or eleven men sat around the table, grimly clutching glasses of dark beer. David sat in the middle, the only one without a drink, looking casual but alert, his eyes smoldering indigo even in the darkness. The man speaking in the slow voice was the tallest and looked to be the oldest—at least fifty. Sores clustered like small clouds over his arms and face.

The door opened, spilling sunlight into the shadows, and I could see that he was younger than I first thought, perhaps only a few years older than my father, but his hunched back and poorly bandaged lesions made him look wizened and weary, like a dying hermit.

"Jack," Smith said, "I know you feel like you owe some sort of debt to the boy—"

"I do," Jack said, interrupting Smith with a sharp look. "David brought my stepdaughter, Sarah, to me when no other of his kind would have. She would have died there and not at home in my arms and her mama's. And for that, I'm grateful."

Sarah. So that was the name of the Rootless girl from the park. An intense sadness filled me at the thought of her death. I wished furiously that I could have been less of a coward and helped her when she needed it most.

The men cleared their throats and looked away. Smith glanced toward the window and I ducked, praying he hadn't seen me.

"Well, it won't matter if the gentry discover our plans," one man said finally. "Not with our new allies."

"What new allies?" David asked.

"Don't tell him."

David sounded irritated. "I know how convinced you are that I am untrustworthy, but I am only trying to help. And if you are trying to reach out to other groups, then I might be able to help you sort out the politics of it all."

"Help us?" Smith snorted. "Because we're too stupid to figure it out on our own?"

"That is not what I—"

"Stop it, Smith," Jack ordered. I got the distinct feeling he was in charge. Smith bit his tongue, though I could almost feel the waves of resentment rolling off him.

"I want it to be clear," Jack said, "that David has my full and complete trust. He was raised as gentry, but his heart is as clear as ours. He grew up caring for and knowing our people in Georgia, and he can help us now. Yes, Smith, you may resent it, but David grew up in the military and went to the best schools. He knows things about the world that we do not. We will listen to him."

"Thank you," David said quietly. "Now please—who are these allies?"

"You know that we have most of the working-class laborers and even some of the middle-class merchants on our side now. The servants are still too comfortable working in the great houses and the farmers do not wish to get involved."

I dared another look inside, wanting to see who was speaking. A thin man with no hair had his hands spread wide, gesturing to a map on the table.

"They sent us a package at first. A letter of goodwill that only Jack here could read, and a pound of jade beads. It was enough to buy medicine and food for all of us for several months. That was two years ago. Last year, they gave encrypted tablets to the Rootless leaders in each city so we could talk to one another. Before the tablets, we used to send messages with our men on the packing trains, but it was difficult for them to pass along those messages when the trains only stopped for a few minutes in each city for track switch overs. Now, we can communicate with our brethren in any city at any time."

Jack spoke again. "Then, last month, one of them visited and we heard what they had to say."

"And 'they' are . . . ?"

"The Eastern Empire, of course," Jack answered.

More silence.

David leaned forward. "You realize that the Empire only help themselves? They may fund you and encourage you, but they will only use you as a tool to destabilize the country. Once you have done that, they will sweep in and take everything for themselves, and they will leave nothing for you."

"You would say that!" Smith roared, standing up. "You would say anything to stop us!"

Smith stopped suddenly, finger still raised from when it had pointed at David. His eyes were trained on the window. On me.

Gasping, I tried to crouch down and sneak away, but Smith was too quick. In an instant, he'd crossed the tavern and reached through the window, hauling me up by my hair. He grabbed my arms and lifted me through the window. A small scream of fear escaped my lips, and when he threw me to the roughly planked floor, I was crying. Bruises bloomed on my arms from his fingers, and I felt as if my scalp had been ripped from my head.

David stood, alarmed. "Madeline?"

"There's another one," Smith said, pointing outside. A few of the others had gone out the door and into the alley, and I could hear Cara shouting as they grabbed her. They dragged her inside, and it took three men to hold her. I saw with more than a little pride that one sported a bloody lip.

"She's a strong one," a man said.

"*Cara?*" David looked incredulous.

"So you know these spies?" Smith demanded. "We should kill them right now before they run back to their manor and tell the gentry what they've heard!"

"I am not a spy!" I cried.

He turned on me. "Then what are you doing here? Did the gentry send you? Did the government?"

"No! I was just—I was just following David." It sounded lame, even to my ears.

"So he led you here? He told you about our meeting? What else did he tell you?" He grabbed my arm again, yanking me up and shaking me. David leaped forward and shoved Smith, fist cocked and ready to strike.

"Enough!" Jack roared, and everyone, including me, froze.

"David, please step back. Smith, kindly take a seat."

David lowered his hand, but Smith still stood, tensed and angry.

"Smith," Jack said. There was a coldness to his voice that frightened me.

Smith pointed at me. "She's dangerous. They're all dangerous. Maybe you don't want to see that, but I do. We won't be safe until she's dead."

Jack got out of his chair, struggling with a cane. But whatever weakness his body betrayed was more than made up for by his expression of fury. He walked up to Smith and spoke ominous rumbling words in his ear, deliberately pronouncing some and emphasizing others with nudges of his cane. Smith slowly paled and pulled back.

"I'll sit," Smith said.

"Good decision." Jack then trained his stone-colored eyes on my own. "You are a Landry, are you not? Alexander Landry's daughter?"

I nodded.

Several of the men hissed. "A Landry within our own walls," one spat. "I never thought I'd see the day."

Jack held up a hand. "She may be a friend yet."

"No Landry is a friend of ours."

"What about this one?" someone said, jerking their head toward Cara. "This is the Westoff girl. The reason our people are being beaten and arrested right now! We should show her personally all the trouble she's caused."

Cara started struggling, and some of the men began cheering.

"But she is David's debutante," I blurted, trying to think of a way to help her. "They just debuted together. She wouldn't tell anybody anything she's heard, I know she wouldn't."

Jack raised his eyebrows and turned to David, who looked just as surprised as everyone else. "Are you involved with Cara Westoff?"

David hesitated, then answered. "Miss Westoff and I debuted together."

Even though it had been my suggestion, hearing the words out of his mouth pained me more than the bruises on my arms.

Cara nodded emphatically.

Jack frowned at Cara, and then at David, as if deciding whether or not to say something else. Finally, he shook his head and gestured for the men to let Cara go.

"We will not harm these girls."

Some of the men protested.

"They deserve it!"

"What if they tell?"

"They may indeed tell, although I hope they will not, but hurting these girls would be the end of us, the end of our hope of building a better life. You see what's happened just on the basis of one attack with no evidence—save for your word, Miss Westoff—"

Cara looked down.

"What would happen if *two* gentry girls were hurt, and we actually *had* done it? Alexander Landry would execute Smith if he ever found out he's responsible for the vandalism. How many would he kill to avenge his own daughter?"

Smith didn't answer, but glared darkly at me, as if everything was my fault.

Jack turned to us. "I would like to speak with you young ladies privately, and then you will be free to leave. Is that acceptable?"

Cara and I both nodded.

"I'll come with you," David offered.

"Excellent. Will you lead Miss Landry and Miss Westoff to my house while we finish our meeting here?"

David agreed and hurried us out of the door, away from the roiling resentment of the men in the tavern. David squinted at me in the sunlight. "Are you all right?" he asked.

"I'm fine," I said.

"I'm not," Cara said. "You have very rude friends."

"Half of their sons and daughters are in prison. They were actively talking treason. You can understand why they would be a little jumpy."

"No, I can't understand. The Empire? A revolution?"

"I thought you, of all people, would be happy to hear it," David said, and Cara flushed a dangerous color.

"Be careful," she warned, and the heat in her voice was palpable. "Now I have just as much dirt on you as you have on me."

David inclined his head politely, as if they'd just finished a game of whist. "As you say." He offered me an arm, which I took out of habit. He offered his other to Cara, who just rolled her eyes.

And then he led us farther into the park, back onto the clean, narrow street lined with tiny houses.

SIXTEEN

"What were you thinking?" David asked after a minute or so of awkward silence. "Smith could have killed you. Any one of those men could have attacked you." He moved his arm and put his hand on my waist to guide me around a small pothole.

"Their leader wouldn't have let them," I said, distracted by his hand. Cara seemed determined to ignore both of us, walking as far behind us as she could without getting lost.

"You mustn't tell anyone," David said. "About what you've seen or heard. Promise me."

"Do you really think I would? When my father would have all of them killed? Even if I didn't agree with them, I wouldn't do that. I couldn't."

David slowed down. "So you do agree with them?"

I slowed down, too. "Yes."

He didn't say anything to this, but his hand began sliding up and down on my waist, as if he wanted to touch more of me. Unable to keep them still, his fingers drummed restlessly, dangerously close to the bodice of my gown. A hot flush spread up my neck. What if Cara saw?

"It's strange," I said, trying to act casual, like men touched my waist all the time. "On our side of town, you always act so—"

"Charismatic?" he answered for me. "Magnetic?"

"I was going to say arrogant."

We walked for a while in silence. When I looked over at him, I saw the same face with the same curved nose and long eyelashes, but it wasn't the same David. His playfulness was tempered. The self-centeredness he wore like armor was gone, replaced with a hushed intensity. His eyes were burning, fervent.

"You are looking at me very strangely," David remarked as we passed another ration station.

"I have lots of questions," I said.

"Ask them, then. I can't have those judgmental eyes trained on me any longer."

I bit my lip. It was all so confusing—his involvement with the Rootless, his strange exchange with Cara, how he had been so protective of me in the tavern today, but so incensed with me at Cara's debut—I didn't know where to begin.

I didn't even know how to feel. With every step closer to Jack's house, my feelings tangled together in an impossible tumult. Envy, shame, guilt, pride, bewilderment, and, strongest of all, that nameless pull in my chest that made me want to walk closer to David, that made things like revolutions and the Eastern Empire seem infinitesimally small.

"Well?" he asked, finally. I opened my mouth to speak, and

then he turned and waved to Cara, who had stopped to retie her shoes. I felt the absence of his hand like an ache.

"Go on ahead," Cara called out. "I'll catch up." Then she flapped her hand to signal that he should keep moving.

He sighed. "My girlfriend," he said to himself.

We started walking again, and I collected my thoughts, pushing the image of David and Cara together out of my mind. There were so many other things to think about, so many other important things . . .

"How long?" I asked.

"How long what?"

I gestured at the Rootless ghetto. "You said you've been helping the Rootless here for two months, but how long have you been sympathetic to their cause?"

"Did you have a nanny?" he asked suddenly.

"I hardly remember her. I had a governess by the time I was four. Father believes children should have education, not coddling."

"In Georgia, our nannies are like our mothers. Certainly my mother was loving and took a large part in raising me—much more than most southern gentry mothers—but Nan was everything to me. She bathed me, dressed me, taught me how to read, took me into the peach orchards to gather fruit for pies. When there were storms at night, it was her bed I ran to. And when Father delayed coming home, it was Nan who hugged me and showed me the new litter of kittens under the porch."

Even over the metallic smell that tinged the air, I could smell that distinctively David scent. Tobacco and spices, with a whiff of something more eastern and expensive, like plums or cherries. He put his hand on my side to lead me around another pothole. The warmth of his hand was palpable even in the June heat. I glanced behind us, wondering if Cara was watching, if she was angry or jealous, but she was more than a quarter mile away. I chewed on the inside of my lip, knowing I should pull away from David, but wanting to move closer instead.

Children ran out in the fields to our side, laughing and chasing a hoop with sticks. They looked remarkably like the children I'd seen playing in the middle-class part of town with the same smiles and shoves and shouts—save for the faint green smudges under their eyes, and the rags they wore for clothes.

"Our estate in Georgia was massive. Some years we would stay at the beach house in Savannah, but mostly we lived in our plantation house south of Atlanta, especially years when the hurricanes were bad. There was this wide avenue leading up to it, lined with live oaks. The house was yellow, with white columns in front and peach trees everywhere. I miss the peaches.

"Anyway, the estate was huge, so I followed Nan everywhere. Except on Mondays. She had Mondays off, and she would sneak out of our room before dawn and go down to the kitchens. She would pack a hamper full of food and steal away before our cook arrived to make breakfast. One day, when I was seven, I snuck out behind her.

"It was hot. Georgia summers are always hot. They are either hot and wet, or hot and dry, and that day a storm was coming, so it was hot and humid. It was so dark that day. Quiet. We walked north, along the road to Atlanta. I could see the skyline, the glass flashing in the lightning. Then Nan turned west and I realized she was going to the Rootless part of the town."

David looked over at the children, who were now running along in front of us, waving and cartwheeling. He waved back and so did I.

"It's different, down home," he said. "With the hurricanes and the heat, it's harder. The rations are smaller. The ghetto itself is smaller." He let go of my waist and shoved his hands in his pockets. A muscle along his jaw twitched.

"It's better here, though," I said hopefully. "Right? They have more food and more room and we don't kill them—"

"As much," he finished for me. "Your people do not kill them *as much*. But you have the right to. At any point, like right now, your father can muster the authority to unleash hell on these people and they have no choice but to accept it. They have no legal rights. They have no place to go and no money to get there. They're not even human to the gentry."

I wanted to answer, to have a response ready that made

us sound better, made me sound better, but I could think of nothing.

"So I followed Nan into the ghetto that day," he said. "I made sure she couldn't see me as she handed out food to everyone she saw. The hunger in their faces—it was feral. Terrifying. And the way they eyed me, and my clothes, and my watch, and my shoes . . . I stayed close to Nan, hoping that if I got robbed, she would hear me. But soon, I felt shame. At my nice clothes and clean skin and full belly. Shame that I had never really noticed the people changing our charges. I didn't even know the names of most of our servants. How had it escaped me that these were people?"

I flushed. Did I know Cook's given name? Or our driver's? Or anyone besides Elinor's? "You were only a child," I tried to say, but he shook his head.

"It doesn't matter. Nan raised me better. Better than to overlook my fellow humans until I was old enough to be in school." We turned a corner and the houses were spread farther apart, with large trees filling the gaps. Almost every tree had a rough wooden swing on it. I felt a twinge—not of guilt but of longing—thinking of my own playthings as a child: china dolls too precious to handle and windup toys imported from Europe. Ivory chess sets smuggled from the East. I'd never tumbled in the grass with friends.

David went on. "Nan went into one of the lean-tos that passed for a house. A small window had been cut out of the particleboard and lined with plastic. There was a sick woman on the floor, covered by a sheet of plastic and with nothing but the dirt for a pillow. Nan knelt and touched the woman's face, pulling out some water and a cloth. She wiped the woman's face and hands, and finally her feet. She took the plastic off and covered her with a soft blanket that I recognized from her own bedchamber in the nursery.

"After helping the woman sip broth and water, Nan sat back on her heels and cried. She must have cried over that woman for the better part of an hour. I eventually realized that the woman had died, right there under Nan's hands, wrapped in her blanket."

A thin track of moisture felt blessedly cool on my face; I realized I was beginning to cry. "Who was she? The woman your nanny visited?"

"Her sister. She had married the man she loved, and he happened to be Rootless. He died just a few years later, but it was too late for her to go back to being a servant or to work in a factory. She had been tainted."

I stopped and pretended to adjust my slippers. I wiped my eyes on my sleeve as discreetly as possible. David stopped too, crouching next to me.

"Have you ever looked into the eyes of someone who has given up? Who has to watch their children fester in fevers and sores, or waste away in starvation? Who has to watch their neighbors killing for bags of weevil-ridden flour and rancid vegetables while they work in estates where food is literally thrown out in heaps? In Atlanta, the penalty for stealing from gentry trash is death. And the bodies strung up on the estates numbered in the hundreds. That is the desperation. That is the abject, blighted, *horrific* desperation of it all. And they live that every day. Every day for two hundred years, they have lived that."

David leaned forward to see my face. "I'm sorry. I just—I thought you would want to know why I cared. Why I helped Sarah in the park that day. Why I give them money, food—whatever they need. Why I have been helping them plan a way to force the gentry out."

I looked at him. "You would be killed if anyone else knew."

"I know," he said. His eyes locked onto mine, no longer bright, but a murky crepuscular color.

"I won't tell," I promised.

"I feel like I'm caught between two worlds, and I can't break through to either side."

"If you're so unhappy, why not join the Rootless? Like your nanny's sister?"

He laughed bitterly. "And leave all my money? The nice clothes and nice cars and nice girls begging for dances? Am I that unhappy?"

I could see the answer as clearly as the night on the balcony when I first talked to him at length. "Yes."

He passed a hand over his eyes. "Maybe I am. When I'm

with the Rootless, it all seems so clear—justice, freedom, and health, regardless of who your parents were. But when I'm home, I find it impossible not to enjoy being the man everyone thinks I should be."

"You're human." I took a breath. "Do you think I don't know better? That I don't notice the incongruity of eating saffron and caviar every night while people just miles away starve on government rations? And have I done anything about it? Have I reached out to them? Have I given them anything I call my own?" I'd never said all that out loud before, or even articulated it that clearly to myself, but I knew it was true as soon as I said it.

David looked shocked … and relieved.

"It is so easy just to give money and supplies," he said. "And anything that's not a real sacrifice for me." He stepped closer, so that his head blocked out the sun and his face was in shadow. I could see every curve and angle in sharp relief. "I've never met anybody who feels the same."

"Are we there yet?" Cara demanded, finally catching up to us. Sweat beaded on her forehead. David backed away from me.

"I'm not taking another step," she declared with a toss of her hair. She gave David a winning smile. "I hope you're up to carrying me the rest of the way."

"That won't be necessary," he told her. "It's right here." He pointed at a stone house that clearly used to be one of the zoo buildings. Real glass filled the windows and a real wooden door hung on antique hinges. The words KANSAS CITY ZOO were etched into the lintel.

David noticed me looking. "They had to force him to live there. He doesn't see why his family deserves a better house than the rest, but they insist."

"Because he's their leader?"

David nodded. "And so much more besides."

SEVENTEEN

As we got closer, I could see two boys at work on the large lawn, stirring a giant vat over a fire. One looked about my age and was tall with hair the color of a rising sun. On closer inspection, I could see that he was the Rootless laborer I'd met in the clinic—Ewan.

The other boy was no more than seven or eight, a laughing, tumbling thing with a shock of hair so red that it rivaled my own. He ran up and started trying to wrestle with David, who easily pinned the boy's arms behind his back. The boy was grinning, but I could see the strength in his wiry limbs as he struggled to get free. He was no stranger to fighting.

"Charlie," Ewan said. "Stop."

The boy called Charlie made a face at Ewan and kept squirming and trying to kick David, who was now tickling him.

"Charlie," David said, "this is Madeline Landry and Cara Westoff. Can you say hello?"

Charlie wheezed out a greeting between giggles, and David finally let him go. He ducked under David's arm and scampered off without saying good-bye.

David gestured to Ewan, who was using a long paddle to prod at the vat. "This is Ewan, Charlie's brother. They're Jack's sons."

Ewan was scowling at me.

No, not at me ... at *Cara*. Cara, for her part, was doing everything she could to ignore him, looking this way and that, even as we drew close enough to exchange words. I could only imagine how foreign it felt for her to be despised so openly. I didn't know if *I* could ever get used to the hatred they had for us. I had thought that Ewan liked me, since he was so kind at the clinic. But perhaps in his element, in his own home, he was different. Or perhaps the continuing raids and ration shortages made him regret sharing his pemmican with a gentry girl.

"Ewan," David said, extending a hand. "Good to see you."

Lines of displeasure creasing his otherwise handsome face, Ewan put his hands in his pockets and jutted a chin out at David. I could only see one sore on his body, hidden in his hairline, and it looked small. It made sense. Changing charges was a lower-risk occupation. Jack's family was better off than most then, if they didn't need at least one of their sons to work as a packer on the trains. Even Charlie looked astoundingly healthy, as if he'd been shielded from as much work as possible. Although Sarah's death proved that even the "safest" job in this part of town could prove deadly.

"This is Madeline Landry," David said, nonchalantly dropping his hand.

I held out my hand. "Remember, we met at the clinic?"

He reluctantly shook it. "I do."

"I haven't seen you on my estate since we met. I've been looking forward to seeing you again."

Immediately, it became clear that I'd made a major blunder. David cleared his throat uncomfortably while Ewan's face filled with heat.

"Looking forward to seeing me back at work again?" he asked.

"Ewan—" David said, at the same time I said, "That's not what I meant—"

Ewan snorted. "Sure, it isn't. You know, if I had it my way, no charges would be changed, and they'd all expire and fill your houses with poison."

And then, before I could apologize, he dropped his paddle and stalked away, leaving the huge vat simmering and bubbling.

Cara gave a choked cough, turning away. When she turned back, her chin was quivering.

This stunned me; Cara never cried, not when she fell off her horse when she was ten or when she'd sunburned so badly that the skin peeled off her back for weeks. She hadn't even really cried after her attack. I gave her shoulder an awkward pat, which she shook off with a violent motion.

"Ewan is a little hostile at the moment," David explained to us. "Sarah, his stepsister, died a couple months ago. They were very close."

"I didn't realize," Cara said, looking truly shocked.

David made a sympathetic sound.

"It must be difficult to lose someone you love," she said, and I admired her attempt at empathy. David touched her arm and she leaned into him. I averted my eyes, focusing instead on Ewan's retreating form. Even though it was laughable in a way, after we'd met at the clinic, I'd thought of Ewan almost like a friend. But maybe the divide between Landry Park and the decaying world of the Rootless was too vast to bridge.

Charlie bounded up to us. "Papa's on his way! He told me to show you into the living room! Follow me!" He sprang off to the house, and the three of us followed, Cara swiping angrily at her cheeks as we did so.

Jack sank into his chair with an audible groan, resting his hands on his cane. His chair was the only one with upholstery; possibly it had once been damask, but it was so patched and worn that it was difficult to say. The rest of us sat in hard wooden chairs that creaked unhappily, louder even than the wood floor, which was visibly buckled in some places. After a minute of sitting, David betrayed his natural restlessness. He stood and started pacing, filling the room with the noise of squealing wood.

The furniture was mostly plain, but a few striking charcoal

drawings were pinned to the walls. A few other discarded gentry items were scattered about—two chipped china teacups, dented brass candlesticks, and a patched silk pillow. A soft pink coat lay across a rocking chair, almost as if someone had been using it as a blanket.

"The drawings are Charlie's," Jack said, noticing me looking around. "I trust you've met my boys," he added, nodding out the window at Charlie and Ewan. Ewan stood with his arms folded, glaring off into the distance.

"You will have to excuse my son," Jack said. "He rather takes after his uncle in temperament. Family first, forgiveness second."

"You have a lovely home," I volunteered, and Jack smiled at me.

"You do not forget your manners, I see," he said. "A true Landry."

"How did you know who I was? Back in the tavern?"

"I'm familiar with the Landrys, and once you've seen one, you can spot them all. You are the spitting image of your father and grandfather, although you have your grandmother's features."

"I hear that often."

"I'm not surprised. The Landrys defy Mendelian genetics with astonishing frequency. Every generation a display of recessive genes. It makes one wonder if Jacob Landry dabbled in more than physics."

I thought of the black roses. "He did. My father told me that he bred unusual plants."

"Yes, but I suppose it must be acknowledged that plants are not people. Perhaps the Landrys are simply blessed to carry such overpowering genes." He coughed a deep, chesty cough that I could feel through the floor. "Now, as pleasant as it is to have visitors that are not keen to talk about war, I am afraid I must move our conversation to a more serious vein. Ladies, please explain why you were in our part of town today."

"I just followed Madeline," Cara said quickly. "It was all her idea."

"You had no wish to come here under your own volition, then?" Jack asked. His voice was pleasant, but something about his eyes made Cara straighten up.

"No . . . I wanted to follow her, and I knew she might come here but . . . no. I wouldn't have come on my own."

Jack leaned his head back, peering at Cara through heavy-lidded slits. Each breath of his seemed labored, laden with phlegm and sputum. "I cannot untell a lie for you, even if it was a necessary one," he warned her. I peered at Cara, wondering if she knew what he was talking about.

She nodded. "I know."

"Mr. Dana?" Jack called. David emerged from the dining room, *creak creak creak.*

"Yes?"

"Could you escort Miss Westoff safely to our gates? And ensure that she arrives promptly at her house?"

David glanced at me. "What about Miss Landry?"

"Come back for her. Miss Landry and I are going for a little walk." A small prickle of fear was at the back of my neck; I knew David trusted Jack, and nothing about him suggested I was in any *physical* danger, but something about his presence made me feel as if I was on a precipice and that a mere word of his could send me over the edge.

"I'm not leaving Madeline," Cara said suddenly. I glanced over at her, surprised, but she stared evenly at Jack. "She's a friend of mine and I think it would be wrong of me to leave her alone in an unfamiliar place."

I did a double take at the word *friend*. Sneaking through the Rootless ghetto was hardly fertile ground for friendship. But I did appreciate the gesture.

Jack thought about her words for a moment. "I believe Mr. Dana can vouch adequately for my relative harmlessness. Can you not, Mr. Dana?"

David nodded to Cara. "It is perfectly safe for her."

She looked at me. "Madeline?"

"I'll be fine." *I hope.* "Thank you."

She shrugged carelessly. "You would've stayed for me."

I suppose I would have.

David came up and took my hand, and warmth spread up my torso.

"I'll be back to get you," he promised.

"I'll be fine here," I said.

"I know. Just please stay with Jack."

Jack shook his cane at David. "Go! I will not let any harm come to Miss Landry."

David and Cara left, and Jack stared at me from across the room. I felt completely naked to him, as if he knew everything about me and my life. Normally, when Father gazed at me with such perceptive intensity, I buckled and dropped my eyes, but Jack's stare was kinder than Father's—warmer, like stones that had been lying in the sun.

"Miss Westoff came because she followed you, and you came because you followed Mr. Dana. Now, putting the assumption that you care for Mr. Dana aside, why would you trail someone who obviously does not want to be trailed? Even a very strong attraction would not induce most gentry girls to pass our gates."

"I saw David helping Sarah," I explained quickly, the words pouring out like rain eager to soak the ground. "In the park several weeks ago. She fell next to me, and I saw it all. David handled the charges himself, he carried them, and then he carried her. He didn't hesitate to help her, and I had never seen anyone do that before."

"And that naturally piqued your interest," Jack said. "If you do not mind me asking, if you saw Sarah fall, then why didn't you help her yourself?"

Now I dropped my gaze, and a shame stronger than any I'd ever felt filled me, hot and nauseating. "I was scared," I whispered. "I was scared to touch her."

My words hung in the hot room, filling up the space until I could barely breathe. I was terrified to look at Jack. Would he hate me? Even though I'd only known him a couple of hours, I wanted him to like me, to approve of me, to invite me back into his company.

"Madeline," Jack said kindly. "Sarah was going to die either way. She was only a changer, the safest job we have, but even that small radiation was too much for her. She was never long for this world. Don't fill yourself with useless guilt. You are a product of the people who raised you, and the fact that you do feel remorse means that you've already shown yourself to be more human than most of the gentry." He stood with extreme difficulty, panting a little until he could lean on his cane. He walked stiffly over to the window, where Charlie still gamboled about in the grass.

"I can't forget what I didn't do," I said. "You say not to feel shame, but it's all I can feel when I think of her."

"I didn't say to forget," Jack answered, still looking at his boys. "Don't forget. Remember every face and every name." He turned to me, his face folded in sorrow. "After these long years, I now believe our freedom can only be born through violence. Violence is a dark and dangerous path, but we will honor every victim as a martyr, and feel their suffering as if it was our own. A spirit cannot be whole if it willfully ignores the suffering of others."

Jack came over to me, his cane clunking against the floor, and offered a hand. "Shall we go for that walk?"

We headed east on a road that dwindled to a dirt trail, well worn but narrow. Trees encroached on either side, sending dappled green light onto the path.

"What do you know of Jacob Landry?" Jack asked.

Quite a bit, given the gentry's adulation of him. "He invented the Cherenkov lantern, and then the nuclear charge. After the Empire invaded, he created the Uprisen and they fought against the dissenters in the Last War. He helped reorganize society afterward."

Jack nodded thoughtfully. "He is a hero, is he not? A visionary."

I felt a twitch of defensiveness. "They say that he stopped global warming with the nuclear charge. If it had not caught on when it did, the world would have been pushed past the breaking point, and the weather would be even worse than it is now."

"And yet the Empire forced America into sustainability well before the Last War. Perhaps such a result was on its way with or without Jacob Landry?"

"I suppose."

"I say this not necessarily to disparage your ancestor—although I will freely admit that Jacob Landry is little liked in these parts—but to probe your perspective. I sense that you're convinced of the injustice of our lifestyle—and perhaps have been so, at least academically, for a couple years—but are still on the cusp of action. Our David—forgive my informality, but I am old and it is a privilege accorded to us—is in the same place. I have urged him to stay where he is, and to keep up pretenses, because he is too valuable to us as an informant. But I think my urgings have come as a relief to him, because he's not ready to divest himself of wealth and comfort and the things that have defined his life for so long."

"But surely he is of more help in a position of wealth?" I asked. "He can give food and money to the Rootless community, and he could not do that if he gave up everything and lived with you. When he's in the military, he'll have even more information that could help your revolution."

"From a pragmatic point of view, you're correct. But I'm not only worried about supporting my community and finding our freedom, but about David himself. And about you, young Madeline."

"Me?"

"How long do you think you can live like this? How long can you dance and twirl in pretty dresses knowing that people are starving and dying? No one can open their eyes to truth and then continue to live as they are. It would tear them apart."

"I guess I try not to think about it," I said in a small voice.

"You see David, so violently lurching between good humor and anger, eagerness and malaise. He's the perfect example: if you do not act according to your conscience, you risk becoming complicit in the misery. And you and David are better than that."

We came upon a large clearing. A concrete shed with metal doors was in the middle, and the trees around us were strangely silent, as if the birds and animals didn't dare to come here.

Jack pushed open a door.

"Welcome to the sorting yards. After today, you can no longer claim ignorance as an excuse."

EIGHTEEN
EIGHTEEN

Inside the doors, Jack handed me a suit of radiation-proof polymer. In the blue-black of the barely lit darkness, I struggled with the heavy sleeves and clunky lead zippers.

"There aren't very many of us working in the afternoon. In the heat of summer, most come in the dark of morning and work until noon. After sunset, they'll come back to finish the day's work. Funny to think it now, but in the winter, I almost crave the warmth."

He pulled on a suit, and we walked down a dark flight of stairs, marked infrequently with Cherenkov lanterns. The first thing I noticed as we reached the sorting floor was the heat. Stifling heat from the crowded sorting platform, where people worked ceaselessly, sweat visible through their clear polymer masks, and heat from the trains, which zipped through at impossible speeds, sending welcome drafts of air followed by waves of steam from the nuclear-steam engines.

I could see that most of the polymer suits had holes or tears in them, and some people went without gloves or boots or masks. I hurriedly checked my own suit, fears of radiation poisoning suddenly overwhelming everything else.

"You are quite safe," Jack assured me, his voice muffled by the mask. "Your suit is one of the newest, purchased kindly by David just last month. Someone must have just left; normally the newer suits are taken right away. At any rate, you would need to be exposed quite a bit longer than a few minutes to contract anything stronger than a headache. Come."

Cane clunking on the floor, he led the way past the sorters hunched over lead bins, cracking apart charge cases like oyster shells and stripping them of their pearl-sized uranium spheres. They were quickly moved into the bins filled with water, where the Cherenkov radiation took effect, sending blue light onto their sweaty faces.

After a bin was filled with three or four uranium pearls, the packers clamped lids on the bins and dragged them to the waiting trains, of which there were always three or four. They loaded the leaking, cracked bins into place, and then wedged themselves alongside for the three-day ride.

"They are only allotted one bottle of water for each day of their journey," Jack said, using his cane to indicate the packers. "And these polymer suits, while efficacious enough for protection, are uncommonly hot, especially in the closed-in tunnels, where the steam keeps the temperature around one hundred degrees. If the men wore these suits, they would be dehydrated within a day, fatally so by the time they reached their destination. Even if they could stay alive in such a state, they would almost certainly be too listless to ride the sharp curves and accelerations safely. The tunnels are littered with the corpses of the men too weak or sick or tired to remember to hang on. And so the packers choose not to wear the suits, and by doing so, they choose a slow death over a quick one."

"Why can they only have one bottle of water a day?" I demanded. "Who would make that rule?"

"That was your grandfather Lewis Landry's idea. He felt that the incidental radiation of the work was not a strong enough check on any radical tendencies that might arise from the Rootless. Since the packers are normally the fittest and strongest of the community, he rightly guessed that poisoning them quicker would stay any attempts at an armed uprising. Such a small thing, a water ration. Yet with enormous consequences."

"But there are no gentry or police here in the sorting yard. Why don't they just take more water? Who would know?"

Jack inclined his head. "A fair question with an unfortunate answer. First, I should mention that the police do venture down here once or twice a year. Those infrequent visits are violent enough to be a deterrent for most of us. Secondly and sadly, there are some in the community who are disposed to tell the police of witnessed infractions in exchange for certain amenities or protections. So yes, every once in a while, a packer dares to violate the rule. And he may not get caught for several trips. But when he is caught—when he is betrayed by his own neighbors—he is never seen again. Often, his family suffers as well, through reduced food rations or forced relocation."

Nearby, one sorter collapsed in a heap. Others came to help her, pulling off her mask and fanning her face. Cankers clustered around her mouth and nose. Her hands were bare, save for the lesions that looked almost like rough red gloves, they so thoroughly covered her skin. When I examined the room closely, I could see several people lying supine. One teenage boy threw up behind me, each heave obviously costing his body some extraordinary amount of pain, because when he finally stopped, he continued crying and crying.

Children—of the poorer families who needed the additional ration card, Jack explained—were there, too. Children as young as four struggled to open the cases and dump the spent fuel into the bins, some without even a shred of polymer clothing to protect them. Without thinking, I pulled off my mask and offered it to the father of a young girl. He was also without polymer clothes, and so I stripped all of it off and gave that to him as well.

Eyes wide, he mumbled thanks, and quickly dressed his girl in as much as would fit.

I felt naked for a moment, wondering if I could feel the radiation seeping into my pores, wondering if I could feel the DNA in my cells corrupting and breaking apart. But I refused to have more fear than the little girl, who now peered at me through the mask with painfully innocent eyes.

Even without the suit, the heat was unbearable. My dress, which had been smashed into the suit, now stuck to my sweaty legs, and my hair was wet enough to curl into ringlets, which clung to my neck and back. The smell of vomit permeated the air. The soft cries of hot and dehydrated children ebbed and flowed in between the clamor of the trains and shouting packers.

After another few minutes, Jack took my arm and steered me out of the sorting yards, and after he took off his suit, we went up into the clearing. The metallic air smelled deliciously fresh and even the hot sun felt cool in comparison to the toxic sauna of the yards.

"Forgive me, Miss Landry," Jack said, coughing and wiping his face. "I wanted to show you more, but in my old age, the heat affects me quicker. I have put in time as a sorter and as a packer, but my people insisted that I take a gentler job once my grandchildren were born. A happy circumstance of my youth made it so that I have lived to see my children reach maturity—most Rootless cannot. I even had the chance to remarry after my first wife died and to father little Charlie." He closed the door to the sorting yards. "But now my second wife has perished, too, and I believe it won't be long before my atoms are reunited with those of my loved ones."

We walked back to his house in silence.

"What do you think?" he asked when we reached his front steps. "Are you ready to help us?"

I paused. The answer was *yes*, of course. How could I not after seeing the sorting yards? After hearing David's description of the Rootless ghetto in Atlanta? But despite what Jack had said earlier about living a double life, I couldn't imagine forsaking Landry Park. "I want to help," I said. "Money, supplies, anything you need."

Jack took my hand in his rough one, and I realized, for the first time, that I had been touching Rootless people all day . . . Smith and Ewan and Jack . . .

"And what about your heart, Madeline? Are you prepared to give up everything to fight with us?"

I kept my eyes on his house. I could see the charcoal drawings through the window. "I can help more if I stay where I am at," I said uncertainly. "I know I can. And I couldn't leave Landry Park—"

"You must make a decision, sooner rather than later, about what being a Landry means. Will you follow in Jacob's and Lewis's and Alexander's footsteps? Or will you make your own legacy?"

"I'll talk to my father about treating the Rootless better," I promised, "and I'll convince Cara to tell the truth about her attack—I can help, I swear."

Out of the corner of my eye, I saw David approaching, the sunset lighting his fair hair on fire.

Jack gave my hand one last pat, let go, and started climbing the steps to his house. "When I was young, I managed to find some unsupervised time in the Landry Park library, whereupon I came across the most extraordinary journals. Jacob Landry's journals. I found quite a different man than is usually described in the history books."

David reached us, looking alarmed at my disheveled and sticky state.

Jack turned and faced me. "I propose a deal: you stay at Landry Park and fight for us there, as David has done from his home. But in the meantime, find Jacob Landry's journals and read them. I think they will help you in your decision. Good night, Madeline."

"Good night. Oh, and Jack?"

"Yes?"

I thought of the unrelenting heat of the sorting yards, the dimly lit anger of the Rootless in the tavern. I had learned more today than I had in years. "Thank you . . . for everything."

"My dear, it is nothing less than you deserve."

David and I started west for the gates into the city.

"He took you to the sorting yards, didn't he?" David asked after a few minutes of quiet walking.

"Yes. Have you been?"

He nodded. "Several times. Every time I go, I bring a new suit or new lead bins, but it never seems to make a difference. It's always just as awful, just as dangerous."

"I don't see how anything we can do will make a real difference," I said, feeling a sudden exhaustion overtake me. "There are so many of them."

"But we have to try, right?"

"Yes." But only twenty minutes removed from the sorting yards, I felt the undercurrent of passivity tugging at me. It would be so easy to go home and soak in a bath of lavender and rose petals and pretend that none of this had ever happened.

The threshold was affecting David, too. I could almost feel his restlessness as we passed through the gates. His stride quickened and his shoulders tensed. I scurried to keep up, trying to unglue my skirt from my legs.

"Do you realize that we're supposed to be the knights, Madeline? The two of us? Against an entire country of people whose lives depend on the system we are promising to destroy? Gawain and Bedivere had it easier than this. They were heroes and the dragons they were fighting were dragons everyone could see and acknowledge. We are fighting something that most people spend their lives ignoring."

"I thought you were the one who believed in knights?"

"I do. What I don't know is whether or not they're worth anything in the real world."

And then he shut his mouth and said nothing more as I hurried to follow him across the city to my estate.

"Is this the last time I'll see you before you leave for the army?" I asked as we reached Landry Park.

"Probably. Yes. I leave in a couple days, and I plan on spending those days drunk and insensate."

I winced. He sounded completely unlike the David of a few hours ago.

He passed a hand over his eyes. "I'm sorry. I've just got a lot on my mind right now, which I'm sure you can understand."

"I should get inside," I said. "I suppose you'll need to get home, too. Or back to Cara."

He laughed a harsh laugh. "Right. My girlfriend. Goodbye, Madeline." And with a bow that was more mocking than polite, he walked off my property and into the twilight.

NINETEEN

It wasn't the last time I saw David before he left. The morning before a train would whisk him away to the mountains, he paid an unannounced visit to my house. Jane Osbourne and I were taking tea in the morning room, discussing her father's latest attempt to marry her to a local manufacturing heir, when David strolled in, trailed by our anxious butler. *Crawford,* I thought to myself. *His name is Crawford.*

Morgana twined around David's legs, purring.

We stood and he bowed. "Ladies."

I didn't really know what to say. After what we had seen two days ago, what we had shared with each other, to be back here in a gentry house, staring at each other over a tray of frosted cakes and teacups . . .

He reached down to rub under Morgana's chin. "Miss Landry, could I have the privilege of taking a turn about the grounds with you? Miss Osbourne is welcome to join us, of course."

"Actually, I was just leaving," Jane said tactfully, and made to go.

I quietly panicked. David and I had gone from outright

fighting at Cara's debut to confessing each other's deepest secrets in the Rootless ghetto. And now that I was acutely aware of how he affected me and how much I cared about him, it made being near him that much worse, because I knew that he would never return those feelings, not as long as he dated Cara. The thought of being alone with him terrified me.

"Oh, no," I told her. "Really, you can stay."

She smiled. "My family is expecting me." She curtsied and he took her hand and kissed it. "Mr. Dana," she said, inclining her head. And then we were alone.

A few minutes later, we were out on the lawn. The sun was out and beating down hard; today was the first of the truly hot days that would dog the city until fall.

I felt acutely aware of the space between us—palpable and electrified. He was dressed in his usual expensive clothes—a well-tailored suit and tie, a charcoal color that set off the starched white of his shirt sleeves, pinned with onyx cuff links. His silky hair ruffled in the humid breeze—a few stray tendrils already beginning to cling to his neck—and the sunlight was catching on his blond eyelashes like drops of gold.

"I thought you were going to spend your last days in Kansas City drunk and insensate," I said, unable to stand the silence any longer.

He squinted back toward the house. "I changed my mind."

"Why?"

"Because of you."

A breathless need blossomed in my chest, razored and painful.

"I wanted to come and give you my apologies for my behavior the other day," he continued. "I was rude and I had no excuse, save for that I was frustrated and confused." He stopped and plucked a small white flower out of the grass. I fought away a blush as he handed it to me.

"I have always known that I would enter the military like my father," he said. "Despite our fortune, we have no estate, and I wouldn't feel my future secure if I didn't have an income. And it's a career that I'll enjoy." A breeze blew through the orchards nearby, sending a storm of fluttering white and pink petals blowing onto the lawn. "I'm tired of what I do here. I'm tired of trying to figure out what's best. What's right, what's wrong. Or, more accurately, what's most right or least wrong."

He looked over at me. "It may sound hawkish or even stupid, but I can't wait to go to a place where there is one enemy—the East—and our days are spent in single-minded awareness of that fact. No more double-guessing, no more subterfuge. The army exists for one reason, and that's to protect us from the East."

"Do you really think the only reason for having an army is to fight against the Empire?" I asked. I looked westward toward Glasshawke, where the many windows winked and flashed in the sunlight. "I think the need for a standing army is only as far away as the closest nuclear charge."

He smiled a tight smile. "Leave it to you to take away my only comfort."

"That's not what I was trying to do," I replied quickly. "I just don't think that any change of situation is going to remove these feelings because it can't remove who you are."

"And who am I?"

I didn't know. Even after he'd haunted my thoughts for weeks, I still didn't know.

He passed a hand over his eyes. "It's okay, Madeline. I can't answer that question either."

We were close to the maze now, walking past the locked door with its peeling paint and bones of history within.

"David . . ." I started, not sure what I was going to say. I never got the chance to find out, because David reached out to touch my grandmother's necklace on my chest, and I froze. I was trapped between the outer stone wall of the maze and David, who held me as fast with a thin gold strand as he would've if he'd had an iron chain.

"I feel so much like I want to trust you," he whispered. "But then I remember that you're a Landry."

His fingers grazed my skin as he placed the cameo gently back against my chest. He stepped away from me and I could feel the gap between us like a wound.

"You can trust me," I managed to say.

"If you had any idea how much I want to." His eyes were earnest, intent on my own, their color making everything around them seem monochromatic and faded.

I stepped closer. "Then do it," I said, half daring, half begging. I tilted my face to his, trying to look confident and assured, like I was a person who could be trusted with anything.

He took my chin between his thumb and his forefinger. "Madeline Landry," he said in a serious voice. His eyes searched mine, and I searched back, my entire world possessed by his hand on my face.

"David," I breathed.

He bent his head down, and—as the summer wind blew silken petals and the scent of fresh crisp fruit around us—he lightly brushed his lips against mine, so lightly that I wondered if it had been a stray petal and not David.

But as I was about to part my lips, as I was about to lean forward and press myself against the expensive suit and the sun-warmed body beneath it, he jerked back, staring at me as if my lips had been covered in poison.

"I'm sorry," he said, his face clouded with—what? Disgust? Regret? Pity? "That was extremely presumptuous of me. A gentleman should not take liberties." He sighed to himself. "Certainly not a gentlemen with a girlfriend."

That need in my chest—a need so like hope—shattered into a thousand pieces.

No matter how much we shared, no matter how many times we locked eyes and I had to will myself to keep breathing, he would always be distant and unreachable.

But he wasn't distant with Cara. He was the one who tried to kiss her at her debut and claim her as his own. No, it must be me. I was the reason that we could never draw nearer than two magnets with the same charge.

"Walk with me back up to the house?" he asked.

I acquiesced, and we trod up the emerald lawn together.

Madeline—

I'd hate to think that your last memory of me would be of my acting so ill-bred. Rest assured that I am normally much more refined.

Your friend—

David

Unlike invitations and library books, which were always printed on expensive paper, most letters were written on tablets with a pen-like stylus, so they could be delivered electronically, but still be written in one's own hand. The gentry, cautious of forgery and rebellion, prided themselves on their distinctive penmanship. Flying loops and spidery letters made it difficult for someone who hadn't spent years with a tutor to copy a signature.

I could picture David writing this letter at his fort in the Rockies. Sitting in his tailored captain's uniform, adding the long flourishes to the word *friend*, perhaps not knowing how it would taunt me. And yet, despite the part of me that begged for a little dignity, I pulled it up on my tablet three or four times a day, hoping to decipher some new meaning in the words. Why was he apologizing for the kiss? Was it guilt about Cara? Was it because he thought I was angry?

Or was it because he regretted kissing me?

I finally responded—sending a note that was at once distant and formal, something that made it sound like I barely cared if he responded or not.

David~

I hope this letter finds you well. I hope that Colorado is as beautiful as they say, and that the army affords you much satisfaction.

Sincerely,
Madeline

TWENTY

Rumor had it that Cara was pining for David, though I had difficulty imagining Cara pining for anyone. And it had only been two weeks since he left—hardly time for true melancholy to set in. But it was said that she rarely left her rooms, that she was seen wandering aimlessly around the castle grounds, that servants found her crying over her tablet in odd corners of her estate.

David. How could one person upset this city's life so completely?

I had told Jack that I would help with money and food, and I meant it, although giving even just a basket of food was harder than I thought. Martha—I had finally taken the trouble to learn Cook's name—kept a faithful ledger of all food purchased and consumed. My mother was nominally in charge of the kitchens, but Father frequently reviewed the accounts to make sure the servants were accounting all things honestly. Martha was nothing if not honest and proud of her twenty-five-year tenure as head cook in our kitchens—and thus, anything more than a couple loaves of bread and cheese would be difficult to take without raising a fuss.

Here, my mother's lassitude toward the drudgery of housekeeping became an asset, and I convinced her to allow me to start setting the menus for breakfast and lunch. She seemed pleased at my newfound interest in household duties, and it allowed me a chance to order a little bit extra for each meal. Not enough to arouse suspicion, but enough for two or three baskets a day, carried out to the maze by Elinor, whom I kept under-informed for her own protection. There, they were picked up under the cover of night and brought back to the hungry mouths on the east side of town.

Money was a different story.

I had never really thought about the exchange of money. I rarely needed to purchase anything myself, and when I did, I only had to leave my name with the shopkeeper or restaurant owner, and my purchase was paid with credit. All around me, food was being ordered from the city, dresses were being purchased and tailored, candles were bought by the crate, wine was rolled into the house by the cask, and books and trinkets of all kinds made their way to me or Mother or Father—yet I never once saw paper notes change hands. Money was everywhere and nowhere at the same time.

I was tempted to give some of my jewelry to Jack to sell instead. But the more I thought about it, the more dangerous it seemed, because if a Rootless was caught stealing the penalty was death. No, it had to be money. Untraceable money.

There was one opportunity during the week, but it was not without some risk. Every Friday night, Father and a few other gentry men—and if my mother's venomous rants were to be believed, Christine Dana—went to the casino for the evening. My father was not much of a gambler, but he was also not one to miss an opportunity to display his wealth, and so he brought plenty of cash with him.

Surely he wouldn't miss a hundred gentry dollars, not out of a few thousand?

So, one Friday evening, three weeks after David's departure, I snuck into my father's bedroom. Unlike my mother's bedroom with its massive dressing room and elaborate bathroom, this was a place I had rarely been. The walls were covered in a deep purple color with crown molding leading to a high trayed ceiling, studded by a massive chandelier. Father had gone downstairs to greet Christine Dana personally—they would drive together to the casino—and had left his tuxedo jacket unattended upstairs.

I had only moments.

I tiptoed across the lush hand-knotted carpet to his armchair, where the jacket was slung over the back. I hesitated, checking behind me. I was alone.

But I still felt as if someone was watching and judging my actions as I rifled through the jacket to find the deep inside pocket. Perhaps it was the ghost of Jacob Landry himself, coming to glare at me as I violated my father's trust. I shook off the guilt and thought about the sorting yards and the torn radiation suits. The Rootless needed the money more than my father, who would spend it all on plum wine and roasted duck and spun-sugar sculptures of mermaids and dragons without a second thought.

That doesn't make it right to steal, a voice said inside my head. *Don't compromise what you know is right.*

But I promised Jack. And I know helping the Rootless is right. And—my hand closed over the fat fold of the money, driving away any other thoughts. I pulled it out, fascinated by how crisp and clean the notes were. Father must have withdrawn them from the bank recently.

I peeled off one hundred dollars—two of the notes, and stuffed the rest back in the pocket. I turned to leave, but stopped, my heart in my throat, as soon as I saw my father standing in the doorway, his head tilted to the side.

He came toward me, the thick carpet muffling his footsteps, and silently held out his hand.

Ashamed, I dropped my eyes to the ground and placed the two notes in his hand. His face was tight, controlled, but not with anger, with consideration.

"Are you stealing from me, Madeline?" he asked finally.

After a minute, I nodded my head.

"Why?"

What could I say? That the money was for the Rootless, to support them until they planned a revolution to overthrow the gentry? And if I lied—said that I'd wanted a dress or a book—he would know I was lying. He knew my every expression, my every tone.

He brushed past me and walked to his jacket. Pulling it on, he prompted, "Well?"

"I . . . I had wanted some money of my own."

He examined my face. "Your needs are provided for, are they not?"

"Yes, Father."

He glanced at his watch. "I have to go." He reached into his pocket and pulled out the clump of money, which he divested of a few more bills. "Here," he said, handing them to me. "Consider this an allowance."

I was shocked. I had expected nothing short of verbal flagellation . . . but more money?

"And perhaps," he continued, "a weekly allowance should be arranged. I can hardly tempt you to remain at the estate if I do not show you the perks of the job, can I?" He left after delivering a swift kiss to my stunned cheek.

And after that night, the Rootless also found money in the baskets of food, and, no longer a thief but rather a keeper of promises, I felt satisfied.

. . .

A few days later, Jamie came over for tea. My cousin seemed to be the only person immune to David's absence, which was a welcome relief. As we picked our way through thin sandwiches and crudités and as a thunderstorm raged outside, I gradually shared my story with him, leaving out David's last visit and the ensuing angst.

"Madeline, you could have been killed by those men," Jamie said, his voice low, though he could barely be heard over the thunder and raindrops on the glass. "And you could have gotten seriously ill. You swear you don't feel any radiation sickness? Nausea, headaches, fatigue?"

I shook my head. "I feel fine. Just . . . confused."

"About what? David?"

"I don't want to talk about David right now." Which was a lie—I did want to talk about him—all the time, in fact—but I didn't know what I wanted to say. That he was frustratingly changeable was a given. That I never knew where I stood with him was a given, too. But I couldn't stop thinking about him, and his conduct made no more sense after hours of musing out loud than it did if I kept my thoughts to myself.

So I decided to keep my thoughts to myself.

"No," I said, "I'm confused about what to do. I know I'm doing the right thing by helping the Rootless with food and money. I believe that their suffering is wrong. But Jack wanted me to leave Landry Park. He talked about how vicious my grandfather was and how wrong we all were about Jacob Landry."

I struggled to find words to express the exact nature of my ambivalence about my ancestor. "But just because Jacob Landry invented something that's being used to suppress the Rootless, that doesn't necessarily make him a bad person. Right?"

"Alfred Nobel invented dynamite," Jamie pointed out. "He was so haunted by its violent uses that he created the Peace Prize to counteract his unwitting contribution to war. Jacob Landry didn't have time to really see how his invention was being used. After all, the Cherenkov lanterns brought light to millions in underdeveloped countries with no electricity. He probably assumed the nuclear charge would be just as beneficial."

I thought of Jacob Landry's bust in the foyer, with the thin mouth and pinprick pupils. "I've never liked the idea of him, but I feel connected to him somehow. Like we can't be untangled from one another. I feel that way about my father, too."

"Feel what about me?" Father came into the room, the lightning outside sending faint shadows flickering across his face. For a terrible moment, I thought he had heard everything about the Rootless and my part in helping them. As quickly as a clap of thunder, my knees and lips lost all sensation.

Thank heaven for Jamie. He stood and bowed, and by the time he was done, I'd mostly recovered myself.

"Mr. Landry," Jamie said.

Father shook his hand and offered him a cigarette, which Jamie graciously took, though he didn't light it.

"It's good to see you, Mr. Campbell-Smith. How is work at the hospital?" His voice was calm. Pleasant even.

"Very good, sir. Very good. I believe I'm able to help many people there, despite our limited supplies."

Father took a seat in a stiff armchair. Even sitting, he was imposing—tall and stern, like a statue of Zeus upon a throne. Jamie sat across from him, his face folded in an expression of nervous discomfort. I sometimes forgot that everything Jamie had—an apartment in the city, an invitation into society, even his job—it all depended on the goodwill of the gentry. The goodwill of men like my father.

Everything I had depended on my father, too. If he knew that I'd gone to the Rootless and that I'd been giving them food and money, he could force me out of the house. Or, since I was the sole scion of the treasured Landry line, he could lock me here like some sort of prisoner, waiting for me to breed a grandchild who was more obedient than myself.

I stared at him from under my eyelids, trying to read his expression.

"Helping the poor is important, in its own way, although I hope that you will focus the hospital's energies on the reproductive clinic. Ensuring that the Rootless have healthy children who can carry on their work is fundamental to our society, in addition to being an emotional solace for them."

Jamie ducked his head. "Yes, sir."

"I don't expect that you will be under that gold dome for

long, Mr. Campbell-Smith. I foresee you in the private gentry hospital or perhaps as a personal physician to one of our noble families, and maybe sooner than you think. So long as you perform admirably at the Public Hospital, of course."

"Yes, sir."

Father lit a cigarette, and the spice of opium filled the air. "While I hate to interrupt your tea, I need a word with Madeline. Privately." The word held an ominous promise.

I felt the blood drain from my face.

"Sir," Jamie said, and rose. He took my hands and leaned down to kiss my cheek. "Be brave," he whispered in my ear.

After he left, Father shifted in his chair, crossing his legs and taking a meditative drag from his cigarette. I braced myself for cold fury, counting the lightning strikes before he spoke.

One . . .

Two . . .

Three . . .

What will he say . . .

Four . . .

"The incident in my room a few days ago has given me cause to consider your future," Father finally said. "I realize that for you to do something as out of character as stealing, there must be something bothering you. Significantly."

I held my breath.

"And then I realized I knew exactly what it was. You feel

that I'm not listening to your needs, you feel hurt that I'm not sending you to the university like you want."

I exhaled so loudly that he narrowed his eyes at me, but I didn't care. He hadn't mentioned the Rootless! He still didn't know!

"I would not breathe a sigh of relief just yet," he said. "You have repeatedly made your case for the university. The teachers at the academy have always raved about your scholastic performance, and over the last few months, the discussions we've had have proven to me how intelligent and prescient you are. I *am* very proud of you, Madeline, for demonstrating the sharpness of the Landry mind, both inside the academy and out of it."

A lump burned at the back of my throat. Father hadn't told me he was proud of me in years, and I hadn't realize how much I'd missed it. His approval.

He gestured for me to come to him. I did, standing before him like a schoolgirl. He examined my face for a moment, before standing and folding me into his arms.

He smelled like ivy, like stone.

Like the house.

"Never forget that I'm proud of you," he said fiercely. "And never forget that I exact from you no less than what my father exacted of me and his father of him and so forth. You may be a daughter, but you have all the steel and strength of the Landrys. What I want for you is to be a rock for your children and your grandchildren, and for the gentry to regard you in the same light they regard your ancestors. You are special, Madeline, and you belong here, on this special estate. You will rule it, and the Uprisen, with an iron fist and an iron mind."

I tilted my head up at him. "You want me to stay here?" I said, voice breaking between gratitude and disappointment.

His face when he looked down at me was the face of my father of years ago, debt-free and affectionate, willing to fold himself into a tiny chair to play at dolls and tea. "It is difficult for me to deny you anything. Give me time to think about it. Give me this year to prove to you how productive and useful you can be—how much there is to learn here at the house. And perhaps, you can prove to me how a university education will be an asset to the family. Agreed?"

This is what I had been longing for—even if it was only a chance, hinged on a condition.

For an instant—a fleeting instant—I almost asked him about Jacob Landry's journals, asked about staying his persecution of the Rootless. This would have been the perfect moment, in one of his rare displays of affection.

But it wouldn't hurt to enjoy my father's approval before I started challenging him. Maybe it would even be easier after I proved how much I cared about the estate. How much I cared about him.

"Agreed?" he asked again.

"Agreed," I said, and buried my face once more into his chest.

Father started my education the next morning. We drove out to our ranches in Kansas to inspect recent cyclone damage and estimate repairs. The next day, it was northern Missouri, where the river had spread flat, muddy fingers over our crops. We discussed growing heartier, more flood-resistant plants, and the costs of levees. I ate dinner at a well-to-do farmer's house, and met his wife and children.

Once we got home, I excused myself for a solitary walk and tucked a thin roll of bills in one of the baskets that Elinor had left earlier.

The next week, Father invited me to lunch with several of the landowners, some of whom were shadowed by their own heirs, most of whom had graduated with me in May. At the table, over glasses of plum wine and bowls of shark-fin soup, the unceasing network of friendships, manipulations, and outright negotiations over marriage unfolded like a kaleidoscope of control.

Patterns emerged. Father and Arthur Lawrence were the most powerful gentry in the city; Harry Westoff was the wealthiest in terms of liquid assets; the Everlys, the Thorpes, and the Yorks were desperate to please and desperate for power, doing favors for anyone who asked in an effort to curry enough goodwill to someday ask favors of their own.

The heirs, close to coming of age, were often present at these lunches and dinners, though none of us were allowed into the inner circle of the Uprisen. That was a privilege only granted once the property passed into your hands. Until then, we all sat in parlors and watched the opium smoke curl out from closed doors down the hall. We sat quietly, our heads filled with finances and loans and the risk of planting too many drought-resistant crops when the year might bring floods, balanced against the cost of renovating estate houses in need of constant care. And of course, the cost of helping the Rootless, if you were secretly playing the part of a corseted vigilante.

I found I liked this group more than I expected. Mark Everly and Navid Thorpe were more thoughtful and intelligent than I'd given them credit for, and were pleasant company. So was Philip Wilder; he and I had something close to a friendship after our lunch at the country club—or at the very least, a mutual respect for each other.

Jane Osbourne was there, levelheaded and calm as always. Even Cara was present sometimes, although never for long. In fact, I was fairly certain she was avoiding me.

In a way, I didn't mind. Without her, it was almost as if David never existed. No need to think of his blue eyes or his rush to protect me in the Rootless tavern. No need to think of the last letter I'd sent him, which had still received no reply, or of his mercurial moods that were impossible to understand.

The end of August brought trouble from overseas: diplomatic clashes with the Eastern Empire, and highly visible military training exercises on both sides. Most of the gentry laughed off the possibility of real war, but my father merely tightened his mouth and refused to downplay the rumors.

"The Empire claims they are defending their trading agreements, but what they truly want is an excuse to finish what they couldn't during their last invasion," he informed me on a car trip to visit another farm. I wondered if Father suspected that the Rootless and the Empire would partner together, but I didn't dare bring it up lest it lead to questions I could not truthfully answer.

The days had turned into weeks and the weeks into months—months of going over ledgers with Father, of meeting farmers, charming the bankers and lenders on the wall screen into extending our credit for just another year, on the faint hope that the harvests would improve. They were all too happy to acquiesce to our requests, to keep the Landry family flush in money even though none of our farms had made a real profit in the last few years.

The months were filled with news headlines about the Empire, about our forts and our army and how strong and prepared they both were. War hovered over the mountains like a storm cloud that refused to rain. I often thought of David, waiting in the mountain fog, waiting for an enemy that he could face and fight without the doubts that beset him here.

All this time, I kept convincing myself that it would be better to wait to speak to Father about the Rootless. Once he saw me as an equal, once I'd proved my value to the estate, he'd listen to what I had to say.

Only once had my guilt turned to more than tiny tugs at my conscience, and that was at the sight of Jack and Charlie walking up our driveway. Charlie skipped and hopped, protesting loudly whenever his father asked him to stay close. I moved Morgana from her perch at the window and raised the sash, taking care to make sure I was alone in the parlor.

"Hello, Jack. Hi, Charlie."

"Watch this, Miss Landry!" Charlie took a running start and then jumped into a flip, landing on his feet with barely a hint of a wobble. "I taught myself how last week, but before I could, I had to learn how to jump really high, so I taught *that* to myself and then started flipping and once I—" he did another flip "—got the hang of it, it was so easy! I can do it all the time now, look!" And again, each flip taking him farther away from the window and into the driveway.

Jack beckoned to Charlie in affectionate exasperation. "Stay near me. This is not our house; you cannot go bounding around anywhere you please. I'm already regretting taking over your brother's duties, even if it was for him to meet with our friends in St. Louis."

Charlie stuck out his tongue and did another flip in the driveway. Jack leveled his gaze at his son, saying nothing, and I was reminded of how quickly Smith quailed under Jack's force of will in the tavern. Jack was used to being obeyed.

Charlie lasted less than a few seconds, and then, knowing he was beat, he shuffled to his father's side.

Jack turned back to me. "Have you made any progress with those journals?"

"Well, I . . ." I fidgeted. "I've been busy. With the estate."

"And Cara Westoff's attacker?"

"It's just been so busy here," I said faintly.

"I see," he said in that rumbling voice. He didn't say anything else. He didn't have to. The disappointment and doubt in his face said it all.

With a farewell nod, he left the window. Charlie waved enthusiastically as they walked around the house to collect our charges.

That night the Lawrences were our dinner guests, and I couldn't help but cast an eye of renewed suspicion on my cousins, who were as rude and raucous as ever. Stuart, Tarleton, and Frank were snorting about some boxing exploit, while the two younger boys, Scott and Oliver, were busy shoving and kicking each other at the table. Arthur Lawrence was deep in conversation with Father, and Aunt Lacey was gossiping with Mother, so nobody seemed to care about their bad table manners. Which meant that nobody would overhear my conversation with the boys.

Maybe I'm not ready to throw my lot in with the Rootless, but at least I can do this. I can prove that Jack's people didn't hurt Cara.

I set down my napkin and turned to the older boys.

"It's a shame they still haven't found Cara's attacker," I said.

"I would find her attacker in a heartbeat," Tarleton blustered. "Give me a day, and I'll get the Rootless talking."

Stuart just scowled.

"What is it?" I asked him. "You don't think you'd be as good at catching a criminal as your brother?"

"What do you think? Use your brain. If months of ration reductions and raids haven't unearthed the criminal, a gentry boy threatening to box them won't either." Stuart leaned over the table. "And no Landry sniffing around is going to help. You'd both do well to shut your mouths and let things take their course."

"And what does that mean, Stuart? Do you have a reason for not wanting her attacker to be found?"

His lip curled. "What are you saying, cousin?"

"I think you know exactly what I'm saying."

"I would like to see you prove it."

Father, finally noticing the intensity of our conversation, called down the table. "Care to involve us in your discussion?"

"We were just talking boxing," Stuart said smoothly. Tarleton nodded.

"I see," said Father, and turned back to Arthur.

We didn't talk much after that, but for the rest of the night, Stuart remained defiant and scornful.

You can't touch me. You can't prove anything, he seemed to be saying.

And I knew he was right.

TWENTY-ONE

Brisk nights had turned into brisk days and the trees were shaking off their leaves when I walked down to the parlor for tea and found my parents arguing. Mother stood behind a chair, tears leaving trails of makeup down her face.

"—won't have the entire city laughing at me," she was saying as I walked into the room. Her voice trembled in such a way that suggested she'd spent the afternoon with a bottle of sake, which was becoming a more commonplace occurrence these days.

"No one is laughing," my father said, not looking up from his tablet. "We have been over this. You're being paranoid."

"I am *not* being paranoid," she hissed. "You think people don't notice that she's over here at all hours of the night? While I'm away? You think that no one sees you out at dinner or the casino?"

My father's mouth pressed into its habitual line. "Maybe it's none of their business."

"It most certainly is my business, though. How dare you skulk around with Christine when it was my family's money that kept your precious estate alive? My money is the reason you didn't marry that whore and then you went and wasted it all anyway—"

"That's enough!" Father roared, leaping out his chair. I shrank back, his rage filling the room. "This is my house, this is my estate, and it belongs to my family! You are nothing! Your money is nothing!"

The silence afterward was thick and vitriolic, punctuated with my mother's sobs. We were frozen: my mother crying behind the chair; my father standing tensely, fists clenched; and me, back against the wall, wishing I could melt into it. Suddenly, all of our tablets chimed, screens glowing bright white and revealing a scrolling news feed.

Steps echoed throughout the marble foyer, sharp and quick, as if someone was running in heels. My mother brought her hand to her mouth to stifle her crying.

"Alexander!"

My father snapped to attention. He walked over to the entrance of the parlor just as Christine Dana tumbled in, black hair messy and tousled, like she'd just rolled out of bed.

"Oh, Alexander," she moaned, burying her face into his chest. "It's David. There's been a battle at the fort and there's no word. There's no word from anyone, and I don't know if he's alive or dead."

A moment passed where I stood completely still, circled by rushing servants as they helped Christine to a comfortable chair and fetched her tea while my father rubbed her hands.

My mother stood as still as I did, but where she could only focus on Father and Christine, my thoughts flew wildly to David. My stomach clenched and unclenched, and an inescapable feeling of panic consumed me.

David. In a battle. When supposedly battles didn't happen anymore.

It wasn't possible that he would leave his world of ballrooms and champagne to die in the mountain mud. It wasn't possible that someone as young as him, as eager to charm, would have his life cut short in his first term of service when everyone so firmly believed war was a thing of the past.

"I just got the notice," a tearful Christine told Father. "It doesn't say anything other than that there has been a battle. When will I know if he is okay? How? How long does it take for them to—to—"

She didn't finish her sentence, but we all knew what she was thinking. How long did it take for them to sort through the bodies of the fallen?

Mother cleared her throat, as if hesitant to speak. "It might be on the news . . ." she ventured.

Christine leaped out of her chair. "Where is the closest wall screen?"

Father led the way, and I trailed behind, wrapped in my own misery. In my mind, I could already see David's blond hair, caked with grime and blood, and the wide-open blue eyes, staring blankly into the East.

Father flung open the door to the viewing room and gestured to a nearby servant, who scurried over to a control panel. Velvet curtains swept back, revealing a matte white wall made of pure marble. There was a slight hum as the nuclear charges kicked on, sending power through the system, energizing the very particles of the stone. Soon, a picture appeared, a field reporter yelling into her microphone as choppers buzzed overhead.

There was a tense moment as we strained to make sense of the noise, struggling to hear the reporter's voice over the din. "We don't know much," I finally heard her say. "But we do know that the brave soldiers here routed the Easterners, and that the government is considering this a victory."

A collective sigh of relief.

"But why would the Empire attack?" I asked. "After centuries of peace?"

"Peace is just another word for preparation," Father answered.

Remembering the Rootless alliance with the Empire, I felt numb. Was this part of the plan? Had Jack known about it? Had David?

"We're told that the true heroes of the battle were two young men," she was saying, looking down at her notes, fluttering in the wind from the helicopters. "David Dana, who is a new officer here—" A chopper landing nearby cut off the rest of her sentence.

Christine slumped back in her chair. "He's alive," she whispered.

He's alive.

"He's a hero," Father said, a little wonderingly. I don't think he thought David had it in him.

I rested my head against the wall, letting the cool stone flush out the fervor. *He's alive, he's alive. David is alive.* I closed my eyes, his face flitting across my eyelids, hearing his quick intense voice in my ears. I might have stayed inside myself that way for hours, but Christine's gasp pulled me from my mirage.

"Is everything all right?" my father asked, brow furrowed in concern.

Christine stared at the screen, now filled with the image of a handsome young man with short dark hair and large eyes. It was a military graduation photo and in it, he stared ahead seriously, as if staring at all the problems in the world he planned to fix. He had broad shoulders and a squared jaw and the sort of regal bearing a prince might have.

The back of my neck tingled. I knew I'd never seen him before, but why did he look so familiar?

"I know that boy," Christine said quietly, hands curled around the arm of the chair. "I was friends with his parents."

"Captain Jude MacAvery was the real hero today," the reporter yelled. "He was the first to know that the Easterners had invaded the valley next to the fort, and he rallied every soldier to fight, leading the charge himself, on foot."

The camera abruptly panned to a nervous-looking soldier standing in front of the fort. A black haze of smoke hung over the scene. Steam and other mists of war rose from the holes blasted through the thick concrete walls, and from bomb craters pocking the dark soil around the compound. The soldier explained how this Captain MacAvery had stopped an Easterner from shooting him, how he'd saved many others with his quick thinking and his quick gun.

Father gestured to a valet standing against the wall. "Arrange for a call to the other Uprisen men."

"Yes, sir." The valet left with a bow.

"With the Rootless in a state of unrest, we need to establish a plan. I don't want the Empire to provide any opportunity for them to revolt," Father explained to me.

I shivered, grateful he couldn't read my thoughts.

"But surely this is the end of it," Christine said, her eyes still on the screen. "They would not be stupid enough to attack us when we've just beat back the largest power in the world."

"They very well might. They're fools."

TWENTY-TWO

"David is coming home for the Solstice!" Christine cheered, scrolling through messages on her tablet at the dinner table. "We should throw a big party for him—to celebrate his victory."

I did my best not to glance at her. I focused instead on tracing the Landry Crest on my plate with a gleaming fish fork. I wasn't going to think about David, who had never responded to my letter, or his soft lips. And I certainly wasn't going to stare at his mother, hungry for any resemblance to her son that would feed that sharp ache I nursed in my chest.

"We could have it at the Lodge," Christine suggested. "Nothing will be more beautiful than the country and the river in all this snow and ice."

My father smiled benignly. "But we would miss all the city festivities."

"Then let's invite the city to the Lodge. Throw a string of balls and feast and hunting parties that no one could refuse."

"Things are uneasy here. If we left our houses unattended, who knows—"

"Stop fretting," Christine said, sliding her long fingers over his. "The Empire has announced a cease-fire and they say negotiations could start any day now. The Rootless haven't made a peep since this summer. Your security systems are impenetrable and the gentry could even hire extra guards. Wouldn't it be nice to spend one night without worrying about the Rootless and the Empire?"

I reflexively wiped away the twinge of guilt that came of thinking about the Rootless. I didn't know what to think after witnessing the battle and all the carnage. I still tucked the extra food into the boxes, but found myself hesitating at the extra cash; the thought of funding something like what I had seen on the wall screen made me sick.

"Come, Alexander. When was the last time the Landrys threw an event that put everyone else to shame? And for a war hero, no less."

"It does sound tempting . . ." my father mused.

"Indeed."

This last comment came from my mother, who sat at the far end of the dinner table with an almost-empty sake glass. At the other end, my father and Christine Dana sat with their heads bowed in conversation, hands clasped together. Christine had become a fixture in our house these past few months since David joined the army, present for every meal, my father's constant companion. She did all but sleep here, and that was because my father stole away most nights to stay at her penthouse. With Christine for company, and me safely at Landry Park and not at the university, Father seemed happier, more relaxed. Once or twice, a smile ghosted across his face. Yesterday he had hummed as we took a turn in the snowbound gardens together.

Hummed.

I enjoyed his recent pleasant moods, but not the toll they took on Mother. Mistresses were commonplace in our city. In fact, in many families I knew, the mistress actually lived on the estate while the wife had her own loft in the skyline. But I realized now that Mother loved Father, loved him like I loved David, and the feeling drew me to her. All these years that she had indulged in clothes and parties, I had never thought to question why. But now I couldn't help but wonder if she had wanted to distract herself from her cold and unloving husband.

Surprisingly, Addison had risen to the occasion. Bored of Cara's newfound reclusiveness, she turned to Mother for companionship, and spent her days shopping with her, soothing her and spreading malicious rumors about Christine. If not for Addison, my mother might have dissipated entirely, becoming nothing more than a revenant with a bottle.

Christine touched my father's hand again. This time, Mother stood up suddenly, chair scraping the floor. "I'm going to bed," she said.

They didn't notice. Wrapped up in their own world, they didn't notice when I left either.

The drive to the Lodge was long and snowy. Several times the caravan of gentry cars stopped so snowdrifts could be cleared. Luckily, we'd sent word of our stay a week in advance, so the Lodge had plenty of time to stock up on supplies and servants. I thought dreamily of a warm bed and an open kitchen, eating warm soup and soft bread by the fire, watching the snow fall on the northern Missouri forest outside. I would not think of the guest of honor. Not yet, when he wasn't scheduled to arrive for another week.

The full name of the Lodge was Victory Lodge, and, fittingly, it had been built by the losing poor following the War. My ancestors wanted an immense country getaway, with hunting in the forest, fishing in the nearby river, and enough space to entertain hundreds. The sprawling building and the surrounding complex of stables, kennels, and barns spread across half a mile of snow-laden hills, nestled against the forest on one side and rich farmland on the other. I could see the welcoming windows of the second story as we pulled onto the long winding drive.

My soup and fire wish fulfilled, I slept peacefully and woke the next morning, determined to stay as out of the way as possible. With my father giving me this time at the Lodge free of estate work, I had unlimited time to read and relax. I didn't particularly wish to waste it playing whist with fifty-year-old women and hanging around the fringes, waiting for David to show up.

I went downstairs to the kitchen to see if Martha needed any help. The other servants seemed a little aghast at my being down there, but Martha was used to my habit of hiding from large groups. She was an extremely efficient woman and not of the mind to turn down help when it was proffered, no matter where it came from.

Thirty apple pies were on order for that night's dessert, and I set to paring and cutting the apples, and was soon flushed from the heat and dusted with flour, which flew in great puffs from the cook's giant mixing bowls.

Then I saw him, standing in the doorway, looking for me.

"Madeline!" David yelled over the din. He pushed his way past the servants, dodging the gusts of flour, smiling. Snow still flecked his navy peacoat and frosted his hair, melting even as he came up beside me.

"I thought you weren't coming until next week," I said, struggling to keep the shock out of my voice. I kept my eyes on the apples I was slicing—now with a dangerously unsteady hand—willing all the conflicting thoughts at bay.

"I escaped early, before I could get pulled into another battle," he said. He ran his fingers along the countertop, his eyes fixed on my knife. "So are you happy to see me?"

"I—"

"Never mind," David interrupted. "There is someone I want you to meet." He turned back to the doorway where a broad-shouldered man in a military uniform was politely squeezing past the servants, ducking underneath the copper pots that hung from the ceiling.

As soon as his head lifted, I knew him. Jude MacAvery. His face had been all over the wall screens and news bulletins, his voice reverberating in speakers across the city. His speeches replayed on countless tablets, including my own.

He stood before me, with his flint eyes and wavy hair, medals glinting in the swinging kitchen lights, and I felt the world tilt on its axis, like a ship unsteady on the sea. I had the strangest feeling of connection, of knowing Jude even though we were strangers.

I extended my hand. "Madeline Landry."

Instead of shaking it, Jude leaned down and gallantly brushed my apple-stained hand with his lips. "Miss Landry, it is a pleasure to make your acquaintance. I'm Captain MacAvery." He continued holding onto my hand.

"Dinner will be soon," David said.

"Yes, of course," Jude murmured. His gaze burned into mine.

David put a hand on Jude's shoulder. "You'll probably want to change out of your uniform."

Jude smiled ruefully. "How right you are." He bowed—

not the shallow bow of an afternoon tea or fencing match, but the deep bow of the ballroom, of a dinner party introduction. "I'm looking forward to more thoroughly making your acquaintance, Miss Landry. Promise you'll sit next to me at dinner. I can't wait to meet the girl David has talked so much about."

David and I left the kitchen as well. On the way upstairs, I turned to take stock of the person I'd thought ceaselessly of for the past six months. Pictures of him—ash-dusted and scratched, his blue eyes fierce in a face covered with mud—had circulated on the wall screens and tablets after the battle, but it was nothing like seeing him here, in person. His shoulders were slightly broader, his arms and back more muscular than they were before, but he was still more slender than strapping, and still wore his clothes with a vain and elegant fastidiousness. The white-blond hair was still silken and longish, and his gait as twitchy and energetic as before. But the quick grin that used to tug at David's mouth was gone, buried under mountain dirt and the bodies of fallen friends.

"Would you like some tea?" I asked, trying to bury my desire to be with him under the pretense of being a good hostess.

"Sounds perfect," he said.

I led him to the library, where we sat on a leather couch, close but not too close to the crackling fire. A maid brought in hot green tea, and I sipped it slowly. Jude had said that David talked about me, and I hoped that meant that he thought about me as often as I thought about him.

It was impossible to tell what he was thinking about at the moment, however, because the tea and fire animated him once more. He was back in one of his livelier moods, talking rapidly about the army and all the things he'd seen and done.

"The army is mostly dull, but the mountains are beautiful and the men are all good men, very brave. Lots of landless gentry boys like myself. And Jude—he is amazing, Madeline," he said, and started pacing the length of the Persian rug. "You should see him fight. Hand to hand, shooting, fencing; he can do it all. Most of the brass in the army can barely get out of their chairs to pour another brandy, much less lead the men in drills and training exercises."

"Is that why everybody in the army is so taken with him?"

"And everyone out of the army," David said.

I flushed. Did David care what I thought about Jude?

"Are you okay? You seem a little dazed."

"I'm fine," I replied quietly. "Just listening to you."

David knelt in front of the couch, his eyes searching mine. "You aren't mad at me, are you? For not answering your letter?"

"I hadn't even thought about it," I said, trying to sound confident, and set the hand-painted china back on the silver tray with a faint *clink*.

He smiled a small smile. "I see."

The fire spat sparks. I wanted to touch him, speak with him, tell him how much I'd missed him. I wanted to tell him how much I'd thought about him and how many nights I'd lain awake whispering prayers to stars and supernovas that he was safe from the East, that the mountains wouldn't fail to protect him.

I opened my mouth, but David spoke first, other thoughts on his mind. "How are they? I haven't spoken with Jack since the day I was there with you."

I bit my lip.

Jack. The Rootless. I would have to tell him that I didn't know how they were, that I'd abandoned Jack in favor of ledgers and the promise of more love from my father.

No, it's because you disagree with their alliance to the East. And you know you could help more with more money and resources. That's all.

But I had also promised to find a way to force Cara to confess to the events of the night she was assaulted, and I hadn't done that either.

"I wish Jack would've told me the East was planning an attack," David said slowly, after I didn't answer. He turned to look out of the window, where snow piled unevenly on the sill. "As soon as our scouts came back saying that there was movement on the other side of the mountain, I knew it had to be the East. And I knew it had to be tied to the Rootless. I realize that Jack didn't know what fort I was at or even how to communicate with me safely . . . I just wish he could have warned me that something like this would happen."

"Did it feel strange to fight them?" I asked hesitantly. "Knowing they were allied with Jack?"

His jaw tightened. "I didn't care who they were allied with. All they want is to control us. They're intent on that one goal. And," he took a deep breath, "they are brutal."

"They showed us pictures of battles at the academy, but to know it was actually happening, on our own soil, just a few hundred miles away, it was different. Scary."

He twisted his mouth. "Try being there. It's much scarier than watching it on a wall screen." There was a darkness to his voice.

"I'm sorry. That was thoughtless of me to say." I wanted to stop, I could tell David wanted me to stop, but a mordant curiosity pressed me forward. "Was it terrible?"

He stood and walked away from me. "It doesn't matter."

"It does to me."

"Does it?" His voice was so heartbreakingly casual, as if he didn't care what my answer was, that I couldn't think of an answer that would preserve my dignity or his. The specter of Cara and our misbegotten kiss drifted between us.

I moved toward the door. "I should go."

"What? Why?"

"I'm tired."

"So rest in here with me. If it means that much to you, I'll tell you all about what it's like to watch the man next to you blown to bits and to see your friend's hand shot off by an armor-piercing round and to have a mouth so full of char and dirt that you can't taste food for weeks."

"David . . ."

He sighed. "Sorry."

"It's completely understandable," I told him. But I had no other words to offer—I'd never been in battle. I had nothing that could assuage his pain.

He threw himself into a nearby chair and stared at the fire. I moved toward him, not sure what I wanted to do—if I wanted to take his hand or embrace him or kiss him. Instead, I touched his hair, still damp from the melting snow, but still soft, still impossibly fine.

Without looking, he reached up and caught my hand. "You should get ready for dinner," he said, but didn't let go.

I nodded, which was pointless, because he couldn't see me nod, and also because I didn't want to leave. I wanted to stand next to this chair forever, listening to the fire pop and spit, feeling my hand inside David's. But then he did let go.

"I'll see you later," I said.

He nodded, still gazing into the fireplace.

Later that night, I begged off dinner, claiming I had a headache from the heat of the kitchen. But it was really because

I had seen the Westoff car pull into the drive as Elinor had helped me wash away the flour and apple scent from earlier. I thought of David and Cara together and I felt sick. I couldn't go down and watch them together. Not yet. Instead, I buried myself in blankets, and, with Morgana warm at my feet, I traced the swirling patterns on my canopy until my breathing slowed and my thoughts with it.

As I drifted gently between sleep and wakefulness, half dreams crept over my eyelids. Kings and queens, knights and princesses. Morgause and King Arthur, locked in an incestuous embrace. Burning castles and knights choking on their own blood.

TWENTY-THREE

Most everyone went on a sleigh ride the next day, but I stayed at the Lodge, curled up in a window seat with a battered copy of *Le Morte D'Arthur*, rereading the part about the marriage of Guinevere to Arthur.

Jude knocked once on the open door, and then entered. "Hello, Miss Landry."

I set the book down. "You can call me Madeline."

He sat in a nearby chair. "When I heard you were not going on the sleigh ride, I thought I would decline, too. I missed you at dinner."

"I didn't feel well," I said.

"Ah."

We sat in silence for a moment.

He reached out to brush a lock of hair off my face. His fingers were calloused, but the touch felt as familiar as my own hand. I was surprised by the presumptuousness of the gesture, but it felt nice, too. Comforting.

"Would you like a tour of the Lodge?" I heard myself asking.

He smiled. "Very much."

We walked through the halls and galleries, filled with hunting portraits and the glass-eyed heads of unlucky game. Despite the hard work of the servants, a slightly musty smell hung about the place, giving it the uneasy atmosphere of an abandoned attic. Jude said little as we strolled, but I filled the silence, mentioning ancestral names and dates, indicating a particularly prized vase or painting—all the while surprised at my own loquacity. Jude sincerely seemed to want to hear everything I had to say.

"Tell me about Landry Park," he requested. "David has told me a little, but I would love to know more."

I never needed urging to talk about my home. So I told him about the long, verdant lawns and English gardens, the constant spray of fountains and the secret mausoleum in the maze. The copper-domed observatory with the largest family-owned telescope in the country, and the sapphire glow when—once a year, on the anniversary of the day the Last War had ended—we turned off all the lights in and around the house and filled every corner and hung every tree with Cherenkov lanterns.

I noticed Jude's eyes lingering on my lips as I spoke. The thought of it sent a not unpleasant shiver down my spine, but then I quickly felt guilty, like I had betrayed my feelings for David.

"Why didn't David stay in as well?" I asked. We were in the front hall now, overlooked by a massive mounted bear. It reared on its hind legs, sharp claws outstretched.

Jude reached out and fingered the bear's fur. "A certain young woman was very insistent that he come sleighing with her. I can't recall her name at the moment."

"Cara," I whispered. "Cara Westoff." Suddenly, the need to be alone pressed on me. Wrapped up in this happy hour with Jude, I'd forgotten to torture myself with images of Cara and David together—nestled under heavy furs, with warm kisses on cold fingers and shared mugs of cider.

Jude looked at me with something like pity.

"How did you and David meet?" I asked hurriedly, wanting to change the subject.

"Ah," he smiled. "He punched me in the jaw."

I hadn't expected that. "He did what?"

"The colonel in charge was one of those old boys who thought that if you came from a good family, you were in the army to make a good living and have a nice uniform. The dangerous parts—patrols, scouting—that was for the poor boys who had joined so they could eat and have a place to sleep.

"David was itching to go on a patrol and get his hands dirty. There had been some misbehaving going on and he had heard the old major saying to someone that, officer or not, the next boy to get himself into trouble was going on an extended patrol. So he waited until we were all in formation the next morning and hit the guy closest to him." Jude sighed. "Me."

"And then?"

"We went on the patrol together. I suppose the major thought I must have done something to provoke a bald attack like that, so to be on the safe side, he punished us both." He paused, staring up at the bear's glittering eyes. "We were out there for a week."

Jude kept staring at the bear. I stared at him. He and David were so different externally—one dark and quiet, the other fair and wild—but there was something alike about them, a soldier-like quality of someone who knew their own strength, who would fight to the death to defend what they believed in.

Both our thoughts were interrupted by the jingling of bells and merry voices. The sleighs had come back. I watched out the window as David helped Cara out of the sleigh, fascinated by the band of skin that appeared between David's slacks and his jacket as he reached into the sleigh bed.

"Is something wrong?" Jude asked, coming up next to me. "You look upset."

My throat squeezed as I watched David help Cara tramp through the snow. "I just wish now I would have gone sleighing," I said.

"If you don't mind me asking," he said carefully, "I was curious as to the nature of the relationship between you and David. It seems he's attached to Miss Westoff, but I know appearances can be deceiving."

I watched as David grabbed Cara's hand to help her into the house. "We are just friends."

I felt my own hand taken into Jude's. "I take people at their word," he warned me. His hand was massive, swallowing mine. "So you are truly only friends?"

"Truly," I said again, my eyes still on the snowy scene outside.

After dinner, most of the guests stayed in the dining room for cocktails and conversation. News of the mayor's death had reached the Lodge that afternoon, and the landowners were already speculating about Rootless involvement. The lighter-hearted of us found ourselves gathered in the cozy parlor, drinking whiskey and spiced wine and playing cards.

The past few months spent serving as my father's protégé had reduced my aversion to these types of gatherings—I supposed that I liked some of the gentry more, knowing them and their business better—and besides, the parlor was the warmest room in the house. That David was here, roundly beating anyone who dared join him and Jude at the whist table, was completely unimportant.

It was also completely unimportant that I'd tortured Elinor with indecision as to my hair and my dress before I'd come down that evening. We'd finally settled on a flowing silver gown with a tight, lacy bodice and high waistline, and Elinor had left my hair down, the scarlet waves gleaming almost to my waist. I'd felt pretty enough until I saw Cara at dinner—in her tight gold dress and dark smoky makeup, her body cozied up to David's. After that, I'd rather wished I would have come down in my infinitely more comfortable day dress.

I'd been talking with Jane Osbourne about her family's plans to vacation in New-New York, when Addison Westoff came to our corner with a sharp smile that signaled danger. A floridly pink dress hugged her waist and hips, stopping short a few inches above her knee. Her hair was up and diamond earrings brushed her bare shoulders. She must have been the only person at the Lodge who wasn't freezing.

"Jane," Addison said briskly. Years ago, Michael Osbourne had refused to do business with Harry Westoff, citing ethical concerns, and the Westoffs had never forgiven him or his children—even gentle Jane, who rarely spoke unless it was to say something nice.

Jane pulled her soft wool shawl tighter around her shoulders. "Good evening."

Addison turned to me. "What do you say, Madeline?" she asked. "Shall we take on the war heroes? I hear you are quite talented at whist."

"Do you think Cara would like to play with you?" I responded.

"I'd much rather watch," Cara said. She stood behind David, looking down at his hand, fingers stroking his hair. Every now and again, she'd lean forward to murmur something in his ear and he'd laugh. I'd be lying if I didn't admit that this had me gesturing at the footman for refills more than normal. And perhaps it was all the wine and sips of warm whiskey, but I almost felt as if Cara and David were up on a stage, so carefully calculated were their movements. David seemed natural enough, mostly focused on his game, but Cara was playing the coquette too emphatically, too assiduously for a boyfriend she already had. Normally, men were only exposed to her cleavage and breathy whispers when she was still pursuing them. I had never seen her act this way to a boyfriend she'd had for six months.

To be fair, she had never had a boyfriend that long, either.

Fortified by spiced wine and something darker—I smiled at Addison. "In that case, whist sounds marvelous."

Addison took my hand. "Come now. Let us see what these brave captains are made of."

I bid farewell to Jane, and Addison and I made our way across the fur-scattered floor to the card table. Jude jumped to pull out my chair and took my drink from me as I took my seat. Addison sat facing me, just as Jude and David faced each other.

"Ladies," David said, inclining his head. "So lovely to see you come to sacrifice your honor upon the card table."

Jude leaned toward me. "I'm glad to see you," he said, as if we hadn't just spent dinner sitting next to one another. I nodded at him, and looked back at the cards, which David was dealing with the sharp, ticking precision of a marksman.

"So, David, I suppose you're grateful to be home?" Addison asked.

Tick, tick, tick went the cards on the table, each lined up precisely on top of the other. "Yes, ma'am."

"And did you miss all of us terribly while you were gone?"

Tick, tick. "Of course."

"And I know you missed your sweetheart, too."

Tick—David looked up, but not at Cara, at me, and his Cherenkov eyes blazed across the table, burning my skin and my thoughts. I wanted to bathe myself in that burn, to let the radiation take my skin and flesh and bones until I was nothing but charged particles dancing in space.

I felt the ghost of his kiss on my lips, felt the ghost of all the kisses I had craved and desired, and all the kisses I had yet to dream of, and then his mouth parted slightly and I wondered if he was dreaming of those phantom kisses, too.

Addison looked from David to me and then back to David and narrowed her eyes. David coughed and resumed dealing, *tick tick tick*, until all fifty-two cards were dealt, and the ending of that moment was as if all the stars in the sky had been extinguished. It took my breath away.

I hid my shaking hands under the table.

"Not good," Addison said as she began arranging her hand. Somehow I knew she didn't mean the cards.

Cara, too, was examining me in a way that made me

uncomfortable, as if she could see my trembling hands and hear the thumping of my heart underneath the layers of silk and lace. Cara placed her hands on David's shoulders and I put a hand to the onyx and ivory cameo around my neck.

"Well, Madeline, you are to my left, and so you must begin the first trick," David said, his voice stiff and formal.

I led with spades, and Addison and I took the first trick. Next, Jude led, and he and David easily took that round.

"Well done," I complimented Jude, who shrugged.

"Communicating during a game of cards is considerably easier than during a battle."

"Speak for yourself," David said, placing a card on the table.

"Cara found the most beautiful white fabric the other day," Addison commented casually. "And I couldn't help but think what a beautiful wedding dress it would make."

David said nothing, but he began rearranging his hand with the concentration of a scholar.

"Do you know somebody who's getting married?" Jude inquired politely.

Addison's eyes glinted in my direction. "Well, I know that young David here must be desperate to make things official with my Cara. What is a military career without a wife to bring to all the balls and show off to the other men? And I hear it's much easier to win a promotion with a wife to help you entertain your superiors."

"I absolutely agree," Jude said. I could feel him looking at me. Was Jude thinking about marriage? *With me?* I examined my cards to avoid looking at him. That was impossible. We had only just met.

David gestured to the middle of the table. "It's your turn, Addison."

"Oh, is it? Now as I play, David, you must tell me about what you and Cara will do after you've wed. Will you come to live at Westoff Castle with us? Or perhaps get a penthouse in town?"

Cara tossed her hair. "Yes, David, wherever will we live?"

He looked up at her. "Are you serious?"

"Of course," she said. She braced her hands on the table, displaying her chest to ample advantage.

Jude, to his credit, looked down at his cards immediately. David did not.

"Are you really trying to force a proposal out of me at a whist table?" he asked her, and out of the corner of my eye, I thought I caught him glancing at me. So that intense moment before the game had been real. I wasn't the only one who'd felt it.

Cara smoldered at him through long, firelight-laden eyelashes. "Well? Wouldn't I look pretty in a white dress?"

David looked incredulous, and I felt a surge of triumph. He wasn't proposing just yet.

Cara laughed suddenly, brightly. "I'm just teasing, David. You know I want my proposal to be a grand production. I've already alerted all the florists in the city that you would be visiting them soon."

With Cara, it was impossible to tell sarcasm from arrogance, as the two were so intertwined.

"Well, I for one can't wait," Addison said. "Since her attack, I've been keeping a very close eye on my Cara to make sure she finds a good gentry boy to help her recover from her shock. I'm so glad that good gentry boy is you."

Something in Cara's face hardened and I had to wonder at the maternal instincts of a woman who would bring up her daughter's attack so callously, so casually, at a card table and in front of a stranger.

Cara leaned down and kissed David and kissed him hard, as if she needed to prove something about herself to David and to her mother. Her golden hair swung like a curtain in front of their joined faces, but just as I felt relieved that I couldn't see them kissing, David reached up to touch Cara's face, his hand moving her hair back. His fingers brushed her cheek in a gesture so tender and comforting that everything in me boiled in a furious black vacuum.

He pulled her into his lap, one armed snaked firmly around her waist, and deepened the kiss, closing his eyes completely.

Jude coughed uncomfortably.

Cara broke away with a small, satisfied smile, and David touched her cheek one last time. It was that gentle, thoughtful caress that made me bite my lip and stare at my cards, willing the fractured emotions inside to stay hidden. I was almost tempted to throw down my cards and walk out.

But maybe spending the last several weeks side by side with my father had awoken the dormant Landry steel within me, or maybe it was the presence of Jude, so handsome and kind and interested.

I put my hand on his hand and he looked up in surprise. "How long will you be staying with us?" I asked.

"At least until New Year, but with the East talking peace again, I may be able to extend my furlough until the first of February."

I tried to remember all the things that Cara did so naturally—to widen my eyes and curve my shoulders and move my head so that the fire caught the light in my hair. "How wonderful. I imagine you will stay with David for most of the time, but you should come stay at Landry Park for at least a few days. Father loves to have military visitors."

"Not to interrupt," David interjected silkily, "but we *are* playing a game here."

Jude apologized and led the trick, which Addison and I took, along with the next two. We were now one round away from winning, and David seemed irritated by this, double-checking everyone's cards at the end of each trick to make sure some mistake in tallying hadn't occurred.

"It's a game of chance, David," Cara said. "Stop taking it so seriously."

He scowled, and I felt a lift of pleasure. *Ha.*

I plucked at Jude's sleeve. "Do you mind getting me another glass of wine?"

He set down his cards and beamed. "I would be happy to."

I met David's eyes with flinty resolve as Jude walked away.

TWENTY-FOUR

The fire in my fireplace crackled in the cozy silence as I finally crawled into bed, the only sound in the room save for Morgana's purring as she lay curled up at the edge of my bed. I burrowed into the down blankets, sticking my toes underneath the cat's warm little body, and was almost immediately pulled into a hazy sleep.

I woke, what seemed like seconds later, to a hand clapped firmly over my mouth. I struggled and tried to scream, opening my eyes to a figure leaning over the bed.

"Shh, Madeline, it's me." I recognized David's voice as the fog of sleep cleared away. The firelight made his blond hair glow orange. "Promise not to scream?"

I nodded, and he released his hand.

What is he doing here? Excitement tensed into a nervous tangle below my navel.

He darted to the door and peeked out into the hallway. Apparently, all was clear, because he came to the bed and deftly lifted me off the mattress. I tried to cling to the blanket—Morgana, angry at being disturbed from sleep, leaped off the bed with a low meow—but soon I was in David's arms in nothing but a nightdress.

Goose bumps emerged all over my arms from the chilly room—and from the sudden intimacy of our position. My nightdress was nothing less than what I might wear during the heat of summer, but still, the idea of being so close to him in the garment I wore to sleep . . .

He must have realized the same thing. As he ran his thumb over my upper arm, his breathing was ragged.

"Put me down," I insisted, remembering that I was still upset about him and Cara.

His pupils were wide in the firelight. "I'd rather not."

"At least let me grab my dressing gown," I said, trying to break the spell, unsure of what was happening.

He tightened his grip on me and his wide smile returned. "No can do. We have furs outside."

"Outside? David?"

"Shh."

He nudged the door open again with his foot and crept out of the room, still carrying me, his feet skillfully silent after months of patrols in the mountains.

"You are as light as a doll," he whispered to me, his breath rustling the curls around my ear.

I shivered.

I grew colder and colder as we made our way to the grand

staircase, our quick passes by the hallway braziers serving only to remind me of how chilled I was getting. Down the stairs we went, bathed in pale moonlight. I could see the red of my hair reflected in David's eyes.

I could kiss him. The mere thought of it made me too nervous to move, too nervous to speak—too nervous even to take a particle of pleasure from being in David's arms.

We approached one of the many wooden doors that led outside. David opened it and suddenly we were standing under the stars, the icy cold freezing my bare arms and nipping at my nose. His boots crunched in the snow as we walked toward the stables, where a single Cherenkov lantern outlined a blue doorway.

The night was absolutely, infinitely clear, and, out here in the country, the stars were so numerous that they almost seemed wasteful. Wanton. As if someone had carelessly spilled a purse of jewels on the road.

"I heard you regretted missing the sleigh ride earlier today," he said as he carried me into the stable. He put me down, and went to uncover another Cherenkov lantern while I hopped from foot to foot on the freezing planked floor. The blue light illuminated a sleigh at the other end. Blankets and furs were piled high in the seat.

He saw me shivering. "Oh God, I'm so sorry," he said, jumping over a pile of rope and shrugging off his tuxedo jacket. He cast it over my shoulders and buttoned one of the buttons, his fingers fumbling against my stomach for a moment. His jacket was silky and warm inside.

"Better?" he asked quietly. The neck of his white shirt was loose and his bow tie was undone. I could see the pulse jumping in his throat.

"Much better," I replied.

He led the horses out of their stalls and began hitching them to the sleigh. The bells on their harnesses began to ring through the stable.

"You didn't have to do this," I pointed out, wandering closer to the sleigh, my feet like blocks of ice. "Really. I'm sure there will be another sleigh ride tomorrow."

"But will it be at midnight? How many people can claim they went on a midnight sleigh ride?"

"I guess not very many," I murmured. *Not many can claim they went on a midnight sleigh ride with you.*

"Besides, you owe me some fun after you humiliated me at cards tonight." He flashed a grin. Suddenly, I didn't feel cold at all.

A few minutes later found us pressed against each other, covered in furs and clutching flasks of spiced mead that David had swindled from Martha's kitchens. It was as if we'd never sat around a card table, twisting in discomfort. Now, with David pressed against me, I twisted in an altogether different way.

David took the reins and we started down the hill, away

from the Lodge. Several hills and valleys away, I could see the cheery lights of the nearby village. The only signs of a road were the solar-powered lamps burning along the edges of the lane—every other landmark was blanketed in snow and ice.

David started talking about the snow in the Rockies, where shaded patches clung to the earth obstinately, even in June. He had never seen snow until this year. "I know it's freezing everywhere else, but I suppose we're too close to the ocean. It's just hurricanes in Georgia," he said. "Or droughts. Or floods. Or heat waves. No snow."

"In Kansas, we get it all. Except we have cyclones instead of hurricanes."

"Tell me a snow story," David requested. "They say the Great Plains get the best blizzards."

"I was never allowed outside when it snowed," I said, remembering years of watching the flakes fall outside the windows. "I got sick too easily."

"Most people prevent that by wearing coats. When they aren't being kidnapped and dragged into the snow in their nightclothes, I mean."

I shrugged. "I was always prone to colds and bouts of the flu, but when I was nine or ten, I started getting a recurring fever. My father blamed it on too much exertion and exposure, so I wasn't allowed out in the cold anymore. But I still managed to catch the fever again—when I was thirteen, I was bedridden for almost an entire year."

"A fever," David said, mostly to himself, looking out onto the snow.

"It didn't have a name—the doctor and my father called it 'the illness' or 'the fever.' My lungs were filled with fluid and I was unconscious most of the time. All I really remember is the pain—like my body was trying to split itself open."

"Are you healthy now?" David asked.

"I haven't had a relapse since then," I said, a little proudly. Much had been made of my illness—at one time, the entire household seemed to revolve around it—and it was nice to know that was no longer the case. The days of fever dreams and needles, needles, needles were over.

A hand brushed past my hand under the furs, giving my fingers a faint squeeze. When I looked over, David was still gazing at the smooth white hillocks and humps that led down to the river.

"Anyway, the snow has been a recent discovery for me, as well," I said, trying to cover up my discomposure. "It was only two years ago that I was finally allowed out in it again."

"A shame." David switched the reins to one hand and took a drink of mead. "It's beautiful."

We didn't talk for a while then, just sat, lulled by the hiss of the sleigh runners on the snow.

. . .

The next day, I sat down by the fire with Morgana and my tablet and wrote a letter to Jamie, who'd gone home to his mother and sisters for the holiday. It took me almost an hour to compose because every other sentence found me staring into the fire, thoughts chasing themselves around like skaters on a frozen pond.

Jane and I still haven't forgiven you for going home to England. The Solstice may be a time for family, but it is also a time for parties and onerous dinners, and we wish we had you here to ease us through the tedium. Cara and David seem more attached than ever, although I am beginning to feel that Cara is putting on an act. Why and for whom, I can't say. I know her mother was interested in snagging David for her, but Cara has always done what she has wanted, regardless of the conse~ quences. As for David, as much as I do not want it to be true, he seems genuine in his affec~ tion toward her.

I should mention that David's friend Captain MacAvery is wonderful in every way. Since you abandoned me during the claustrophobic winter, he has been keeping me company. For a hero, he is very grounded and attentive. Most of the girls here are chasing after him, and it is easy to see why, although I am not sure I share their enthusiasm for captain~capturing. He is such a kind friend and very handsome.

I must go. Mother is insisting that I come down for charades. I think she does not want to face the drawing room with Father and Christine by herself.

Come back soon~
Madeline

TWENTY-FIVE

That night, after an endless evening of drinks and charades, I paused while closing the curtains in my bedroom, surprised to see David and Jude outside in the snow. David smoked his usual cigarette, while Jude pointed up at the stars, talking in a low voice that I couldn't hear through the glass. David said something, and Jude let out a hearty laugh, causing David to laugh, too. A feeling of peace settled over me watching them. The bond between them, so strong, so natural and brother-like, had kept us safe in the mountains. As long as they were together, the Easterners couldn't touch us.

Then David went inside, leaving Jude by himself in the cold air. I watched him for a while. There was something so purposeful and calm about everything he did, the very sight of him was reassuring. He looked up at my window and a tiny part of me wanted to duck.

Why? It was my house, and I had a right to look at my guests. Instead, I raised my hand in a little wave. He smiled and gestured for me to come outside and join him.

Still corseted and clad in red velvet from dinner, I slid my feet back into my ballet flats and went outside.

Without asking, he pulled off his cape and draped it over my shoulders. I smiled in thanks, but couldn't help but compare it to the intimate warmth of David's jacket.

"Good evening," Jude said, after he'd clasped the cape around my neck.

"Good evening," I replied.

"Shall we go for a walk?"

In answer, I slid my arm through his. As we walked, I could see his dress shoes slipping on the snow, but he still held out his arm to support me. It was much easier to relax when Jude was touching me than when David did. None of the nervousness or suppressed desire crackling under my skin, just the faint tingle of connection I got whenever I looked at him.

"I hate these big gatherings," he said, the crunch of the snow punctuating his words. "All the people wanting to talk to me about the war. People think the military is all flashy uniforms and bravery. I would give anything to have everyone stop congratulating me on our victory. Do they even know how many men died?"

I looked at him, expecting to see bitterness on his face like I had on David's, but there was only exhaustion.

"And it's not over yet," he said, more to himself than me. "The Empire will not stop, not now when everything they want is so close."

"I think my father is more worried about the Rootless."

Jude nodded. "Another concern. But I believe they will see

the wisdom in restraining their anger. Even if they were to start a revolt, they aren't organized or educated in martial tactics. How could they hope to win?"

I turned my head to look back at the house, to the window I knew was David's. "I don't know. Maybe if they had help."

"I have sympathy for them. They live a hard life." He closed his eyes and rubbed his forehead. He had longer eyelashes than David's. Longer and darker. "If it came to it, I suppose I'd be bound to military oaths to defend the gentry. I wouldn't enjoy suppressing them, but it would take something tremendous to make me abandon my command and betray my country."

Betray. That was a strong word, wasn't it? But it was true. The Rootless weren't legally considered citizens, and so helping them overthrow the gentry would be treason. I pulled Jude's cloak closer around myself, thinking of the thousands of people who'd died with the pronouncement of that word.

"Do you enjoy fighting?" I asked, changing the subject.

"You know, David asked me that same question in the mountains and I couldn't answer him, never having fought in a battle before. Now that I have, I suppose the answer is yes. I don't enjoy killing or hurting people, but when I stop someone from killing or hurting one of my men, or when I turn a rout into a rally . . . yes, I enjoy that."

"You're brave."

He shrugged. "Bullets are just lumps of metal. A flash of

pain or a quick death. But being a coward—that's something that eats away at you slowly, from the inside. That's what really scares me."

"What is it like? Fighting?"

"Loud. Muddy. I thought it would be like what we learned in Officer School, two civilized armies marching at each other, firing in volleys. But the Empire doesn't march. They swarm. There were tens of thousands of them and when you shot one, five more sprang up in his place. With all the mud and smoke, it was impossible to tell who is who. There were times when I almost shot one of my own men, because he looked as sooty and filthy as the others.

"There was one man, good as dead, holding his innards and trying to crawl to safety. I thought he was an Easterner, so I left him behind. But when we collected the bodies, I recognized him. He was one of ours and I left him there to die like a beast in the mud."

"He might have died anyway," I commented.

"That is not the point."

And then he went silent, reflective.

"Your father, is he in the military?" I asked, hoping to distract him.

"No," Jude said flatly. "He's dead. Three years ago, he went on a diplomatic mission to the Empire. He left on a Monday and the following Friday I received a box of ashes." After a moment, he added, "My mother is dead, too."

I wanted to ask if his father had died in an accident or if he'd been murdered by the Empire, but I didn't. Something about the long strides Jude took told me all I needed to know.

"I imagine you have heard endless empty sentiments," I said. "So I will just tell you that I can't conceive of how hard it must have been to lose your family and I'm sorry."

We stopped at the wooden fence and turned to see the Lodge lit up—a beacon of warmth and light in the endless fields and forests of the Midwestern winter. "You are so lucky. You have a strong, powerful father. A beautiful mother. I'll confess I am jealous of you, Madeline, and of all the Landrys."

I put my other hand on his arm. "You are welcome to stay with us anytime you like."

A cold wind began to blow, whistling fiercely through the trees and over the pond. Jude began to walk again and I let him pull me along, bowing my head into the wind. There was a moment when I thought I saw the glow of a cigarette near the stables, but the swinging Cherenkov lanterns made it impossible to tell what was real and what was shadow.

When we reached the door, the weary look on Jude's face had passed, but something else had replaced it, a determined gaze that I wasn't sure I felt entirely comfortable with. He reached out and trailed a finger along my neck.

"I should get you back to your bed," he said.

TWENTY-SIX

Despite the warmth of my bed after the chilly walk across the grounds, despite the soothing sounds of a house at rest—crackling fires, Elinor breathing heavily in the next room, Morgana purring—I couldn't sleep. It might have been the lingering afterglow from my sleigh ride with David last night, or perhaps it was the way Jude's hand had held onto my own as he bid me good night outside my door. Like he wanted to hold on to me forever. The thought wasn't pleasant, but it wasn't *un*pleasant either, as if the satisfaction of being wanted canceled out the disappointment that the wanting was coming from the wrong man.

Whatever it was, I couldn't sleep, and that is why I heard the footsteps in the corridor and saw the moving blue light of a Cherenkov lantern under my door.

It was close to three in the morning, too early for the servants to be rising and too late for straggling drunks coming from downstairs. But someone was up and about, walking into the main part of the house. It could have been anyone, any tired servant fetching a late snack or extra blanket for a gentry guest. But I wanted it to be David. We hadn't been alone since the night before, when he took me from my room dressed only in my nightgown, and I needed to talk to him, needed to hear his voice, needed reassurance that whatever moment had flickered between us at the whist table was real and hadn't withered away with one of his changing moods.

I slid out of bed and wrapped a soft woolen robe around me, finding my slippers with my feet. I opened the door as silently as possible and stole out into the hallway—without a lantern of my own. I didn't want to be seen, and besides, I hardly needed it. I wasn't intimate with every corner and stone of Victory Lodge like I was with Landry Park, but it was still a Landry house and I still knew it well enough to make it around in the dark.

They had already descended the stairs and made for the gallery by the time I reached the central staircase. The gallery! It had to be David; no servant would need anything from the gallery. It was merely a long corridor fronted by windows on one side and by paintings on the other, the monotony of the room broken up by mounted animal heads and three separate fireplaces, none of which were lit at the moment. The largest painting hung in the very middle; it was a portrait of Jacob Landry at a desk, a gray cat curled at his feet. Even from here, I could see the sightless glare of his painted eyes.

The snow reflecting the moonlight made the entire gallery unnaturally light, throwing long shadows across the floor.

But as I crossed into the gallery, the moonlight streaming in through the windows revealed long, golden hair and a striking green ball gown.

Cara.

Still unaware of my presence, she leaned against a wall and slid down, until she was crumpled in a pile of emerald taffeta on the stone floor. And then she laid her head against her knees and began to cry.

She would die of shame if she knew I was here, witnessing her moment of stolen privacy, but I couldn't leave her like this, alone and crying under the stern faces of my ancestors. I tentatively stepped over to her, unsure whether I should announce myself or wait for her to notice me. Instead, I sat down beside her and draped my arm over her bare shoulders. She stiffened, but didn't look up.

"I should have known you would be here," she said into her knees. "You always find me when I least want to be found."

I simply squeezed her shoulders and, after a moment, she relaxed. I could tell by her ragged breathing that she was still crying, but she seemed content to have me here, and so I stayed, watching the ephemeral winter clouds whisper over the moon.

Finally she raised her head and wiped her eyes. "Okay. I am finished now."

"Okay," I said, and removed my arm, suddenly uncomfortable at the intimacy we just shared.

It seemed like something of our childhood had crept over us slowly since her attack, that sense of being forced together, despite being different—almost like we were related by blood. I hesitated to name it friendship, but deep down, I cared about her. And as she gave me a watery smile before she used my robe to wipe her nose, I got the sense that she cared about me too.

"I am sorry, Madeline," she said, tears brimming at her eyes again. "I am so sorry."

"I was awake anyhow," I told her.

"No, not this. About everything else," she said, and gestured toward the windows. "About my attack. About your house getting ruined. About . . . other things. You were right about always being dragged into my troubles, except this time, I didn't mean to. I didn't want you to find me in the woods that night any more than I wanted you to fall in love with David after he and I had already met. I just wanted you to stay away so you wouldn't get hurt. But instead, you're in as thick as me." She looked over at me. "Please be careful, Madeline. You must be careful."

As she went up to wipe her eyes again, I saw it: the dark blue-purple of new bruises ringing her upper arm.

"Cara . . ." I whispered.

She followed my eyes down and gave a trembling shrug. "A couple hours old. They don't hurt anymore." She stood and brushed off her dress. "I should probably get some rest before Solstice Day tomorrow. Good night, Madeline."

I stayed there for a moment after she left, staring at the Cherenkov lantern she'd forgotten on the floor. Who continued to torment Cara? And why?

I picked up the lantern and walked out of the gallery.

The morning of the Solstice was cloudy and dark. I woke to find an embroidered stocking hanging from my mantel. The cat didn't stir as I slid out of bed and ran over the cold floorboards to grab the bulging sock. After dinner last night, I had given Elinor gifts to cache in others' rooms—a watch inlaid with a jade atomic symbol for Father, a bottle of strong perfume for Mother, and, despite my worries that I'd look overeager, a book for David. *Le Morte D'Arthur*—a leather-bound copy with hand-painted watercolors inside.

I'd also ordered a gold sash from the village for Jude to go with his red dress uniform. It felt wrong to give David a gift but not Jude.

My stocking contained the usual baubles and bright things. Earrings and necklaces and bracelets and other jewelry bought with borrowed money. A small package wrapped in heavy paper came with a tag inscribed with Jude's square hand. I unwrapped it and my heart rose to see a small miniature of Landry Park, done in painstaking detail.

Once I heard you describe Landry Park with such effusion, I knew it was near to your heart. I sent David's valet to commission the miniature in Kansas City, and it just arrived. From the images I see on my tablet, it seems to be a fair likeness. If it's not too forward of me to say, I hope that I get to see your fine home in person soon.

— Jude

It was a fair likeness indeed. I could even make out the brass telescope in the observatory. I crawled back into the still warm bed, cradling the miniature in my hands. Something about the texture of the brushstrokes made the house seem much more alive than it was in shiny, backlit tablet pictures. *I knew it was near to your heart.*

Indeed. Who would Madeline Landry be without the observatory and mausoleum and wide green lawns?

Behind the house, set into the cloudless sky, a faintly golden atomic symbol caught the light. I sighed and set the miniature aside.

There was nothing else in my stocking. Nothing from David.

I flopped back on my pillow, startling Morgana enough for her to open one eye to see what the fuss was about.

It was stupid to think he would have given me a present.

I felt so embarrassed and exposed, having given him a gift that he would probably toss aside. I rolled facedown on my pillow, trying to bite down the humiliation, and my hand brushed against something. I sat up and lifted the pillow.

It was another miniature, this time one of the poster in the Rootless ghetto, with the Rootless smiling vacantly at their nuclear charges and sacks of food. Except, instead of the gentry man behind them, it was me. The atomic symbol crowned my scarlet hair, which ran down my shoulders like blood, the ends of it brushing the tiny heads of the Rootless.

I dropped it as if it had burned me.

Was it from David?

Had he put it in my room while I'd been asleep? His hand reaching under my pillow, his breath on my face while I'd slept obliviously on?

I curled my knees to my chest and laid my head on my arms. *He knows. How little I've done for the Rootless.* A flare of anger followed my guilt. *But it's not as if he's dropping his life to join them either.* It could just as easily be him in that picture.

"Miss?" someone said out of the darkness.

I gasped and pulled the blanket up to my chest.

Charlie, Jack's son, stepped out of the murky corner by the bookcase. He wore the same clothes I'd seen him wearing in

June; his feet were wrapped in filthy rags and the glistening skin between his nose and his lips revealed a recent bout of flu. He looked cold even now by the fire, covered in goose bumps, his lips a faint blue.

"Charlie!" I lowered my voice, paranoid, not wanting Elinor to hear. "What are you doing here?"

"I delivered that, miss," he said, pointing at the miniature of me. "Mr. David had me make it for you."

"You made it yourself?"

He nodded proudly. "Mr. David gave me the paints and the canvas and a picture of you. It took me every day for five days—I'm not used to paints, since we normally just have charcoal in our part of town. But after a couple days, I got the hang of it. Mr. David told me how to use the post and even gave me money to send it here, but I wanted to come myself to see you open it. Do you like it?"

His face was so eager that I couldn't bear to tell him the truth. That it horrified me. Shamed me. That I never wanted to see it again. "It is beautiful," I said instead. "You are so very talented, Charlie."

"Thank you, miss," he said happily, cheeks glowing pink. "I could make you more—not of those, but of any picture you'd like. I've gotten really good at dogs, especially if they're old dogs because they don't move very much."

"I would love that, Charlie, but you shouldn't have come here. The Lodge is solar-powered. We don't have Rootless in the countryside. If they find you here, they will think you are up to no good."

"That's what my father said, and he forbid me to come. Mr. David did too." Charlie admitted. "But I wanted to see you open your present and I wanted to see Mr. David again. And I got to ride the freight train most of the way here, and it was filled with fresh fruit! I had apples and oranges and even cherries."

"This is dangerous, Charlie. Very dangerous. Coming here was a huge risk."

He crossed his arms. "Why haven't you come back to visit us?" he asked. "Mr. David only came back to have me paint that picture, and you haven't visited us since the summer. How come?"

I opened my mouth and then closed it. None of the easy answers about political alliances and the necessity of keeping up pretenses held up in Charlie's poor, runny-nosed, and painfully, painfully sweet presence.

Because I am selfish, Charlie.

A knock at the door interrupted my conversation. Panic rushed through me and I gestured violently at Charlie to hide. He slid swiftly under the bed.

"Miss? Your father would like to see you in his study."

"Come in, Elinor."

She came and dressed me in the elaborate Solstice morning dress my mother had chosen the night before—another velvet, blue this time—after she'd laced me into the stiff Renaissance-style corset. I counted the seconds as she pulled the stays tight, hooked the buttons on my gown. After she styled my hair and left, I knelt on the ground and looked under the bed. Charlie grinned out at me as if he thought it were a game.

"Charlie, you must stay here. Use my sink to clean up and find some blankets, then *stay hidden*. My father would be furious if he knew there was a Rootless hiding in his house."

"I'll be safe, I promise."

"Don't go looking for David. I will bring him to you."

"Yes, miss."

Feeling as if I were leaving something more dangerous than an expired charge unattended, I left.

Please stay hidden, Charlie, I willed him.

I went downstairs to the study, where Father sat behind a large desk, stuffed game trophies peering at us from the walls and corners. I ignored their blank glassy eyes and focused on meeting Father's as evenly as possible. I could hide Charlie from him. I was made of the same stuff he was.

Mother was there too and, for the first time in weeks, I couldn't smell the now-familiar whiff of alcohol on her breath when she kissed my cheek. Her hair and makeup were fresh, and she was actually smiling.

"Madeline, do you know who has just been to see me?" Father asked, lacing his fingers together and leaning back in his chair.

I shook my head, desperately hoping it wasn't a guest who had noticed a Rootless hiding about the house.

"Captain MacAvery. He came about you."

The quivering panic in my stomach subsided; Charlie was undiscovered for the moment. Whatever had Jude visited Father for? Our unchaperoned walk last night had been technically a breach of etiquette—young people weren't supposed to sneak off together, the purity of gentry heirs had to be ensured, et cetera et cetera—but it happened all the time and usually no one cared. David and I had been alone more than a few times. But perhaps Jude had been secretly shocked at my behavior, shocked enough to tell Father.

"He came to ask my permission to be your escort at your debut." Father looked enormously satisfied and I felt enormously stunned. Jude had asked me to debut? Surely my flirting hadn't been that good.

Mother came out of her chair and hugged me tightly. "We are so happy for you, Madeline darling," she said. I tentatively hugged her back. I'd forgotten how gentle she could be. I buried my face in her neck.

"I must confess this has exceeded my wildest hopes," Father added. "Captain MacAvery is a national hero and is bound to advance to the highest ranks of the military. In addition to his very considerable money, you would be entertaining generals, politicians, presidents more frequently than we do now—maybe even dignitaries from other nations."

I let go of Mother and looked up at Father. "What?"

"Captain MacAvery left no doubt in my mind that a proposal would be imminent. I, of course, encouraged this."

Wait . . . what? "A proposal? But we have only known each other a week!"

"Marriages have been arranged while people are on separate continents, Madeline. Your own grandfather was married in a proxy marriage where his bride's father stood in for her. A week is much more than many are given. And you two seem to enjoy each other's company. Or were those two other people sneaking off for a stroll last night?"

"How did you—"

Father waved a hand. "It is my property, Madeline, and you are my daughter. I know everything I need to."

"I can't marry him without knowing him better. I don't even know his middle name!"

"It is Jacob," Mother volunteered.

Father leaned back in his chair, his fingers steepled together. "How would you feel knowing this? That if you agree to debut with him, agree to be his wife, I will change the Landry deed and my will. You may attend the university and still inherit Landry Park, as long as you are engaged. I imagine Captain MacAvery would be amenable to waiting a few years until you finished your studies. He seems quite taken with you."

I worried my lower lip with my teeth.

"I find this a rather elegant solution to all of our concerns. You get your education and Landry Park, the estate gets more money and prestige, and I get the security of knowing our line will continue, albeit a little later than I would like."

I felt that I was losing the battle somehow, sliding helplessly into my father's trap.

Helplessly or willingly? It was true that marrying somebody handsome and kind hardly seemed a steep price for everything I'd ever wanted.

Except . . . "What if I want to marry somebody else?"

"Like David Dana?" Father laughed. "He seems otherwise occupied with Cara Westoff. Besides, Captain MacAvery is a better match in terms of money and influence."

I passed a hand over my eyes. "I need to think about it."

"You do not have a choice," Father said. "We marry who we must for the good of the estate."

Mother looked away, a hand pressed against her chest.

"I am not marrying Jude MacAvery just because you want me to," I said. "If I do it, it will be my choice."

"Whatever makes you feel better," he said.

I didn't have an answer for that.

After being dismissed, I tried to push the thought of Jude away and focus on Charlie—specifically the issue of getting Charlie safely home. But as I climbed the stairs back to my room, my father's voice echoed again and again: *you do not have a choice.*

He couldn't force me to marry. He wouldn't.

It wasn't that I didn't like Jude. I did. He was kind and genuine and very good-looking. If I was the type of girl who dreamed of getting married just to be married, then Jude would have been the perfect husband. But as it was, I still didn't want to marry at all, unless it was to—

I stopped my thoughts right there. It didn't bear thinking about.

When I got back to my room, I flung myself on my bed, oblivious to the miniature that was still there. Facedown in the downy quilt, I became aware of the empty silence of my room. I sat up.

"Charlie?"

I slid off the bed and looked underneath it. No Charlie.

"Charlie? It's Madeline. It's okay to come out now."

Nothing. I'd been stupid to think of containing a cartwheeling boy under a bed for over an hour. Even Jack could barely contain him. Why did I think he'd listen to me?

I swallowed my panic and tried to think. He'd probably gone looking for David, who was on the other end of the Lodge. I would just wander around, pretending to take a turn in the corridors until I found him. If he had washed himself up, he could pass for a stable boy or gardening servant, although with his clothes in the state they were, I doubted it.

I pushed open my door and started looking, passing several laughing houseguests on their way down to the vast

Solstice lunch. Even from up here, I could smell the sweet, sticky breads and fried bacon being carried to the banquet room.

Lit with an idea, I picked up my skirts and hurried down to the kitchens, where Charlie sat on a countertop swinging his legs while Martha fed him scraps of turkey and roast peafowl.

"Oh, Charlie," I said, coming up to him. "You scared the blue lights out of me."

"Sorry," he said, chunks of food tumbling out of his mouth. "I smelled the food and couldn't help myself."

"I shouldn't have left you so long," I said, feeling suddenly exhausted. "Let's get you back to my room, and I will try to find David for you." I piled a plate high with warm bread and meat, and offered him my hand.

Cook helped him down from the counter, and he looked so small in her large arms that a surge of protectiveness ran through me. I had to keep him safe. For Jack and for David. And for me.

"I hope you know what you're doing," Martha said to me as I took Charlie's hand.

"I do, too."

Leaving Charlie alone again seemed like a bad idea. I told Mother that I had come down with a sudden stomachache and needed to rest for the remainder of the day. I also sent a message down with Elinor for David to come visit me in my rooms. She came back an hour later, saying apologetically that she hadn't had an opportunity to speak with him, as he was so busy playing games and drinking.

Charlie was restless, but still sick and a little fevered, and by the time night began to fall in the early evening, he was ready for sleep. I made a nest of blankets and pillows for Charlie under the bed, and within minutes, he snored softly, more comfortable and warm than he'd been his entire life. I read until midnight—hoping somehow that David would know to come find me—and then tried to sleep too, trying not to think of Jude or marriage or the stowaway boy under my bed. After five or six fitful hours, I gave up and pulled back the covers. I stood up and looked out the window.

Blue swathed along the black backdrop of night, heralding the coming dawn. Suddenly, I wanted to be outside, in the cold, more than anything. Charlie was sound asleep—surely he'd be safe if I left just for a few moments. He would never even know I was gone.

I dressed hurriedly in riding pants and a sweater, pulling on a coat as I left my room. My boots I waited to put on until I reached the door outside, not wanting to wake anybody else.

The dark and cold felt so clear, so clean, that I could've stayed there forever. Instead, I walked over to the kennel building where my father kept his hunting hounds. On days when a hunt wasn't held, it was a servant's job to exercise the dogs by running them around the grounds. It was something my father and I had done together when I was a little girl, before the estate had started to truly suffer, and he'd grown distant. I pushed the button that unlocked the kennel doors, and the dogs rushed out, tails wagging, the green lights on their collars blinking.

They bounded eagerly around my feet as I walked toward the northern field. I could see the dark blot of the frozen lake in the distance. A weak and pink sun started to shimmer out of the rolling low hills.

The breaths puffed out of my mouth in white clouds.

Up and over the hill, Jude MacAvery came walking, an unbuttoned uniform coat flapping around his waist. The dogs ran to him, barking and gamboling around him, and he knelt to rub their necks and scratch behind their ears. I had to admit—he looked very handsome.

I stood completely still as he approached me. Charlie seemed very far away right now. So did Jack and David. Jude was the key to everything I had wanted before I met David and Jack. With Jude, my lifelong dream could be achieved. I could have them both: the university and Landry Park.

Jude stopped in front of me and held out his hands. "Madeline, the day I met you, I felt like we'd known each other our whole lives. Will you allow me to escort you to your debut?"

Maybe it was the cold air or the nosy dogs or the now-blinding sun, but it was hard to think clearly. David was never going to ask me—the image of him kissing Cara at the whist table flashed before my eyes—and a debut wasn't a marriage. And right now I could see the dawn in Jude's eyes. I took his hands and responded with a single word.

"Yes."

TWENTY-SEVEN

As soon as I'd answered, blue lights began flashing around the house, a siren blaring. The emergency system had been activated, signaling for the local police to come to the house.

Charlie.

Without a word to Jude, I started running for the house as fast as I could, the breaths stabbing in and out of my chest like icy knives.

Oh no oh no oh no.

If anything happened to Jack's son, it would be all my fault.

Inside, the Lodge was pandemonium. Women were hysterical, men were yelling, servants were rushing for anything they thought would help: tea, opium, brandy.

I shoved my way through them all to the upstairs hallway, hoping against pitiful hope that my room was undisturbed and Charlie still safe. But it wasn't.

He wasn't.

Several servants held him pinned to the ground while my father, Arthur Lawrence, and William Glaize stood over him.

The crowd of agitated guests made it difficult to elbow my way into the room, but I did it, ignoring their protests and warnings. Inside my room, Elinor sat in an overstuffed chair, looking stricken. Another maid chafed her shoulders and murmured soothing things in her ear. When she saw me, she started crying.

"I'm so sorry, Miss Landry," she said, face wet and miserable. "I'm so sorry."

Father turned to me, his face so full of undisguised fury that I took a step back. But the anger wasn't for me. "He . . . *it* . . . was in your rooms. Your maid happened to find him stashed under your bed, no doubt planning to hurt you as soon as you came back. Fortunately, she screamed in surprise, alerting us all to his presence."

Elinor started crying harder. She must have realized, too late, that a Rootless boy, cleaned and wrapped in my blankets, was clearly there under my protection.

"Likely he would have killed us all after he killed you," my uncle Lawrence said.

"No! I'd never—" A servant clamped a hand over Charlie's mouth.

Father glared at him, then turned to me and tugged me into a hard hug. "You are safe," he said, "by sheer chance. If you had been hurt, I would have been devastated. More importantly, the estate would have been devastated."

I flinched at that.

"I have no doubt this boy is connected to those who vandalized our house and who attacked Cara last spring. His people are likely connected to the death of the mayor. He must be punished."

"He is just a boy," I said, trying to sound calm. "What harm could he have done?"

"He looks to be seven or eight. That is quite old enough to kill, if he's clever."

"Look at him! Would the Rootless really send a child seventy miles to take on a house full of people?"

"They are not like us, Madeline. They do not think like us."

I didn't know what to do. I could argue with my father until I was bluer than a lantern, but he would never bend. I could reveal that I had been harboring Charlie and hope that my Landry blood would protect me from the worst of my father's anger. But would it ultimately help Charlie? I supposed I had to try anyway.

"What is going on?" David asked from the hallway before I could frame my thoughts into words. He pushed his way through the crowd around my door, and as soon as he saw Charlie, his body sagged against the doorframe. "Oh my god," he whispered. "What the hell happened?"

"What the hell happened indeed," Father said acidly. "The Rootless have crossed the final line. Lock the boy up and prepare our return to Kansas City. If he's to be made an example of, it must happen in front of his conspirators."

"What's all the fuss about?" Cara came into the room and gasped. "Cha—"

I kicked her swiftly. She shut her mouth and glared. But David cast me a grateful look. He wasn't ready to reveal our connection to Charlie yet. Not before we could figure out how to help.

The servants hauled Charlie to his feet—a short distance—and shoved him roughly out of the room. When he turned his head to look at me, pleadingly, I saw a lifetime of fear in his eyes. And I felt the weight of the atomic crown on my head.

"What are we going to do?" I asked. The three of us who knew Charlie had managed to snag a car back to Kansas City together, leaving Jude in a limousine full of fawning girls, which he seemed less than happy about. Charlie, handcuffed like a violent criminal, barely tall enough to look out the window beside him, was riding back to Kansas City in a local police car.

David stared at the farmland rushing past, his legs twitching as he ran his fingers through his hair over and over again. Cara was more affected than I would have anticipated, shakily pouring herself glasses of gin and chewing on manicured fingernails.

"David?" I prodded.

"How could you keep this from me?" he finally asked, eyes still on the snowy fields.

"I sent Elinor down with a message for you, but you were too busy with the festivities to pay her any mind."

"Do you think for a moment that I wouldn't have come up if I had known he was in your room?"

"I didn't exactly know how to tell you, okay? If I had written a note, she probably would have read it, and I didn't want to burden her with something like this. If you would not have been so intent on spending all night drinking and dancing, you could have seen him."

"And then what would you have done, David?" Cara followed up. "Sent him back out into the snow?"

"I would have found a better place for him to hide!"

"In a house full of people? With every room full? There was no better place than my bedroom," I said.

"There was the nuclear shelter."

Every gentry house had a well-stocked shelter underneath it in case of a nuclear attack. Food, water, medicine for up to a year. As far as I knew, no one had ever used them for anything other than tornadoes since they'd been built. "Father would have found out somehow. He knows everything about his property at all times," I insisted. "I did the best I could."

We sat in silence for a while.

"What are we going to do?" I asked again.

"I don't know, Madeline, what do you think we should do?

Since you felt so capable handling this situation on your own before?" David's voice was as flat as the steel-gray clouds outside.

I hoped he could feel the anger I was radiating right now. I hoped it was burning him. "Why are you angry with me? You were basically the one who brought him here with that present."

"I told him to stay away," David groaned. "I told him to mail the thing. I never imagined that he would run away and jump on a train."

"He's hotheaded like his brother," Cara said softly.

David and I ignored her. "You should have planned it better," I accused him.

He threw up his hands. "I just wanted to do something nice for you. And somehow that makes me a terrible person?"

I thought of the painting—the Madeline with cold eyes and the atomic crown. "It was a terrible present," I told him, my voice shaking.

"I thought a Landry like you would like it."

I was so furious I couldn't even form words. He went back to staring stonily out the window.

"I think we should try to break him out," Cara said into the tense silence. "We just have to distract the constables or something—or maybe we could bribe them."

"Even with your money, it would be hard to bribe an officer under my father's control," I pointed out tiredly. "No amount of money you could give him would be worth his life. And trust me, if he ran, my father would find him."

She tossed her hair. "Well, we can't just leave him to rot in jail."

"Or worse," David added. "Who knows what your father will do."

I sighed, and picked at my white coat. "There is no other way. I am going to tell my father the truth."

David sat up. "Not about the revolution?"

"Of course not! I just meant about Charlie hiding in my room. I'll invent some story about meeting him someplace in town, and how I was friendly to him, and that he wanted to bring me a Solstice present."

"You really think that will help Charlie?" Cara asked doubtfully.

"And you really think your father will buy that?" David asked.

"If Father knows beyond a doubt that Charlie was not there to hurt anyone, he will have to let him go."

David shook his head. "It won't make a difference. It's all over now."

The car dropped Cara at her house right as she received a message from Addison saying that the stress of the thwarted Rootless attack was too much for her and she was leaving straight for an airport to join her husband in New Miami.

"Oh, thank God," Cara murmured.

"You won't miss her?" I asked distractedly, thinking about the task that awaited me at my own house.

"Are you kidding? I hope she stays in New Miami for a year."

"That's healthy," David remarked from his corner of the car.

Cara's teeth chattered as she climbed out of the car. "Lord, I miss my pink coat. It was so warm."

Pink coat?

Where had I seen a pink coat before?

"Cara, I saw your coat ages ago." I paused. "At Jack's house."

"What?" She seemed at a loss, and then tossed her hair over her shoulder, as if to cover her discomfort. "You must be mistaken."

The door closed abruptly and I sat back, trying to piece it all together. It all made sense. She *had* worn a coat outside the night of Marianne's debut, and it had been taken by Jack or by another Rootless and then given to Jack. But why?

Maybe her attacker had been a Rootless all along, and Cara had been telling the police the truth. But why would she lead me to believe it was someone else?

And to confuse matters even more, I saw Ewan rounding the corner to the front of the house as we drove off, a leather charge satchel slung over his shoulder.

"That was Charlie's brother going in," I told David. "You don't think he'll hurt Cara, do you?"

"He's probably going inside for charges," he said dully. "She'll be fine."

The last time I'd seen Ewan, he'd been so angry and vicious. I couldn't imagine how furious he'd be now that the gentry had his brother.

"But last time we saw him, he was so bitter. He made Cara cry."

David caught my look. "Trust me, Madeline. She's safe with Jack's son. I would turn the car around if I thought anything different."

We drove down to the skyline penthouse where David and Christine lived, passing glaciers and mountains of dirty city snow.

"David . . ." I said as he opened the door, wondering if he knew the truth about Cara and her coat.

"How I am going to tell Jack that I let his youngest son be captured?" he asked before I could start, running another hand through his hair as he stepped out onto the sidewalk.

"I don't know."

The door slammed shut, and he vanished inside the building. I leaned my head back on the soft leather seat and tried not to take David's nettled words personally. He was upset. We all were.

At home, Jude greeted me in the foyer with a bow and a soft kiss on my cheek. "You must be terrified. Almost attacked in your own room," he said.

I set aside thoughts of Cara for the moment. "I'm holding up. Do you know where my father is?" There wasn't a moment to waste.

"He's busy at the moment, but he asked me to give you the wonderful news."

I pulled away from Jude. "News?"

"He would like for you to debut next week. Isn't that fantastic?" Jude took my hand in between his own, the leather gloves on my bare skin cold to the touch. "When I asked him, just yesterday, if I could escort you to your debut, I thought it would be months before we were dancing in your ballroom together. But now it will only be days."

I blinked at Jude. A debut? Now? When my father was terrified of a rebellion? After Charlie's capture, I could barely wrap my head around the idea of any light-hearted activity, much less a debut.

Besides, a week spared no time to put together a party of this size. Cara's debut with David had seemed hasty and it took them at least four weeks to plan. And Jamie would hardly have time to cross the Atlantic, and so my closest friend would be missing from what was supposed to be one of the most important days of my life.

"But the guests from out of town . . . ?"

"That's why your father is so busy. He is personally inviting all of his friends from across the country." Jude tucked my hand in the crook of his arm. "I have met with the president and countless admirals and generals, but a party full of the Uprisen . . ." he shook his head in happy disbelief. "It is amazing."

It couldn't be a coincidence. Charlie captured and my debut happening so quickly. Especially if my father was finally gathering the Uprisen after months of delay.

"Excuse me, Jude," I said politely, and extracted my hand from his arm. "I will see you at dinner." And then I hurried down the hall, my button-up boots leaving brownish snowmelt puddled on the marble.

I doubted Father would be in the library. With Jude, my mother, and me in the house, he'd want more privacy, most likely in his study. The light of a wall screen flickered through a crack in the door. I pushed it open, expecting to find my father conferencing with someone but instead found an empty chair and a screen showing a view of the foyer where I just was. On the screen, I saw Jude examining the paintings and sculptures, still in his wool coat and gloves, as if waiting for someone to take his coat and formally invite him to sit. It was eerie to watch him—oblivious to being watched—and to know that I'd been on that screen just a minute ago.

Sunlight filtered in through heavy wooden blinds. It had been years since I'd really looked around my father's study, and I'd forgotten how dark it was, even in full afternoon light. Dark wood panels echoed a dark wood desk and dark wood shelves, all watched over by a massive portrait of Jacob

Landry. Old books of science and history lined the shelves, interrupted here and there by brass bookends in the shape of atomic symbols and glass paperweights with frozen purple galaxies inside. Two ivory-handled guns were mounted on the wall, hanging over a glass case with the very first lantern prototype Jacob Landry had built, the kernel of radioactive material long since removed.

I was about to leave when something caught my eye: three old books on a low table near the case, on their side and topped with a silver model of the Large Hadron Collider, a paperweight in the shape of the machine that had sparked Jacob Landry's research into the potential of private atomic power.

Checking the hallway to make sure I was alone, I lifted the model and took the books, surprised at how soft the old leather was. Replacing the model as quietly as I could, I left the study and took the stairs two at a time up to my room.

These had to be Jacob's journals.

TWENTY-EIGHT

The journals ended up having to wait, and so did talking with my father. Mother came up to my room, throwing off her coat and scarf and pulling me into her arms, as if I'd just survived a car crash. The smell of ivy-scented soap and gin overwhelmed me.

"I'm fine," I said, trying to wriggle out of her grip. There were so many things to do, and I felt the heavy desperation of knowing how impossible all those things were.

Mother caressed my hair. "To think that you could have been hurt! Killed!"

"I was in no danger," I told her plainly. "Mother, can't you see how blown out of proportion this is? How obsessed Father is with punishing the Rootless?"

A flicker of something was behind Mother's eyes and she looked away, turning her head toward the door.

"Mother . . . ?"

She stood quickly. "We must dress for dinner. I'm so glad you're safe."

I couldn't ponder this new mystery because it was time for our meal, and then drinks with Jude after that, who seemed reluctant to let me go anywhere without shadowing me. But after the festivities, finally, I caught a moment alone with Father, who was by himself in the library.

He had lit an opium cigarette and was reading a book by firelight, his face creased in concentration. "Ah, Madeline," he said, noticing me. "What is it you wish to discuss? Your debut?"

"No, I—" my voice failed. Standing in front of him was like standing in front of a mountain, preparing to beat my hands against the stone. I took a deep breath and remembered Charlie's frightened eyes. "I need to talk to you about your prisoner."

"The boy?"

"His name is Charlie."

Father stiffened. Outside, the wind blew louder, rattling the windows in their frames and sending soft storms of snow against the glass. "You have my attention," he responded slowly.

"I knew he was in my room, Father. I was hiding him. He was not there to hurt me or you or anyone." I took a deep breath, trying to steady myself. "He just wanted to give me a Solstice present."

"And why would a Rootless boy of no account give a gentry girl—a Landry girl—a Solstice present?"

This was where I had to be careful. "We had met outside the Rootless gates when I got lost one day. He helped me find my way back to a part of town that I knew." I kept my face earnest, but not too earnest. I tried not to lick my lips or breathe too quickly or look away as Cara did when she lied.

Father sat completely still, absorbing my story. "So you met a Rootless boy with whom you spent one afternoon, and he was so taken with you that he wanted to travel seventy miles in the freezing snow and wind to give you a present."

"Yes, that's right."

"And what was this present?"

I hadn't expected this. What would he think if he saw the miniature, with me as the benevolent atomic ruler? Would he be pleased by it or sense its darker undertones? "It's a picture of me."

"Ah. It would not be this picture, would it?" He held up the miniature.

Surely he could see the sweat on my forehead, could see my dinner dress beginning to stick to my sides and my back.

"I found this on your bed with your other presents when we discovered the boy in your room. The miniature of Landry Park was quite fine—I rightly surmised that Captain MacAvery had commissioned that piece. But this one," he held up the miniature, and in the firelight, the atomic symbol glittered, "is such a curious work. For one, I wonder at the message, inserting your face into a poster created to foster a sense of peace and belonging. And secondly, I also wonder how a Rootless boy came across oil paints and canvas? They are so expensive. One must only guess that they were stolen."

"They were not," I said quickly. "They weren't stolen."

"So he bought them? Or he was given them?"

I cleared my throat. "He bought them. With money I gave him for helping me home."

"I see."

The fire crackled loudly, making me jump.

I saw Father mark that jump away in his mental ledger. "What do you want, Madeline?"

"I want you to let him go. He didn't do anything wrong—he doesn't understand all the rules yet. He's just a boy!"

"When you were four years old, you could recite portions of Tennyson and Malory. You cannot expect that I will allow a youth of twice that age to claim the ignorance of a child."

"I know that you're worried about our safety and the security of our estates, but you have to see that Charlie did nothing willingly wrong." I walked closer to his chair. "Please."

He placed his cigarette in an ashtray, letting the ash burn its way to the end of the butt. "I will consider letting this boy go."

"That's it?" I asked. "I'm not in trouble?"

"Should you be?"

"No, but . . ."

"I do have certain expectations, however." Father slid the miniature across the low table between us, where I caught it under my fingertips.

"I expect you will redouble your efforts to this family and

to the estate. I expect you will prove to the world at your debut how happy you are with Captain MacAvery and how willing you are to be obedient. I expect that all the contact with the Rootless will cease and that you will remember where your loyalties lie."

I almost wanted to ask *what if I don't?* but I kept my mouth shut. He saw the resistance in my face anyway.

"And if you do not do these things, I suggest you take a lesson from your grandmother, who protested her husband's treatment of the Rootless, and who consequently never left this house again, not even to visit her dying sister and mother. The garden was the closest she came to the outside world."

I shivered.

"If there is one more hint of your involvement with the Rootless, of communication with them, or sympathy for them, you will say good-bye to your freedom. The university will be closed to you. The city will be closed to you. And I will keep you in this house until you have provided our line with another heir. Am I clear?"

"Yes, Father," I whispered.

"You must choose which place you wish to be—free and at the university or chained to this house," he said, leaning back in his chair. "I'll see you in the morning. We have a lot of work to do if this debut is to happen next week."

. . .

The seven days leading up to my debut were blurry and endless. I found myself in baths, scrubs, and massages. My nails were polished in three different shades of cream before my mother was pleased. Gardeners and decorators turned the house into a war zone—piles of flowers and ribbon, bundles of candles, and large swaths of cloth made walking through the house all but impossible. And after hiring twenty cooks from the city, the kitchens seethed with activity from dawn until midnight.

The journals sat under my pillow, safe for the moment. With the Uprisen guests arriving, Father spent most of his time in the dining room or the library in the company of his comrades, and hadn't spent enough time in his study to notice the missing books. But I'd had almost no chance to read them with the constant preparations.

I managed to dash off a letter to Cara and to David, asking them if they'd heard from our friends and telling them of my father's agreement to let Charlie go, but I didn't hear back. Even though I was used to David's random silences, it still gnawed at me. Even one line, one word from him would help thaw the glumness that clung to my bones like damp in winter.

Jude came to our house at every opportunity, eager to dine with the Uprisen, eager to drink with me and walk with me in the snowy garden. As pleasant as his company was, Charlie's captivity and David's noncommunication occupied my mind and left no vacancy for trifling concerns such as our forced courtship. Whenever I asked Jude about David, he shrugged and said that beyond breakfasts at the penthouse, he barely saw him. So David was spending his days and evenings elsewhere—probably with Cara, I supposed.

And after the week of fog passed, I woke early in the morning, the January wind wailing around the corners of the house, at times slow and mournful, other times shrieking and screaming like a banshee. I pulled back the covers and watched goose bumps travel up my legs. Outside the window, I saw workmen arranging solar heaters in the pleasure garden.

It was really happening. I was debuting tonight.

TWENTY-NINE

The dress was a dream.

The bodice fit snugly around me, softening the angles of my frame and spilling down into a full skirt lined with silk flowers. The lower half of the dress opened in on itself, revealing ivory chiffon and tulle sparkling with crystals. It was so beautiful that even the sour-faced seamstress smiled as she laced up the back, and I couldn't begrudge the dress the thirty minutes it took to button and hitch and lace and steam, so that no wrinkles shamed the China silk.

Elinor was just approaching me, ready to pin up my hair, when the door to my bedroom opened and David stepped inside and leaned against the doorframe. The maid and the seamstress froze. I stared.

"What are you doing?" he asked, all levity and friendliness, as if he hadn't spent the week ignoring my messages.

"We are pinning up miss's hair," Elinor answered for me. "And you shouldn't be in here."

"Ah. I just wanted to speak to Miss Landry about her father's prisoner." His hands were in his pockets and he looked like the David from before the battle—emitting charm and spice and canine grins. His eyes raked over me, sending blood rushing to my cheeks, to my thumping heart. "Leave it down," he told me, his gaze trained on my hair. "It would be a crime to pin it up." Then he left as suddenly as he had appeared.

I stared after him, a tight sensation in my chest.

"Miss?" Elinor asked.

"Leave it down," I said hastily, ignoring the part of my mind that begged to me *forget about David*. "Don't put it up."

She raised her eyebrows. "Most ladies wear their hair up to debuts, miss."

I took a deep breath. "I don't care."

She shrugged and put down her pins. Slowly, with a brush and palms covered in ivy-scented oil, she smoothed and arranged my hair so that it spilled gracefully over my shoulders and down to my waist. Then, with the precise concentration of a sculptor with a chisel, she inserted the ancient tiara that my mother had worn to her own debut.

There was a knock at the door. It was Mother and Father, standing together as they had before the Danas came to the city, united as they had been when I was a little girl.

"It's time, Madeline," Father said. The stone-faced dictator of last week had been replaced by the image of a gentleman. His tuxedo was crisp and perfectly tailored to fit his tall frame. His red hair was combed back. A bright red rose and an ivy sprig were pinned to his lapel. On the other lapel glittered a platinum brooch wrought in the shape of our family crest.

And Mother, standing beside him, looked the part of the ideal gentry wife, with the train of her beaded gown spread around her feet and her dark hair held up with ruby-encrusted hairpins.

My father held out his arms to me and I allowed myself to be embraced, hating how much I loved the feeling of my father pretending to love me—and just not the Landry blood inside me. He kissed me on the forehead and said, "You look perfect."

The illusion of perfection—that's all he wanted. He didn't care how cracked and confused I was inside, as long as I played my part. I wondered if he'd released Charlie yet, but was too scared to ask.

We walked to the end of the hallway, where the voices of the guests spilled up the stairs in a champagne-scented din. Jude stood waiting, in his scarlet uniform, hands clasped behind his back, like he was presenting himself to a superior officer. His eyes widened at the sight of me and he strode forward to take my hand and kiss it. It was like something out of Camelot, a knight and his lady.

Except I'd always pictured David as my knight.

Father nodded his approval. "Let's give them some privacy, Olivia," he told Mother, who sniffled.

"My little girl," was all she said as he led her away.

Jude still hadn't let go of my hand. "You look beautiful."

"Thank you," I said. For once in my life, I did feel beautiful. I did enjoy the feeling of silk on my skin and jewelry heavy in my ears and on my wrist. But hearing it said out loud seemed . . . scripted. Unreal. *This is what every man says to every woman at their debut,* I thought. *And now perhaps, he will say it again, and then say how happy he is to be here with me. I wonder what David would have said to me—*

"You are truly lovely. I'm so glad you accepted my offer."

Jude leaned in and swept his lips past mine, and I stayed completely still. He took my whole face in his hands, so gently that his fingertips tickled my jaw, and kissed me harder, his mouth firm and warm. It felt nice, in a distant, premeditated sort of way.

I wished I was kissing David.

I wished I knew if Charlie was safe, and that Jack knew I was sorry.

Jude pulled away, looking dazed and triumphant at the same time.

"Are you ready?" he asked.

Too troubled to do anything but nod, I placed my hand on his arm, and we descended the stairs.

Ivy trailed everywhere—around table legs, over portrait frames and mirrors, and even on the chandeliers high above the ballroom. A fresh green smell filled the room, drowning out even the smells of the banquet tables so piled with food that they threatened to sag. There were roast turkeys, peafowl, Cornish hens, and two suckling pigs. Veal and prime rib and lobster and Atlantic flounder flaking and drenched in herb butter. Delicacies from the East obtained at exorbitant cost, even after the battle: shark-fin soup, steamed bamboo shoots, and piles of peanut noodles flecked with peppers.

The dessert table was crowned with a giant spun sugar swan, sitting serenely in a lake of taro ice cream, kept cold and solid by a hidden nuclear-powered freezer underneath the tablecloth. Waiters circled the room with aperitifs and hors d'oeuvres. A few hours from now, their trays would be loaded with cigars, cigarettes, and sake.

I searched for David and saw a flash of white-blond hair in the corner of the room. But the shuffling of the crowd and the incessant tug of Jude's arm made it impossible to catch David's eye.

Mother stood on the dais by the band, giving an uncharacteristically coherent and concise speech, while Jude caressed my fingers with his in small motions that no one could see. My pulse was racing, and I had a sick, anxious feeling in my stomach; I didn't want to be here anymore. Would Jude try to kiss me again in front of the guests? And David?

The band struck up, the crowd applauded, and Jude pulled me out onto the ballroom floor. I remembered how I felt dancing with David at Cara's debut and my body lit with fire at memory. I hoped I could dance with him at least once before the night was through.

"Are you happy?" Jude asked into my ear.

"Yes," I lied, acutely aware of all the eyes on us. Of my father's eyes.

Jude bent down and kissed me again. It was a good kiss, deep and soft, with his arms strong around me, although I still felt only a tithe of the desire I'd felt when David ran his thumb down my arm. My dress swirled around Jude's feet as we stopped midspin, and the guests cheered and clapped at this display. When I opened my eyes, I saw David first among the crowd, next to Cara, his face a cipher.

Jude and I broke away from our kiss when the music ended. Suddenly we were surrounded by men and women, eager to fill our dancing lists. I danced with cousins and classmates, boys I'd known since childhood and strangers who were visiting relatives from the East Coast.

And then, without being aware of how it happened, I was dancing with David. His hand was flat against the back of my corset, pulling my waist toward him. We stepped in time to the music, our heads turned away from one another.

"Well, Madeline, you've finally debuted. Everyone is raving about your dress, and Jude is in love with you. Is this what you wanted?"

"No. I want Charlie to be safe. I want this all to be over."

"You seemed pretty confident that your father would free him. I've passed the message along to Jack."

"What did he say?" I asked fervently. "Was he angry with me?"

"Jack is never angry with anybody. Well, unless they are the Uprisen . . . or the government . . . or the military. I will rephrase: I don't believe Jack would ever be angry with *you*. He said he knew you had done everything you could and he wanted to thank you. He hopes that once he has Charlie back, you will come and visit him."

I was almost too relieved to keep dancing. "I was so worried. If something happened to Charlie, he could never forgive me and I could never forgive myself."

"Could you forgive yourself for letting Charlie die a long, radioactive death instead?"

"What?"

David changed tactics. "Jude told me that your father was amending his will. Jude is too good-hearted to realize what's going on, but I put two and two together. Your father offered you the university in exchange for a marriage to Jude, didn't he?"

I didn't answer.

"Madeline, what are you doing?"

"What are *you* doing?" I countered. "One moment you're not speaking to me, the next you're waltzing into my dressing room or giving me marriage advice. I can't keep up with you."

"But you *do* want to keep up with me," he said with a grin.

"Stop," I said. "This is not a game to me, no matter what it is to you."

Moving in time with the other girls in my line, I held my

skirt in one hand and turned so that my back was to him. He pressed his hand against my stomach, and we began to step in small circles. "It's not a game to me either," he said as we turned. He pulled me close. "I'm sorry if you ever felt that way."

His mouth was very close to my cheek. If I turned my head now, our mouths would meet.

"Are you being serious?"

He sighed. "Look—I was upset about Charlie this week, okay? And then I found out you were debuting with Jude, days after it was already decided, and I felt a little confused about all that." He stopped and my heart skipped, then started again at a breakneck pace.

Confused? I have spent the six months twisted in longing and jealousy and hopelessness, and now he decides to feel a little confused?

"David," I said very clearly, "it's none of your business whom I debut with or why. And I'm tired of you treating this—us—like a joke."

"Oh, there is an 'us' now?"

"This is exactly what I mean," I said. We slowly stepped in a circle around each other. "You know there's something between us. There has been since we met at Wilder House. But it's like it's nothing to you. Do you have so many people that you care about that you can afford to be callous to them? Because I do not."

"Madeline—"

"You've treated me like I don't matter, like I'm perfectly willing to have my feelings trampled on a ballroom floor while you pursue whomever you please. Let me tell you one thing, David Dana, it won't happen again. I won't watch you kiss Cara and then saunter back to me with more flirting and more lies. I'm done hoping for something you are clearly too selfish to give." I tossed my head back and raised my chin. It felt so good to tell him that.

He looked indignant. "I am *not* selfish."

"Please," I snorted. I wanted to say more but he held a finger to my lips.

"Hush," he said, "for just a moment. Let's go back. You said that I made you hope for something—what are you hoping for?"

I didn't answer.

"Because," he whispered, "I hope for very much when I am with you."

I meant to ask him about Cara, about why he chose her, but the words left my mouth as ghosts of a breath I could barely breathe, for at that moment, he pulled me closer.

His hand slid against the small of my back and I was pressed against him, forced to look up and confront his sharp, handsome face and his deep eyes. A wordless ache claimed me, consuming me, and my mouth parted in surprise at the sudden and knife-edged power of the feeling. He leaned his head closer to me, and I could see his lips parting too.

And then abruptly, the dance ended, and I was aware of how utterly inappropriate this was, me dancing so intently with David when I was supposed to be debuting with Jude. David looked very much like he wanted to hold on to me, like there was more he wanted to say, but Jude came forward to claim me for another dance.

"What were you and David talking about?" Jude asked as we began moving in a line of dancers. His voice was possessive and his grip was firm; I was suddenly aware of his height, of the muscles heavily layered under his expensive tuxedo.

"Nothing of any importance."

David watched me from across the room. He tossed back a glass of whiskey and set it on a nearby tray. Jude and I walked in a circle with the other dancers, then came together for a spin. When I found my place in line again, David was gone.

Hours later, the debut concluded with a shower of gifts and handshakes from the guests. Jude gave me one last kiss on the patio, where the solar heaters had melted the snow off the atomic symbol, making it glisten under a thin layer of water. The lavender glow of the city washed the snowy lawn and garden in dark purple shadows.

"I want every night to be like tonight," Jude said, looking out at the park. "I want us to be together like this, always. I feel as if we belong together, here at Landry Park, like all of this is meant to be. Don't you?"

I murmured a quiet assent.

Jude kissed my head. "I have been thinking about our future, Madeline, and about what we could do together. I want to be a general someday, like my father, and to do that, I will need a partner like you. A woman with impeccable breeding and an impeccable estate."

I pulled away, startled out of my thoughts. "Sorry?"

He took me by the shoulders. "I want you to be my wife. Ever since I met you, I knew you would be the perfect partner for me. I need someone who is smart, but quiet. Pretty but not flashy. An heir in her own right, but willing to use her resources to help me and my cause."

I struggled for words, unable to process what I was hearing. "Your cause?"

He nodded. "I want our military to be as strong as it was before the Last War. I want to strengthen the mountain holds, and then, when the time is right, take back the land that the East stole from us two hundred years ago."

"That's impossible. We have a treaty. And anyway, the Empire is stronger than us. There would be no way to beat them."

"That's what our leaders said when the East swarmed the mountains. But I did it, didn't I?"

So he had. And he so looked the part of the hero, with the broad shoulders and square jaw. I could almost imagine him succeeding, pushing the East back with the force of his will.

But. That didn't mean I was ready to marry him.

"Who knows? Maybe I could be elected president someday. Especially with your Uprisen connections."

"Jude . . ."

Jude let go of my shoulders. "Please, just think about it. We would make a wonderful team."

Of course, I knew that this was part of the bargain struck with Father. That Charlie's safety and my future and maybe even the stability of the city rested on my ability to convince Father that I was a dutiful daughter. But I couldn't speak the words; I couldn't accept a proposal I didn't want, not when I could still so clearly see David's lips, parted and close to mine. "I don't know if I want to be part of a team, Jude. I want to marry somebody I love, if I marry at all."

Jude came closer, and I could feel his warmth through the chilly air of the patio. "Madeline, I love everything about you and your life. What else do you want?"

"I want you to love *me*."

For a moment, he said nothing, and my words hung around us like a charged, electric fog. "I think what you really want has already been claimed by Cara Westoff," he said pointedly. "And I know you'll see reason soon. I am willing to wait."

He bowed and left, the expression on his face icier than the wind outside.

THIRTY

Finally I was free to shed the embroidered silk heels that pinched my feet and the tiara that dug into my scalp. My parents had long since retired to their separate bedrooms, and our Uprisen guests had also taken to their beds after their customary smoke in the library.

Music and laughter wafted up from the kitchens. The servants, Elinor included, were downstairs enjoying the remaining food and drink, and many of them would have the day off tomorrow. Unfortunately for me, I couldn't unfasten my dress and unlace my corset without help. But I didn't feel like dragging Elinor from her party just to help me change into a nightgown. I curled up on my bed in a pile of crystals and silk and tulle.

I watched the moonlight dance off the embellishments on my skirt and held up my hand to watch the prisms dance across my fingers. What was Charlie looking at right now? The same moonlight through the bars on a jail window?

And David? Was he with Cara?

I adjusted my head on the pillows, and a hard lump reminded me what was hidden underneath. The journals.

I sat up, ignoring the corset jabbing me in the ribs, and

ripped the pillows off my bed, sending a stray feather or two floating into the air. The journals lay underneath, exactly as I had left them, brown and age-stained, smelling slightly of dust and smoke.

I got up and checked that my door was locked, and then rustled my way back to the bed. Hiking up my skirts, I climbed back onto the tall mattress and opened one cautiously, not sure what I expected. It looked exactly as I'd expected a centuries-old journal might—brittle pages, faded brown ink, and the sort of narrow slanted handwriting that suggested the person who'd written on these pages had been meticulous and exacting.

I began reading. The first journal contained mostly diagrams and equations, detailing Jacob Landry's exploration of nuclear physics and his initial attempts at creating a stable source of light for people unconnected to the power grid. He hoped to light every village in the Southern Hemisphere and make the entire globe glow blue. It was hard not to pick up on the occasional note of avarice in his words—he mused upon the buying power of third world governments and the benefits of limited trading with China and the nations under her sway—but amazing to think how groundbreaking his work had been at the time.

I moved on to the second journal.

October 13th, 2021
The Cherenkov lanterns have finally reached Africa,

and news is promising. At least three hundred villages are lit, if not more by the time I write this, and increasing numbers of governments are contacting Landry Enterprises to purchase many more thousands. And the world thought American industry was dead after the Chinese invaded! If anything, the Chinese have helped Landry Enterprises. Just ten years ago, we were just a single lab, with only two or three technicians helping me develop the lantern, wearing those irksome masks to protect against the airborne flu—which the Easterners still claim they had nothing to do with. Now, after the turmoil in the economy and the famine and the war, I own almost all of the established power plants in the country. And with the displaced people from the West Coast, finding cheap employees has been easy, making the production of thousands of lanterns quick and inexpensive.

The protests are starting up again—unfortunately—as they did after the recession and before the war. Income inequality, they say. A work ethic inequality, I reply back. Why do they stand outside my offices with their signs when they could be finding work?

His tone and his diction reminded me of Father. The brilliance, the efficiency . . . the indifference to the less fortunate. The same indifference I had felt within myself from time to time. I stretched out onto my stomach, ignoring the creaking of the corset, and propped myself up on my elbows.

November 2nd, 2021

Have heard from a local source that people are leery of the lanterns—worried about radiation. We've done everything in our power to demonstrate that the polymer casing provides complete protection for an entire year. All the customer needs to do is send the lantern back to us once the year is through, and we'll replace it. There is negligible danger as long as they use the brains nature gave them. Although some of these people—like these protestors I am staring at right now, chanting below my window—probably have brains no bigger than the uranium pearls inside the lanterns.

November 7th, 2021

Several of the African governments have called, concerned about the more remote villages not being able to trade out their lanterns before they decay and start emitting radiation. I fail to see how that is Landry Enterprises' problem. They simply need to build a better infrastructure.

Besides, I have other matters to consider. The treaty with the "Eastern Empire," as the Chinese and their allies are now styling themselves, has just been ratified by Congress. Several of my senator friends have encouraged me to sit in on the negotiations and give some of my suggestions. The Chinese, now with Korea, Japan, Russia, and the OPEC nations under their thumb, perceive themselves as the new superpower and caretaker of the globe, and as such, are concerned about environmental practices. They are calling for an extreme reduction in carbon emissions over the next three years, and have cut off our supply to foreign oil to show they mean business. Within months, our coal mines and power plants will shut down.

It is a shame for my friends in the petroleum and coal industry, but this opens a vacuum in the American energy industry that I hope we can fill.

November 8th, 2021

Just got off the phone with the vice president. It seems an addenda was added at the eleventh hour about large-scale fission plants . . . the type of power plants I own. He is appropriately apologetic, but I made my anger no secret. I have no idea if the Chinese or if a cadre of congressmen who oppose me are responsible for this. I am working to uncover the truth.

But necessity is the mother of invention, they say. Nuclear power is not banned outright, only large-scale plants. Granting that the Empire honors their treaty and gives America autonomy from this day forward, I believe I can work within those parameters.

I remembered the treaty from my days at the academy. It was designed to avoid catastrophic climate change—or so the Empire claimed—but it also had a conveniently weakening effect on many of the world's major economies. Of course, the Empire was nothing if not ruthlessly efficient; if they could save the world by hamstringing their enemies, so much the better.

I skipped ahead a few months, until I saw the words "nuclear charge."

March 15th, 2022

The protestors seem determined to live outside my building. They've brought in tents and portable toilets. The stench of the toilets is horrific. But one must imagine that these types of people were quite malodorous before leaving the West. They seem the kind that protested artificial soaps and hot showers even in better times.

The nuclear charge is close to completion. Using the polymer casing from the Cherenkov lanterns, I was able to create something like a miniature fission reactor in a case no bigger than a shoe box. The customer would have to install a small turbine and a small water tank inside their homes, but the cost would be no more than a few thousand dollars and the whole system would take less room than a coat closet. They would pay more for the charges, but without coal or gas for electricity, what else will they do? Wind power is clumsy and unsightly, solar panels are still fragile and expensive, and few have access to hydroelectric power.

It may just work.

April 1st, 2022

The problems with the lanterns continue. A recent death was linked to radiation poisoning after some simpleton failed to dispose of the lantern after it expired. This would be difficult enough, but the nuclear charge uses the same casing. If I used a more permanent casing, the charge would be too heavy for the average person to lift, much less send in to our warehouse and have one sent back. I am working with all the contacts I know: my friends in Washington, my friends in the media, and my friends in the banks to convince them of the safety of my lanterns and my charges.

But I am sensing a pushback. They are listening to the fear of radiation instead of the facts. No amount of literature I send them seems influential enough.

I sat back for a moment. No book or teacher had ever mentioned that the charge was hailed as anything other than a marvelous idea and the savior of the American way of life. Having seen the sorting yards, I couldn't help but wish the people who doubted the safety of the charge had won the day.

Or did I?

I rolled onto my back and stared at the ceiling. The small crystal chandelier threw delicate shadows across the crown molding. If there had been no Cherenkov lanterns, no nuclear charges, then there would be no Landry Park. I might have never met David—or Jude or Jamie or Jane. I might never have been born.

June 27th, 2022

I have received word that I've been nominated for the Nobel Prize in Physics for the invention of the Cherenkov lantern. Still, bad media plagues the lantern, and the charge, too, although it has not yet been released. The coal plants are beginning to shut down and hydrogen-powered cars are beginning to show up on the streets. The clock is ticking. I need those charges to be ready by the treaty's deadline.

July 3rd, 2022

A solution has been revealed—and by the protestors of all people.

The camping toilets they use for waste management need to be emptied periodically to keep from overflowing. As one can imagine, this looks like a terrible job. The tanks holding the waste are filthy and rank from sitting in the Kansas City heat, and they are so heavy as to need to be dragged along the ground, causing the substance to slosh out of the tank's opening over their hands and feet.

However, the volunteers are treated like royalty. They get the best tents, the first round of sandwiches and bottled water, the privilege of using the two makeshift showers first. They are heroes, and so the odiousness of the job is outweighed by the rewards.

I feel convinced that this could be applied to the nuclear charges. A well-paid workforce could be employed to change out the charges and bring them to the warehouse. We could offer great benefits . . . vacations, retirement, the middle-class dream. And once the customer realizes that the weight of responsibility of remembering to change the charges themselves is no longer theirs, and once they see how healthy and happy the charge changers are, they will listen to reason.

I turned the page slowly, again feeling my entire education shift under my feet, and all the certainty of facts I knew cracking under the weight of new information. Jacob Landry had considered paying volunteers? The textbooks taught that the Rootless were given the job of handling charges because they were the descendants of the worst of the plebeians in the Last War. But this job was originally meant to be safe . . . prosperous.

August 5th, 2022

Will they ever invent a new chant? I've been listening to the same shouts for months.

I've been assured that the Nobel Prize is mine for the taking, but I don't know if it will be enough. With the up-ended state of everything, people seem more reluctant than ever about the charges, even when I proposed the idea of a workforce. My friends in the financial sector pointed out the cost of insuring such workers and of the intense medical screenings they would need periodically, in addition to the sheer number I'd have to hire.

It would be rather expensive. Even if I raised the prices of the charges, the workers would cut sharply into my prof-its.

August 5th, 2022, later

I've seen another solution.

It was the last entry, written in stark black ink, as if he'd grabbed any pen nearby to catalog this one thought.

I've seen another solution.

I felt cold fingers in my chest just reading it.

I grabbed for the third and final journal, my nails scratching at the paper in my hurry to open it. A stiffness had crept up my back and shoulders, locking my arms and neck like my corset locked the rest of my body. A nauseous urgency riled my stomach. The next journal didn't start until a few months later, and it only had one entry.

December 25th, 2022

Today is the day we begin. At this moment, I can't help but think of the curious behavior of the observed particle. Unobserved, it exists in multiple states at once. But once it is viewed, this particle, without any sentience whatsoever, commits to one destiny. I feel like since the invasion, we've all existed in multiple destinies. I've played the part of inventor, lobbyist, and now strategist. And now we are ready to reveal our true selves to the public, to commit to one, glorious path.

After weeks of planning in the mausoleum I had built, we are ready. It was almost ridiculous how quickly my peers saw the brilliance of it all, and the more unenthusiastic were lured by an opportunity to invest in Landry Enterprises before the nuclear charge becomes ubiquitous in American homes.

We're calling ourselves the Uprisen. One of the congressmen came up with it; he seems to like the idea that we are the oppressed ones here, fighting for what we believe in. And so now—with the military, the banks, and the government with us—we will begin. While the protestors and the others celebrate with their families, we will begin.

...

I closed the journal carefully with shaking hands, taking care to set it gently on the bed and not to drop it on the floor. Jack had been right about Jacob Landry. He hadn't cared about climate change or helping people in poverty. If anything, it sounded like he hated the poor. Or maybe just held them in the same regard as one holds a fly or an ant. To him the displaced and hungry protestors were nuisances. Pests.

And so he—what? I still couldn't wrap my mind around the fact that Jacob, whose face haunted every wing of this house and the cover of every history textbook at the academy, had invented a war for money and power.

That meant Landry Park was built out of violence. This whole house—the whole beautiful, ancient marble and stone house—was the product of one man's insatiable greed. I looked around, as if expecting the walls to look back at me, as if they were displeased with the information I now possessed. I wanted to run all the way to Jack, tell him that I understood now. The imperative to shed everything that connected me to my family and this house almost propelled me out of bed and out the front door, but I couldn't. It was night and it was freezing and I wasn't brave enough to barrel through the worst parts of town at this hour, unaccompanied.

I would go first thing tomorrow morning.

I turned off the light and lay down, every breath marked by the rustling of my dress and the straining of my corset. I felt as if the house were watching me, as if I would open my eyes to find the walls closer to my bed, the chandelier closer to my face. As if Jacob Landry was reaching his hand out to me, through time and through whatever veil separated life from death, not to comfort me but to grab me and hold me tight, to pin me down until I suffocated under the weight of the Landry legacy.

THIRTY-ONE

THIRTY-ONE

I was dreaming of the mausoleum, of a pen scratching against paper in the yellow haze of incandescent lights. Deep burgundy hair, large hands.

It was Jacob Landry writing in his journal.

I tried to leave, but I couldn't run in my debut dress. The skirts grew and grew and my shoes pinched and I was stuck next to Jacob, struggling and reaching for the door. He turned to look at me and *smiled* and his teeth were small and pointed. I still couldn't move.

And then suddenly I was in a bed, in a long nightgown, burning with fever. Father stood over me with a syringe, *tsk*-ing at my groans, and pushing the gleaming needle into my arm. "We have all been through it, little Madeline," he whispered as fire filled my veins. "Every Landry before you."

I opened my mouth to scream and flames spilled out, burning my face, my bed, my father. I would burn alive, like a witch tied to a stake, and my father would hold the syringe all the while.

Something jarred me out of my dream and into my dark bedroom, where Elinor was wrapped in her night robe, looking distressed. She held a Cherenkov lantern in her hand.

"You have to wake up," she said, helping me sit upright. "Something bad is happening to that boy."

The grogginess fell like scales from my eyes. "Charlie?" I swung my legs over the side of the bed.

Elinor brought over boots, wool stockings, and my long red coat. "I'm not sure what Mr. Landry is doing, but several of the maids were called to serve him and the Uprisen men an early breakfast, at four thirty. Then they were ordering cars and having valets bring portable solar heaters."

"What time is it now?" I asked, yanking off the silk and lace stockings from last night and pulling on the warmer woolen ones.

Elinor clucked her tongue at my dress, turned blue-purple by the light of the lantern. "Almost five thirty. They are going to the memorial around Liberty Park. You'll have to change, Miss Landry, you can't spoil that dress in the snow."

"There is no time. It will take you twenty minutes to undo all the laces and buttons and bustle hooks. Unless you want to cut it off me."

She looked sick at the thought.

I took the buttonhook from her and started buttoning my boots as quickly as I could. "You said Charlie was involved?"

"I heard your father on a call to the local justice of the peace, telling him to release the boy to his custody."

I stopped, hardly daring hope. "So they are releasing him?"

Elinor shook her head, laying a dark hand on mine. "Your father is summoning all the Rootless to Liberty Park as well. I heard him. And I heard him mention the gibbet cage."

The gibbet cage. Jacob Landry's preferred method of execution during the Last War: forcing people to swallow a packet of radioactive material and then locking them in a metal cage to die. Usually the prisoner died within hours, burning from the inside out, but there were some who held out longer. They were the ones who died of exposure. They'd shown the old news clips in the academy; images of limp bodies and bleeding mouths flooded my mind.

If the room weren't already dim, it would have darkened. I heard a buzzing noise that seemed louder than Elinor's voice and my own thoughts.

He wouldn't hang a boy in the gibbet cage. He wouldn't.

Elinor was helping me to my feet, feeding my arms into the sleeves of my coat, pressing gloves into my hand.

"You have to go," she was saying. "Go!"

I made for the door, too stunned to try to make sense of the tornadic whirlwind of thoughts, protests, pleadings. "Call David," I said faintly. "Tell him everything."

"Yes, miss."

"And that book on the table?"

Elinor handed it to me. One of the journals—the first one with the equations and plans and designs for the lantern.

"Do you know how to scan things into a tablet?" I asked suddenly, an idea taking fire.

"Yes, miss. Of course."

"Those other two books, scan them into my tablet please. It should be next to my bed. Once you have finished, I need you to send it to everyone on my contacts list. And send it to all the people you know, all the servants, all the middle-class. Send it from my address so no one can trace it back to you."

"Yes, miss."

I walked into the hallway and down to the foyer, where Jacob Landry's bust cast its sightless eyes on me. Without a second look at him or the house, I rushed out into the snow.

With so many houseguests from out of town, finding a car was easy. I had the driver stop at the edge of the park, and took the rest of the trip by foot, my boots slipping a little in the soft snow, the hem of my skirt and coat soon caked in it. The trees were dipped in shining glass and the whole park sparkled in the pinkish dawn light. The branches were so weighted with ice that they drooped wearily, with icicles as long as daggers hanging from their tips. I found a wide tree to shield my bright red coat from view.

At the top of the hill, I could see the crowded top of the war memorial. High above us, a stone tower held aloft a bowl of flame and at its base was a terrace that looked out over the skyline. To the south, the large lawn held thousands of silent people, hemmed by a border of wary police. The Rootless. They were rimmed with bristling constables, who stood facing inward, holding riot shields and batons. They all had guns. They all had gleaming canisters strapped to their backs—smoke bombs perhaps, or tear gas. But there were still far fewer police than Rootless. I suppose—as always—Father counted on fear being the true deterrent.

On the terrace, my father stood among a row of his Uprisen friends and—shockingly, heartbreakingly—Jude. To his credit, Jude looked unhappy, keeping his normally confident gaze on his shoes and twisting his hands behind his back. I hoped that he didn't feel he had to be here in order to gain Father's approval and secure my hand.

Behind Father was the gibbet—a post with a wooden bar across the top. From the wooden bar hung a cylindrical metal cage, much like a birdcage, save for the crudely thick metal bands and large bolts. Charlie was huddled underneath the gibbet in handcuffs, tear tracks plain on his now-dirty face. A black polymer case rested next to him, containing the radio-active waste he would swallow later. The gibbet food.

Father stepped forward to the edge of the terrace, holding his tablet in his hand. The tablet sent his voice to the speakers set up around the park. "My friends, I have asked you here today to share some troubling news. For generations, we have coexisted peacefully, each playing our part to keep this great nation stable. And most of us are content in these roles." The snow gave his speech a muffled quality and made the scene feel distant. Surreal.

The Rootless crowd looked blankly back at him. I couldn't see Jack or Ewan anywhere. But Smith was in the very front row, and even from this distance, I could see the tense set of his body, the shoulder-width spread of his legs, as if he were an animal about to pounce.

"It's no secret to the Uprisen that there has been a—shall we say—*restiveness* among the Rootless as of late. Anger and fear and revolt are infecting our happy lives like a cancer, mutating and growing, poisoning everything we have worked so hard to accomplish. And although we have done as much as we can to be your benefactors—to feed you, and clothe you, and put you in a position of usefulness that your ancestors rejected—the time for altruism is over. The time for discipline has begun."

Charlie started crying, a pathetic sound that shattered me. I moved forward, but a hand clamped around my mouth.

I moved my eyes to see David, his eyes determinedly on the platform. He held a finger to his lips, and I nodded. He moved his hand.

"Stay here," he whispered.

"I have to do something," I whispered back. "I can't just watch."

"I know." Against the snow, I could see the barest trace of gold in his hair. "Stay here for now. I am going to try and get Charlie. When the moment is right, I will need a distraction. Can you do it?"

"David, if they catch you—my father will not hesitate to put you in that thing." I didn't mention that if he got caught—if we failed—then a similar fate would await me. My father would never forgive me abetting open defiance, for undermining his power in front of the Uprisen and the Rootless. But it was as if my soul had turned to glass in the frozen morning. I couldn't feel anything for my father anymore, least of all a desire for his forgiveness. Not after this.

David tore his eyes off the terrace and reached out to brush a gloved thumb across my cheek, sending chills skittering across my skin, chills that had nothing to do with the snow.

"You are so brave," he said.

"You are, too."

"Not like you."

I had the paralyzing premonition that this was good-bye, that David would be seized the moment he emerged from the snow and that these would be the last words we shared as free people.

"Be careful," I begged him.

"If I don't come back . . ."

He took a step closer. Clouds of steam from our breath mingled between us. I could see the violet streaks in his eyes.

"Then I'll go with you," I vowed. Even to the gibbet. I would not stand by as David sacrificed everything; I too would finally play my part.

"Madeline . . ."

His hands were on my waist. I felt everything fade away to snow and white fire; my inhibitions, my fears, my revolutions—gone at his touch. I slid my hands up his arms, up to his neck, and put my fingers in his hair. It was as silky and as fine and as light as it had been in my daydreams, like holding sunlight between my fingertips.

"I want to kiss you," he said, his mouth very close to mine now.

That white fire was dancing from his hair to my hands to my chest to my stomach to my lips—

"I've wanted you to kiss me again for a long time," I whispered.

"Then I shall." And he did. His lips were on mine, warm and spicy and smoky. Something needy and hot pulled at my stomach, and I pulled him closer, kissed him harder, breathed him in deeper and deeper until I saw stars and static at the edges of my eyes.

His hands slid under my coat, and his lips found my neck and my hair, and now there were galaxies, a million infinitesimal stars pricking at my eyelids.

"I love you," he said breathlessly. Then, without warning, he was off. He crouched, moving from tree to tree, edging closer to the stage.

I pressed a hand against my hammering chest, the other to my mouth. I had to wait now, even though my pulse pounded and my heart thrummed with adrenaline and something lighter, something that could pull me up into the clouds if I let it. Up to the sun.

He'd said he loved me.

I had to wait.

The Rootless waited, too. There were no hisses or shouts from their ranks. They stood still, shoulder to shoulder, making no sound save for shuffling feet and ragged breaths in the cold.

"We do not take punishment lightly. I would not have built this gibbet and brought you all here if I was not convinced of the absolute danger of this anger you have harbored against us." Father flung an arm back at Charlie. "I found this boy under my daughter's bed, on what was supposed to be the merriest of holidays, the celebration of light against darkness." At that, the sun finally glinted between the skyscrapers of downtown, sending shafts of blinding light dancing across the glazed trees.

David was almost to the terrace now. No one seemed to have seen him. Then Jude looked up to the sky, as if pleading with the dawning sun and still-visible moon to send him back to the mountains, where the morality was as clearly drawn as a line on a map. He lowered his gaze and his eyes widened as he saw David.

I felt a thrill of panic. Jude was a soldier, loyal to his government and to the gentry. He was here of his own free will, willing to watch Charlie killed in a barbarous method that hadn't been used in two hundred years, yet I knew he was a good person and David's best friend.

David and Jude locked eyes, and I could see Jude wrestling with himself. After a second that lasted hours, Jude gave the slightest of nods, then deliberately turned his head away.

My father continued. "We cannot tolerate the cold-blooded murder of our own. And so, here with a representative from our noble army"—he indicated Jude—"and the circle of the Uprisen, we are determined to crush this insolence once and for all. What happens to this boy this morning will happen to each and every one of you if you do not find it in your hearts to serve."

He turned, nodding to the constables, and then David turned, looking at me. He was at the side stairs to the terrace, squatting behind a row of shrubs. The next move he made would be seen by everyone in the crowd, including the police.

It had to be done, Charlie had to be saved, but I granted myself a moment to say good-bye to the university, to my father's affection, to my freedom. When my father saw the scarlet-coated girl emerge from the snow, it would not be his daughter, but someone who had permanently cast her lot with his enemies.

I squeezed my hands into fists and willed myself forward.

THIRTY-TWO

"I will not serve!" I yelled. My voice carried across the snow and ice, and bounced off the stone and concrete of the memorial, reverberating back to me in a fractured chorus. Thousands of Rootless eyes turned to me. My father's hand dropped to his side, and for once, he looked completely at a loss for words. Of all the contingencies he'd planned for, he'd probably never considered that his daughter would come tramping through the snow in her debut dress, shouting at him.

"I will not obey you," I shouted. I moved my feet forward, toward my father step by slippery step. "And if your own child will not listen to you, how can you expect them to?" I was almost to the front of the crowd. All eyes were on me as David crept up another stair. His head was visible now.

"Charlie is innocent. All of these people are innocent. All they want is to be free and to be healthy, just like we are."

"Madeline," Father said, the shock in his face slowly changing into stone. "You don't know what you're talking about."

"Don't I?" I held up the journal I'd put in my coat pocket. "I know all about Jacob Landry exploiting the people displaced by the Empire's conquest. I know that he invented a war to justify enslaving those people into handling the charges for free. I know that everything I have been told about the nobility of the gentry is a lie."

Behind me, the Rootless grew restless. Murmurs and whispers swelled through the crowd, and I heard the constables grunt as the crowd pressed forward. Smith actually shoved one of the men holding him back.

For a moment, Father said nothing, his steel eyes locked onto mine.

"I have sent the pages of the journals to everyone I know. To the press."

"The Uprisen own the press," my father scoffed. "You can do no damage there."

"Maybe, but some people will see the truth for what it is. And now that I know the truth, I can't go back. I can't pretend it away. What we are doing is *wrong*, and I won't do it anymore."

His expression hardened. "Then you will be punished along with everybody else." He came to the front of the terrace and knelt so that his face was very close to mine. The Uprisen and the police around Charlie all leaned forward to hear my father speak.

"I never wanted to be like my father, Madeline, but you have given me no choice. It broke my heart to see my mother locked in the house like a bird in a cage, and it will break my heart to do the same to you. You could have been such an asset to our family." He shook his head, as if saddened by the waste. "All I have ever wanted was to see you ready to rule over Landry Park. Why can you not see that this is what you are made for? To be my heir? To lead the gentry and to take your place among the Uprisen?"

My throat constricted and I looked down. Maybe I wasn't made of glass after all. Disappointing Father was almost more than I could bear.

Charlie, I told myself. *Think of Charlie.*

Seizing the moment of my father's inattention, David darted forward and took the steps three at a time, pushing past a constable and grabbing another's arm while he fumbled with the constable's belt for the keys to Charlie's handcuffs.

This was all that the crowd needed to stir from their empty silence. With a roar from Smith and a surge from the very back of the crowd, they pushed forward, and then the line of police holding them broke. Several constables fell down, and more starting throwing canisters into the crowd. I heard the loud, quick pops of a gun, but there was no way to tell where it was fired.

David quickly dispatched another constable coming toward him, and then moved to unlock Charlie's cuffs. More constables came behind him, and I cringed, thinking this was the end of David's rescue, but a crimson army uniform moved into the navy and brass swarm. Soon Jude was fighting the police, and David had Charlie in his arms. David was right about Jude's fighting ability—even in his stiff uniform, he easily dodged and blocked strikes. Once he even laughed out loud at a constable throwing wild haymakers in his direction and then sent the man flying with one shiny-shoed kick.

Only a handful of constables remained in front of the Rootless, firing guns and swinging clubs, but the crowd moved forward like an inexorable tide. Shots rang out and people fell, but still they kept coming, improbably, impossibly, fearless in the face of bullets and beatings.

Father stood, assessing the situation. The Rootless were moving to the terrace, their faces enraged. Jude and David were making easy work of the police fighting them for Charlie. The Uprisen were backing away slowly, discreetly using tablets to summon cars as they crept off the terrace.

Father jumped off the terrace with an ease that I wouldn't have thought possible and grabbed me by the upper arm. "We are going home," he said between clenched teeth. *"Now."*

"No!" I said, wrestling. "No!" But he was too strong for me. He jerked me down the hill, and I slipped and fell in the snow.

"Come on!" he yelled, yanking me up. Behind us, the Rootless came like a wave of embodied fury.

We lurched down the hill where our car waited on the street.

"Please," I said, out of breath. "You're hurting me."

"Would you rather be dead? You think that mob cares

whether or not you support them? They will rip you to pieces just for being born gentry."

"Such anger, Alexander," a familiar voice said. "Shame to see that you have not grown out of it."

It was Jack, shuffling painfully between us and the car. He stopped and leaned on his cane, considering us. Ewan prowled behind him, looking like he was ready for any excuse to tackle my father to the ground.

To my surprise, Father stopped and stared, and all the anger and determination in his body evanesced away like ice under the sun.

"Stephen?" His words trembled. His hands trembled. "Stephen?"

Jack squinted at him, putting both hands on his cane. "Yes."

"Brother . . ." Father breathed.

I peered into Jack's face, mentally comparing it to the serious-eyed man in the hallway of Landry Park. The little hair he had was white, not red, but the eyes were the same. The long, solemn features, though covered in sores and burst capillaries and sagged with age, were identical. In fact, underneath the layer of disease and exhaustion, he looked a lot like Father. "You are my uncle Stephen?" I asked.

Jack kept his eyes on Father. "Stephen Landry was the name I was born with. It's a name I've since left behind, just as I have left Landry Park."

"How?" Father asked, searching Jack's face. "And why?"

I remembered the reason for Father's haste, and looked back to see the Rootless only a few feet away from us. At the terrace, Jude was holding Charlie's hand while David used his scarf to dab at the blood pouring freely from his own nose.

"But you died! They killed you! We found your coat bloodied and buried!" Father was panting in short, uneven breaths now. The bright sunlight illuminated a sheen of sweat on his forehead. And then the mob reached us. Jack held up a hand and a few men stepped out from the crowd and seized Father by the arms. Smith wrapped an arm around his neck.

Father didn't even try to resist.

"You found poorly hidden evidence of my new life," Jack explained. "When I left Landry Park, I left in the middle of the night, from my bedroom window. I fell into the thorn bushes below, and bled the whole way across town. I hoped you would never find that coat. I hoped you would assume that I ran away."

"Stephen, why?" Father squirmed a little to peer into Jack's face. "Father was never the same after he thought you died. He never could forgive himself for not keeping you safe, for not protecting Landry blood. I know that is why he died so soon after you left. Do you have any idea how hard we searched for you? What we did?"

Jack frowned. "I know that you tortured my friends, trying to extract a confession from them. I know that you raided my new home, burning houses and beating women and children to try to find my body. But I made sure you would never find me. Almost nobody within the Rootless knew who I truly was, and the few who did know would have rather died than give me away. Because they are stronger than the gentry, Alexander. You still do not understand that, do you?"

Father's eyes flitted around. There were no constables in sight and the last of the Uprisen cars were speeding away from the park. He was alone and in the hands of the Rootless.

"You were about to put my youngest son—your own nephew and the son of an eldest child, a Landry heir more central to the line than your own daughter—in the gibbet cage and watch him die. For what? Did you think that would stop us?" Jack limped forward and I realized that he was even taller than my father, his figure naturally broader, even after the ravages of radiation. "On the contrary. If you would have succeeded in killing Charlie, I would have killed you myself."

Father opened and closed his mouth. "Stephen—"

"You're lucky that your daughter and young David were here to stop you. Had I not a tablet in my possession and had David not contacted me to tell me he planned to spirit Charlie away from his execution, I would have asked my people to unleash their strength upon you and your fellow Uprisen. I would have done so a week ago when you took my son had David not relayed your promise to Madeline that you would let him go. I decided to bide my time, in hopes that you would act on your word. You did not."

"I—"

Jack's voice trembled with fury. "I would have burned everything you love to the ground before I would have let you kill my son." Jack closed his eyes, breathing noisy, chesty breaths. "You must answer for it, Alexander. You must answer for it all now. But your daughter does not need to see you die."

Ewan, still prowling, looked like he disagreed.

"And it is for my dear niece's sake that we will pursue a more elegant solution, which perhaps for you will be worse than death," Jack said. "Our laws dictate that the eldest child of a family controls the estate, even after a lengthy absence. Perhaps even after a supposed death. And as I am still the eldest, I will claim my birthright today."

Father paled. "You can't be serious."

"Oh, I am quite serious, little brother. I have restrained myself during your despotism for years, thinking the route I had chosen was the only way. But I can't wait another day for our allies to swoop in and liberate us. It is time for humanity to return to Landry Park."

"You can't," Father said, and struggled against Smith's grip. "Landry Park is mine. And it will be Madeline's after me."

"I think you will find the legalities are on my side. And if not, then my people will help fill any loopholes." Smith and Ewan both looked very eager to fill any loopholes in question.

"My friends in the East will be delighted to witness this transition. They are very invested in what happens to the gentry."

"Traitor," Father said through clenched teeth.

"As for Madeline," Jack said, as if he hadn't heard, "she will have a place at Landry Park for as long as she chooses. And she *will* have the right to choose."

Father slumped, and I allowed worry to slice at me.

Father without Landry Park? Landry Park without Father?

"There is one last thing," Jack added, voice thoughtful. "I have dispensed my justice, but I can't speak for all the heartbreak you have caused these people. So your daughter and I are going to leave now, and within an hour, you will be delivered *alive* to Landry Park. But I can't vouch for what will happen in that hour."

The wind whipped Father's white scarf around his face as he stared at his brother. "You can't hurt me, Stephen."

The Rootless tightened their grip on him, one of them clapping a sore-riddled hand over his mouth.

I stepped forward, but then caught sight of Charlie on the terrace, shivering in Jude's coat, tears of terror still on his cheeks. I looked into the haunted eyes of an entire group of people who'd been robbed of loved ones, beaten, starved, made homeless, and arrested—all thanks to my father.

But hurting him now would make them no better than he was.

I ran forward and threw my arms around him. "I love you,

Father." I could feel the expensive silk of his scarf against my cheek and smell lingering traces of opium smoke.

"My Madeline," was all he said. And then I felt myself pulled away—gently but firmly—and I looked up to see Ewan's grim face.

"Please," I asked Jack. "Please do not let them hurt him."

"I don't lead the Rootless like your father leads the gentry, Madeline. I'm not an autocrat. They have made it clear they want revenge and that they will take it, no matter what I say. All I could ask of them is to spare his life, and believe me, even that was hard won. It is out of my hands."

He met my eyes and I shivered, for the knife-edge inside them was exactly like Father's.

And then the crowd swallowed my father, like the ocean swallows a stone, like the snow swallows sound. Hands passed him on to hands, and backs turned, and as he thrashed, more took hold of him, pushing his body closer to the center of the crowd. I pushed forward after him, but the mob pushed me back, and soon even the distinctive red of his hair was gone. I stopped, my heart pounding.

"Come," Jack said.

"I can't leave," I whispered.

"It is happening whether you leave or not," Jack said. "Would you like to watch? Or leave, knowing that he will live and be with you in an hour?"

Then Ewan, Jude, and Charlie were there, and David, with

his blood-soaked scarf and slightly swollen nose. They herded me toward the street, and reluctantly I went, sending silent prayers up to the stars, now hidden in the rosy glow of a winter morning.

THIRTY-THREE

Jamie joined us at Landry Park—fresh from his journey from England—and was astounded to find so many Rootless milling about the estate, and me tending to David's nose. He quickly took charge of David's and Charlie's minor wounds and hypothermia, gathering blankets and warm tea while I explained what had happened since I'd last written. Jude helped where he could, mostly hovering over David, looking uncomfortable whenever a Rootless person passed by.

But before we could discuss anything at length, the front doors blew open in a storm of noise and January wind, and several men came through, carrying Father's body like a sack of grain, his arms dragging to either side of him. Running out of the drawing room, I just was in time to see Father carried up the wide white stairs to his bedroom.

He made a cracked, viscous moan, and I wanted to rush to his side, to hug him and tell him I was sorry, *so sorry*, but I couldn't make myself. I was afraid to see his face. I was afraid to see what the Rootless had done. I was afraid he'd open his eyes and all I would see was anger, and I would know that I had lost my father more certainly than if he had been killed.

Instead, I walked slowly over to the doors and pushed them closed, shutting out the snow and the cold. Enough snow had blown in that I could see faint footprints revealing the gleaming marble underneath. The snow looked like white ashes.

I looked around the foyer, lit as it was with winter daylight, and felt a cold fear that I would never see the house the way I wanted to again. I would never see it as simply beautiful, as simply ancient, as simply a part of me. And then I felt a fear about that fear—why, after all I had learned, was it so hard to let my perception of Landry Park go? Would I always be a gentry at heart, caring more about things than people?

I walked toward the stairs and climbed the first step. My fingertips brushed the cold marble of the banister and I found myself clutching the railing, feeling off balance, like everything was being ripped away from me. My father, my house, my life. . . .

In this light, the bust of Jacob Landry was almost shadowless, and so was the tiny atomic symbol underneath it, the symbol that comprised our family crest, that decorated our home, that reminded us that our power and wealth and legacy rested in the unseen forces of colliding and splitting matter.

It was a symbol that meant everything to Father, and I used to think it meant everything to me. But now I knew that it would haunt my dreams, possibly as it had haunted Jack's, knowing all the misery that had stemmed from one man's decision to misuse a gift of enormous power. Tears burned at my eyes, and I wasn't sure who—or what—they were for. I stared at the bust for several minutes, my thoughts wandering from my father to Charlie to David, from Cherenkov lanterns to journals to the atoms themselves. Atoms that comprised the banister I was holding and the bust I was looking at and the air I breathed.

And then—on this sprawling estate, in this large house, on the brink of a revolution—I was reminded of the power of the small. Small ideas, small acts, small people. After all, it was the furious industry of those tiny atoms that fueled the stars, stars that then nourished planets, and planets that then nourished life. No matter how small I felt, how infinitesimal my feeble gestures seemed, I was part of a larger chain, a larger system, and so help me, I *would* bring order to this chaos.

I turned away from Jacob Landry and started up the stairs.

Jack was in Father's room with Ewan, and Jamie was by the bed with his tablet, using it to take readings of Father's breathing.

"Is he all right?" I asked Jack.

"He is alive, as I said he would be," he said, and gestured to Father. I approached the sleigh bed, where Father had been dumped on top of the silk, hand-embroidered duvet. His coat, gloves, and shoes were missing, and the raw red of his feet and hands made me think they'd been stripped away shortly after

I left. His eyes were closed, but he was writhing slowly, his hands grabbing and clutching at the duvet.

And his mouth—

"What happened to him?" I cried, going to the side of the bed and taking his hand. He clutched at my fingers with a steel grip.

"I will send for my doctor bag," Jamie said, looking queasy. "We may need to call for a surgeon."

Jack's face was a statue's, but there was a trace of sadness in his words. "I believe they chose to give him a taste of his own medicine, so to speak. They pinned him down and forced the gibbet food inside his mouth for several minutes. Not enough to kill him, but enough to burn his mouth. Enough to give him severe radiation poisoning and probably cancer."

Father's mouth was more than burned. The lower half of his face was unrecognizable—dark brown with blisters covering his lips and tongue. Bloody ulcers were beginning to form at the corners of his mouth, and smaller burns stretched down his chin and neck, as if he'd thrown up radioactive bile.

"Father, it's Madeline," I said, brushing the hair away from his forehead. "Jamie is going to help you, okay? He will be back any minute and he will fix you."

Father's eyes fluttered open. He reached up to touch my hair, and then closed his eyes again with a groan.

"A shame," Jack said.

"He was about to do the same to Charlie," Ewan reminded

his father. "If we hadn't stopped him, you'd be watching this happen to Charlie right now." But even Ewan looked a little sick at the sight of my father's ruined face.

Jamie came back not ten minutes later, hurrying in with his bag. "I have called the gentry hospital to arrange for home treatment," he said breathlessly. "They should be here within the hour." He set the bag on a nearby table and began pulling out syringes of morphine and vials of anti-microbial medicine. "We will need to clean the wounds as best as possible, and then cover them with a dry dressing. Necrosis of the tissue will set in within a few days, and we don't want to risk sepsis. We will also need to order cellular scans to estimate the level of DNA damage and cancerous cells."

"Will his mouth heal?" I asked. "Will he be able to talk with his tongue and throat burned like this?"

Jamie prepared a syringe of morphine and then eased it into Father's thigh. After three or four minutes, his squirming stilled somewhat, and his breathing deepened. Jamie nodded, and began dousing cotton pads in anti-microbial fluid. "There is always a chance," he replied finally. "But at this point, I think it doubtful that he will ever eat or speak or smile again."

That night another snowstorm came like soft, soft music. When I woke, even the ice in the trees was covered with a thick blanket of white. Cold seeped in along the baseboards and through the frosted windows. The house was muffled and empty, bereft of the guests that had filled its rooms the day before. All the Uprisen had fled back to their homes, probably conspiring over their next move, searching for a new leader now that Father lay wordless and suffering, a prisoner in his own home.

I pulled on a warm dress of ivory angora and went downstairs, where I found Mother grimly contemplating a chunk of bread in the morning room.

"Your uncle has given the servants a holiday," she said, poking at the bread with a knife. "When they come back, he wants to talk about a pay raise. Regular days off."

"Mother . . ."

She burst into tears. "Your father, darling, your poor father. Your cousin says he doesn't know if your father will ever heal properly and that he probably has cancer. What will those Rootless do to you or to me when they have the chance?"

"They had the chance with me," I reminded her. "And they did nothing. It was only Father they wanted."

"Here they are gloating and nattering about justice, when they are nothing more than violent criminals. It makes me sick. I can't see how one brother would let that happen to another."

If the brother in question was about to kill his son . . . But I agreed with her. I felt the same shaky nausea as I did after seeing the battle on the wall screen a few months ago. So much violence, so much destruction. "Where is he? Uncle Jack?"

"Back at his hovel, I suppose," she said. She pushed her plate away. "Preparing to invade our home and kick us into the streets."

"He promised me a place to stay," I told her. "I am sure you can stay, too."

"But who would want to? After what he let those animals do to your father? And with that awful journal of Jacob Landry's circulating around? The Rootless are refusing to change the charges, the working poor and the middle class are in an uproar, and now that awful man is in charge of Landry Park. Oh, Madeline, why couldn't you have just left all this alone?" She put her face in her hands. Even despairing, she was beautiful.

I sat next to her and put my arms around her slender frame. She leaned her head on my shoulder.

"Everything was going so nicely," she said sadly.

"For you. Everything was going so nicely for you and people like us. But it could not go on forever. Isn't it better that Jack takes control now, rather than have the Empire help the Rootless overthrow the gentry?"

"I don't trust a man who deals with the Empire," she answered.

"Desperate people make desperate choices."

"Then why didn't he just stay?" Mother demanded. "Stay and inherit Landry Park and then administer whatever social changes he wanted to then? Why fake a death and then come back to claim his birthright?" She stood up. "I'm going to lie down. This day has already exhausted me."

"Mother?"

She stopped and turned, her dark eyes and dark hair lovely in the pale winter light. I thought of the night of Charlie's capture, of the flash of agreement I saw in her eyes. "Didn't you ever feel that Father was unjust? Didn't you ever wonder about the suffering of those around us?"

"Your father has always been just—it is what the Landrys pride themselves on." She answered quickly enough, but I could see her hands balled in her skirt. I stood and went to her, staying silent.

She pulled me into a fierce embrace, pressing my cheek against hers. I could feel the lingering tears on her face.

"I hope you never know what it is like to love a man like your father," she whispered. With a swift kiss, she left, the silk skirt of her dress making a pleasant swishing on the marble floor.

I stayed in the room, watching snow drift idly outside. That Mother loved Father, I had always known. But that she felt it a burden, I had never considered. Under her plum-colored dress, under the silk chemises and fragrant oils and lotions, beat a heart that I realized I barely knew.

Laughter echoed in the hallway—a girl's laughter—and a *shh!* noise that was followed by scuffling feet. Curious, I got up and walked into the hallway to see Cara pressed against the wall, kissing someone with ferocious intensity. Someone who was decidedly *not* David.

I gasped, and she heard me, breaking apart from her paramour.

"*Ewan?*" I asked, flabbergasted. "Cara? Why are you here?"

"Oh, I spent the night last night," she said, as if that answered all my questions.

"I should go," Ewan told Cara, and pressed his lips to her cheek. "Bye, love."

She smiled her stunning smile and moved her fingertips in a wave. "Good-bye."

Grinning, Ewan walked past me. "Cousin," he greeted me with a nod.

Shocked, I turned to Cara, waiting until Ewan was out of earshot before I erupted. "Cara, what on earth is going on? Ewan is Rootless! And you're dating David!"

"That did not stop you from kissing him yesterday in the park."

I blushed, ashamed and a little grateful that she didn't know about the other kiss. "I didn't mean for that to happen—we were scared and he was about to save Charlie and it took me by surprise," I tried to explain.

"Like I care." Cara started walking, and I scurried to walk beside her. "David told me himself after everything settled down. I can't believe it took this long, either. I would have gone for it ages ago if I were you."

"What?" I was so confused.

"Please. Did you think I was really dating David Dana?" she scoffed.

"Yes! You debuted with him. And at the Lodge, you kissed—"

"And other than that, how often did we kiss? Did we ever seem like we were madly in love?"

"While he was gone, you were so withdrawn. Everybody said you were heartbroken over David being in the mountains. I just assumed . . ."

"You assumed wrong." We stopped at a window and looked out at the snow. Ewan was trudging down the driveway, already covered in white dust. "Look, David came to me, okay? Last spring. He knew. He *knew*."

"He knew about what?" I watched her follow Ewan down the path with her eyes, and then the truth began to connect. "You and Ewan."

"David found out when he started meeting with Jack that Jack's son was in love with a gentry girl. We each had something the other needed. I needed him to keep his mouth shut about Ewan, and he needed the appearance of being a normal gentry boy. He needed to look happy and carefree, and I could help him with that. In public, of course, which ended up backfiring once Ewan heard that we were dating. You saw him at his house. I thought he was going to throw me into that laundry vat. He wrote me a letter telling me never to speak or write to him again. After that, I—I was upset. I didn't care about anything else if I didn't have Ewan."

Cara and Ewan. The idea was ridiculous, and yet it fit together with everything that had happened this year. "How did you meet?"

"The first time he came to change the Westoff charges, he couldn't find his way into the house, and we met face-to-face on the patio. I didn't realize he was Rootless at first because he was so healthy and strong. I thought he was a servant and I teased him a little about being so quiet. He told me that it was because he had heard I talked enough for an entire city. Then I dared him to kiss me."

"Did he?"

"Of course."

"Like that poor servant boy when we were girls."

She shrugged. "Ewan's the only person who has never treated me like a princess or a concubine. He made me feel strong. He made me feel like I could do anything I wanted." She sighed. "He made every boy that wasn't him seem frivolous and spoiled. After we ran into each other two or three more times on my estate, we started meeting in secret."

I struggled to imagine Ewan—the tense revolutionary, the angry rebel—falling in love with a spoiled girl like Cara. And Cara—who had never once expressed any sympathy for anyone less fortunate than her—how had she found herself craving the company of a charge changer?

She noticed my expression. "What?"

"It is just that you two . . . do not seem to have much in common," I said delicately.

Ewan was long gone, but Cara continued staring out the window, as if she had vision that could penetrate through all the snow and houses and trees that separated the sight of Ewan from her eyes. "You know, at first, I think we hated each other. There wasn't much, um, *conversing* when we were first meeting up, and neither of us wanted to talk about it or us or anything at all. And not only would I walk away resenting him, but I would feel ashamed of myself. All those things they tell us as children, about our responsibility to marry someone of good gentry stock, about how purity of breeding is what kept our world from sinking into another war—" She shook her head, brushing away the echoes of her memories. "I believed it my whole life. But there was nothing weak or craven about Ewan—not at all like how they describe the Rootless in school. He was strong and gentle and before I knew it, I wanted to do more than touch him. I wanted to know him. And you know what? I don't think anyone, not even one of his fellow Rootless, had ever wanted to know *him*. To them, he was a soldier. A strong body. But to me, he is so much more."

I felt a heaviness weigh on me as I thought of all the unfair things I'd thought—and said—about Cara. This whole year, she'd been risking everything to see the man she loved.

"So you were meeting secretly. And then you were going to see him at the Wilder debut. Wearing your pink coat."

"It was supposed to be easy," she said, suddenly flaring into emotion. "He took a friend's job that day to collect the Wilder charges. No one would miss me at the ball, and I had already hinted to a few people that I would be occupied with Philip Wilder. We would be able to spend a few moments alone together, while the rest of the city was occupied."

"What happened?"

Cara sat down on the bench under the window. When she looked up at me, her eyes were wet. "Mother."

"Addison?"

"She followed me. She had noticed that I'd been acting differently, sneaking out at strange times. She followed me to the grove and found me with Ewan." Tears clung to her eyelashes and dripped down her cheeks. "I made him run as soon as we heard footsteps, but he left his bag, and he still had my coat in his arms. . . . Mother was so angry. Said I was destroying my chances of having a healthy gentry heir. Said I was disgusting. That Ewan was vermin. She hit me, and I fell into the brambles nearby. She hit me again and again."

I shuddered. I couldn't imagine living with someone who had hurt me so viciously, who continued to hurt me afterward. And I couldn't believe that there were times when I had almost liked Addison, with her acerbic wit and keen observations. But then again, there were times when I loved my father, and he left lacerations of his own, even if they couldn't be seen.

"Cara . . ."

"I was too surprised to fight back, and then she left after I screamed, and you came. It all happened so fast. Your father was so intent on hunting down the Rootless, and the bag was right there and I knew my mother would . . ."

"But they could have hurt Ewan," I pointed out.

"I was hoping they wouldn't. There are so many other Rootless . . ."

"So it was okay if lots of innocent people got hurt as long as it was not the one you cared about?"

Her voice was fierce. "I'm sorry, okay? I didn't know what to do or what to say, and no matter what I did, my mother would be able stop it." She drew a shuddering breath.

I put my hand on hers.

She brushed a lock of hair away from her face, the tear tracks still glistening on her cheeks. "Ewan was furious that I lied, that I protected my mother. He wanted the whole world to know how corrupt and violent the gentry could be. He wanted to go to the constables or to your father. He knew that he would most likely be arrested, but he accepted that, too. In fact, he told me he would rather be arrested and killed than watch his people suffer."

"So why didn't he step forward?"

"Jack," she whispered. "He forbade Ewan to speak. He said

that the more the Rootless suffered at the hands of the gentry, the more it primed them for their great revolution. He said that it was a pain akin to a birthing pain and that the pain was necessary for a new world."

I saw with some surprise that my hand had tightened around Cara's; my fingers were white and bloodless.

An echoing clunking and shuffling announced Jack coming down the hallway, and Cara and I both started, dropping each other's hands. I swallowed back this new uneasiness and met his gaze with what I hoped was a composedly polite expression.

He smiled at Cara and me. "Hello, ladies," he said. "I see we are all relieved that yesterday's unpleasantness is over?"

"Yes," Cara said.

"My son seems especially happy," Jack mused. "I wonder why. Hmm."

"Jack?" I asked. "I was wondering if I could speak to you?"

"Of course," he rumbled.

I stood up and took his arm. "Miss Westoff," he said with a tilt of his head. She inclined her head in response. He steered me back south, the direction of the foyer.

"What would you like to talk about?"

"You."

We walked slowly to accommodate his limp.

"If I am not mistaken, you want to ask why I went to the trouble of running away and spending years among the Rootless planning a revolt with foreign help, only to come back to the very place I left."

Or why you let your people suffer to encourage their hatred of the gentry. Or why you let my father be maimed in the name of vengeance.

"You are very astute," I remarked instead.

"I have been accused of worse."

We passed the bust of Jacob Landry. Jack paused to examine him. "Madeline, may I ask what your first reaction was upon reading those journals?"

I thought for a moment. "Shock, I guess. Horror. Fear."

"Fear? That's interesting. Jacob Landry is dead. Why should you fear him?"

"I do not know." I thought back to two nights ago, trapped in my debut dress, trapped in my house, trapped in my father's will. "Except it seems sometimes like he is not really dead. Like his wishes still live on through my father and everyone who listens to my father."

"And in you?"

In me? I wanted to object, but when I considered it, I'd spent my life doing nothing to help the Rootless, and even after seeing the sorting yards and meeting and befriending them, I'd still taken the first chance at a Landry life when my father offered it. That fear then—could it be the fear of becoming like my father? Like Jacob?

"You see," Jack said, turning away from the statue, "I had

been meeting with the Rootless for a few years before I read those journals. Something tugged at me watching them. I knew something was wrong. My father crushed them tighter and tighter in his fist, killing more and more, and it never seemed to satisfy him. It was never enough to make him feel safe, and the funny thing was that I never felt safe either.

"No matter how many women I bedded or how much wine I drank, I felt as if this life were tenuous. Precious. It all hung on a delicate thread, and sometimes, I found myself secretly grateful for my father's tenacious hatred. I was like you, Madeline, and David, too. I wanted my comfortable life and a comfortable conscience. I could decide on neither."

We were in the ballroom now, the wall of windows and glass doors giving a breathtaking vista of the snowbound world.

"And then you read Jacob's journals," I guessed.

"Quite right. And I felt everything that you felt. Especially the fear." He flicked a switch on the wall, and the solar heaters began melting the snow on the patio. "Especially the fear."

"You see, I could feel everything that Jacob felt. Disgust for the helpless. Lust for power. For money."

"But he was inhuman," I said, shaking my head vigorously. "You are completely different—" But then I stopped myself. I didn't know if Jack was completely different. Not anymore.

"Don't make a caricature of him," Jack said. "Jacob was passionate about many things. His family. Science. When you read the journals looking for the man and not the legend, you will see it. He doubted himself, and he doubted his inventions. He could have made any number of choices, even after the Last War. What makes him cruel is that he continued to choose abuse and power, despite his doubts. Even when he could have turned back."

"You were not going to make the same mistake."

Jack nodded. "Quite right. I felt acutely aware of his blood in my veins, of his genes shaping my mind and my emotions. I was made of the same stuff and surrounded by the same temptations, so how could I hope to choose differently? If I were in charge of Landry Park and the leader of the Uprisen, I feared I would never leave Jacob's legacy behind. So I removed myself from the estate, and chose a new name, and in doing so, committed myself to the maintenance of my conscience. I have never regretted it."

"So why now?"

"An excellent question." Small lakes formed in the snow, forcing tiny rivers of icy water down the steps. "I had felt for years that we needed a true uprising. With the help of the Empire and with much careful planning, I felt we could succeed and hopefully with minimal loss of Rootless life. After all, what army would dare fight the Empire for long? With them as allies, we could finally shake off the yoke of the gentry. But your father forced my hand. He had Charlie, and I damn well was not going to wait for a foreign army to stop him. My first instinct was to have my people attack, to pretend submission and then swarm the terrace at the last instant. It would, of course, have little likelihood of working, and would probably result in many deaths, and war for the whole country, if the Empire belatedly came to our aid.

"But then David messaged me on the tablet I had been given by the Empire. He was coming to help. We might have a chance to stop the execution and overwhelm your father. But how to stop him from striking back at us? From hunting Charlie again? And punishing you and David? And then it occurred to me that I *did* have the legal power to stop him, still, after all these years, thanks to the gentry's foolish obsession with birth order."

Chunks of snow were sliding off the patio now, carried by the water underneath like icebergs, revealing the platinum symbol below.

"Do I possess the self-control I feared I lacked as a younger man? That remains to be seen, but now I have children who are Rootless, and one may hope that one's children's well-being is a sufficient incentive."

Jamie approached us, and Jack fell silent. "Madeline, can we talk?" Jamie asked. "It's about your father."

THIRTY-FOUR

Jack, who was feeling stiff from the cold, opted to stay downstairs, but Jamie and I climbed up to Father's room. Inwardly, I prepared myself for the sight of his ugly wounds, but it was unnecessary—clean white bandages had been wrapped around the lower half of his face. He was tucked under several blankets and surrounded by black beeping machines that showed diagnostic interfaces of all his body's systems. A nurse in white nodded at us and left the room.

"Jamie? What is this about? Is Father okay?"

"Yes. More than okay, actually."

Jamie walked up to one of the machines and pulled up a screen showing three-dimensional DNA strands, spiraling slowly like a ribbon in the breeze.

"This is your father's DNA. When we ran tests on his cells to determine if any had become cancerous, not only did we find no trace of pre-cancer, but we saw a type of DNA that we had never seen before." He zoomed in on part of the strand, and used his finger to highlight part of it. "I don't know what it is, but it's seamlessly grafted onto the rest of his genetic code. And what is more, we found that the DNA was repairing itself."

"Is that strange?"

"DNA repair happens every second of every day—repair from toxins and UV rays and the like. But repair at this speed and efficiency from a radiation injury so severe? I have never heard of anything like it."

"Does this mean that he will make a complete recovery?" I asked. "Does this mean he will be healthy again?"

Jamie shook his head. "I don't know. I'm going to ask to use the university's laboratory to examine this further. It's fascinating. I wish there were still geneticists who could help us, but I don't know of any, not around here in any case."

I sat on the bed and stared at Father. I wondered if he knew about his strange DNA, and if he knew that he was going to be all right. That some strange mechanism that lived within his cells was going to save his life.

I held up my hand, pale and slender in the faint light, and examined it. I shared the Landry name and looks with Father. What else did we share?

The next week, Father and Mother were removed to the Lodge, along with several nurses and equipment to help in Father's convalescence. Father was sedated and placed on a gurney. When they loaded him into the ambulance, I realized that I couldn't see his mouth under the bandages and had no way to see if he was healing as well as Jamie claimed.

I kissed his forehead and sent him on his way with as many good wishes as I could muster.

Mother opted for the limousine. I hugged her good-bye.

"Your father and I will be back," she said, wrapping her fur coat more tightly around herself. "Once your father wakes and regains his strength, Landry Park will belong to him once more. The Uprisen will never acknowledge Jack as their leader."

"Maybe," I said. She looked around the house one last time and sniffed in disapproval. I watched their car leave with a mixture of regret and relief.

But I knew she was right. Jack had plans, of course. Plans to pay the Rootless fair wages and give them legal rights. Plans for hospitals and schools. Plans to build solar panels and wind turbines. Plans that sounded idyllic and utopian, but made me wonder if they were going to be subsidized with blood and suffering.

And now that the Empire had all but revealed their alliance to the Rootless outright, I knew it wouldn't be easy. The government would never stand for a revolt funded by the Empire and the Uprisen would never stand for an attack on their way of life.

Rumors began to swirl of tanks and plans on the other side of the mountains. Jack seemed certain that it was all for our benefit, but I could not summon up the same confidence. I could only remember the horrible pictures from the battle last year.

"We will prevail," he said one night at dinner. "Perhaps within a few months, this city will change. And when it changes, the country will see how much better things can be."

Nobody else at the table was listening. Cara and Ewan were whispering and nuzzling at one end, while Charlie was drawing a picture at the other, his tongue sticking out in concentration. Despite a dip in his exuberance and a certain twitchiness in response to sudden noises, he seemed okay. He was alive. Now Cara and Ewan were tracing each other's features, as if they'd never seen a thing as wondrous as a face before. Jealousy pinged inside me.

"Excuse me," I said. "I think I'm tired."

"Go rest. We have been very busy these past two weeks."

I set down my napkin and left the dining room for the staircase. Someone stepped out of the shadows and bowed. My heart lifted. *David.*

But it was Jude, smiling and square-jawed and dashing, but Jude all the same. He offered an arm and I took it. In the insanity of the past fortnight, I had forgotten about my debut, about his determination to marry me and have me be his perfect military wife.

"Sorry for the surprise, but I wanted to speak to you alone. Just for a minute."

"Of course."

We walked up the stairs, our footsteps muffled on the lush carpet.

"David told me that you and he had kissed."

I stopped. "Oh, Jude."

"And that he had feelings for you."

"I am so sorry," I said. "I never meant to lie to you."

Jude shrugged, but I could see the pain in his face. "I won't pretend that it doesn't hurt. I had thought, at least, I had hoped—" and here his fingers found my ring finger. "I would have been a good husband, you know," he said softly. "Anything you wanted, I would have given to you. Anything." He leaned in and kissed my hand, his lips warm and dry.

A curious sense of regret tugged at me, along with the feeling I had when I first met him, of having known him before. Maybe I had been wrong in thinking he only wanted me for a partner in his ambition. Maybe he did really care for me.

I swallowed something I didn't know was in my throat, feeling my chin quiver.

"Go get your coat," he said, indicating my bedroom. "I will wait here."

"Why should I get my coat?"

He smiled, a real smile, even though it was thin and small. "Because we are going outside and I'd like to keep my cloak on this time."

Once I was clad in my coat, Jude led me downstairs and outside, where, in the light of a Cherenkov lantern hanging from the front of the house, David sat in a large sleigh. Two horses stomped impatiently in the front.

"Madeline!" David said cheerfully. "I've got enough sake to float this sleigh to St. Louis."

"I forgot my gloves inside," Jude said, and disappeared back through the door.

David jumped easily out of the seat and came toward me. "Did he mention . . ."

I nodded, unable to bring myself to talk about it directly.

David looked downcast. "I had to tell him. We don't keep secrets from each other."

It seemed to me like Jude had kept my debut a secret from David for long enough, but if male relationships were anywhere near as complicated as the relationships I had with the women in my life, then I knew loyalty could coexist with doubt and omissions and outright lies.

"I understand." David reached for me, and I couldn't help it, I reached for him, too. His lips were just as warm, just as searching as they had been the other day in the park, and the same white fire as before lapped at everything with insatiable flames.

"Why didn't you tell me?" I asked hoarsely. "About Cara?"

His eyes dipped. "It was not my secret to tell. I could not risk another soul knowing that our relationship was fake. Initially it was to protect me, but then I began to suspect the truth about her attack."

"Addison," I said, remembering her pointed words in the parlor at the Lodge. So that's why David had kissed Cara like that. To protect her from a second incarnation of Addison's wrath.

"I couldn't let her hurt Cara again." David kissed me again, softer, his lips light as snowflakes on my cheeks and nose. "But you have to know how much it pained me."

"Cara said that you wanted someone to help you seem normal, a girl to complete the gentry bachelor lifestyle." I looked down at the snow swirling around his black shoes. "Why Cara? Why not me? I am rich, I come from a good family; I mean, I am a—"

"—Landry," David finished for me. "You are a Landry. And I did not know I could trust you until the day you met Jack, and even after that, there were times I was not sure. You have no idea how like your father you are. Not only in the way you look, but in the way you carry yourself, the way you radiate ambition."

"I am not ambitious," I protested.

He traced my lower lip with his finger. "You are. You are full of this . . . zeal. And I could never tell what that zeal was for. Was it for the gentry? Or for something else?"

He tilted my face toward his, and I could feel the bite of the frost-scented breeze on my upturned face.

"You were not like any gentry girl I'd ever met. You were sharper, more perceptive. You were like looking through a telescope at the galaxies. I felt dizzy and small just seeing you. I wanted nothing more than you, which was terrifying, because I spent most of my time vacillating between what I wanted for my own life."

"To be gentry or Rootless."

"It is over now," he breathed. "I do not have to wonder any more. About myself. About you."

I slid my hands around his face. "No more ambivalence."

His lips touched mine as he spoke. "No more lies," he promised.

The cold air nipped at the heat between us as we separated just in time for Jude to emerge with his gloves.

Jude helped me into the sleigh, and then climbed in himself, his hand squeezing mine one last time before he let go. David hopped in the other side, all energetic bounce again.

"The Rootless and the working class are calling us heroes," Jude said, settling into the furs and blankets. "All three of us."

"Still don't believe me about modern-day knights?" David asked me.

"I'll believe it when I have a statue next to Jacob Landry's."

Jude offered me a flask of wine. "Then I will make sure that happens."

"And I will make sure that it's a full body statue. Maybe naked," David said, taking the reins.

Snowflakes appeared out of clouds so thin and transparent they could barely be seen, and David used his thumb to wipe them from my face. With the skyline glassy and lit up behind us, and the stars glittering above us, David urged the horses forward, and we rode south together.

And even though I knew it would be beautiful, covered in snow and ice, bathed in starlight, tall and majestic in the face of upheaval and heartbreak, I didn't look back as we drove away from Landry Park.

ACKNOWLEDGMENTS

First of all, I want to thank my incomparable agent Mollie Glick for taking a chance on my book when it still needed lots of love. Your sharp eye and keen business sense have been my life raft through this entire process. Thank you.

A huge thank you to Nancy Conescu, who is kind and wise like Glinda the Good Witch. You knew this book better than I did—you knew what it needed and what it didn't need any longer. Thank you for your patience and insight.

To the entire Penguin team, especially Stacey Friedberg and Courtney Allison. You are the brilliant people who do brilliant things. To Kristin Smith, for making the most mouthwateringly gorgeous cover imaginable. And to Kathleen Hamblin, another ray of brilliance. You guys deserve all the chocolate in the world.

To Gennifer Albin for the hard words and practical advice and 2:00 A.M. pancakes; to Robyn Lucas for the cheerleading and marketing help and plot fixes; to Laura Rahimi Barnes for all the honest encouragement and the late night G-Chats, and most of all, for being my book fairy. To the WrAHMs: there has never been a wilder, funnier, smarter group of lady writers out there, and I am so honored to be among your number. To Lucy Stark, Melanie Harlow, and Tamara Mataya, this table flip is for you.

To Ashley, for all the free babysitting and encouragement and for hiding from imaginary bears with me when we were on a mountain in Albuquerque. To Denise, for the beautiful author photo. To the Bu, for reading my baby novels in high school and college. To Alyssa, Jill, and Amanda, who keep me well adjusted, and to all of my colleagues at the Johnson County Library—you make being a librarian fun.

To my grandparents: John, Kay, Ed, and Sandra—your nurturing presence has allowed me to thrive. To Kathie and Milt Taylor, for constant babysitting and support; to Dana Hagen and Eddy Bisceglia, for all the love. To Renee Bisceglia, who took me to the Central Resource Library as a girl and let me check out more books than I could carry. To Doug Hagen, who took the time to read to me every night and who told me to make the Hagen name proud.

To Noah and Teagan, who stayed up late to give me hugs and kisses after I came home from "writing stories." And most of all to Josh, who never let me quit, who always believed in me, and who brought me snacks and beer and *Doctor Who* when it was needed. I wouldn't be writing this if it weren't for you.

ONE

It was the shouts that caught my attention.

I had been looking over the menu for tonight's dinner—roast goose and lobster—when I heard the noise come from outside, where the gardeners had been rolling heavy solar heaters into place and shoveling snow off the wide gravel walks. Curious, I went through the ballroom to the patio doors, hoping to find the source of the commotion.

For the first time in the month since I'd stood up to my father at Liberty Park, the estate bustled with activity. On my way through the ballroom, I passed servants carrying fresh bundles of flowers, neatly pressed linens, crates of long white candles for the candelabras and chandeliers. I made a quick mental note of the progress as I walked, trying to calculate how much more still needed to be done. The dinner my uncle and I were hosting tonight was to welcome the Rootless and the gentry together, to try and demonstrate goodwill on both sides. How well the Rootless would adapt to sharing a table with their oppressors remained to be seen, but I felt hopeful that tonight would be a turning point.

Tonight was important.

The men were gesturing emphatically to one another, and I could hear them arguing even before I opened the glass doors that led outside. A rush of cold damp air hit me, cutting through the filmy silk dress I wore. "What's going on?" The frigid air made my voice unusually sharp. I took a breath and changed my tone to something softer, more polite. "I heard the shouts. Is everything okay?"

One of the men, the head gardener, touched his hat respectfully. "Good afternoon, Miss Landry. There's really nothing going on here, just an unexpected complication."

But I'd already stepped out onto the patio, shivering, snow soaking through my thin slippers, and now I could see what the men were concerned about: an ugly red stain in the snow, right on top of where the platinum atomic symbol was inlaid into the stone.

"We were clearing off the patio," he said, "and we noticed a heap of snow in the middle. We started shoveling and found this."

"It looks like blood," someone said.

"It looks like a *lot* of blood," another added.

I came forward to examine the stain closer. It did indeed look like blood, a vivid crimson that eerily matched the color of my hair. Darker in the middle and surrounded by bright splatters, the stain was large and deep. When a gardener used his shovel to scrape away a section, the snowmelt lingered in scarlet puddles on the patio.

The wind picked up again, ruffling my hair, and the scent of something metallic and salty blew with it. "Do you think this means that someone is hurt? Have any of the servants reported injuries?" I asked.

The head gardener shook his head. "None of the staff has been hurt. And it would be difficult to hide a wound that produced that much blood."

"Could it have been an animal?" I asked. "Maybe a fox or a wild dog cornered something." I felt a flutter of fear as I thought of my cat, Morgana, who habitually wandered outside.

"But then where's the rest of it? No carcass, no bones. Not even a trail showing where it had been dragged off." The gardener shook his head, and I relaxed a little. "No. Whatever bled here was *carried* off and then great pains were taken to cover the blood back up. A person did this, Miss Landry."

I took quick stock of the patio. Four gardeners, two solar heaters, and various assorted shovels, spades, and ice picks. Muddy bootprints were everywhere, mostly leading from the south side of the property where they'd been clearing the garden, and one leading from the east side, where the gardening shed abutted the carriage house. Ignoring the head gardener's noise of protest, I walked around the blood and down the steps, the snow scraping against my bare legs as I sank in up to my knees. At the bottom, I could see no footprints other than those that clearly belonged to the gardeners. There was no disturbed snow on the lawn, no trace of blood anywhere else. It was as if whatever—no, *whomever*—had bled into the snow had then simply vanished.

I trudged back up to the gardeners. "How long since the patio's last been cleared?" I asked.

"The night of your debut," he said.

That made sense. That was the night before I'd confronted Father and everything had changed. "So it's been a month," I said. "Could this could have been here since then and no one would have noticed?"

He shook his head. "Someone would have seen it, surely. And besides, it snowed last night, and the snow piled on top of the stain was freshly disturbed. It must have happened today."

The thought made me intensely uncomfortable. Mere hours ago, someone had spilled what appeared to be torrents of blood right outside the ballroom of the most important estate in the entire city, and no one had noticed. Had someone been mutilated? Killed?

Please let no one have been hurt, I begged the fading sky. *Please, please, please, no more, no more blood, no more pain.*

I thought back to my father, bloodied and hands knotting in pain, when he'd been rescued from the Rootless mob at Liberty Park.

And along with the thought came a stab of fear—a rapier prick of fear really—sharp and small and gone in an instant.

"Should we tell your uncle?" the gardener asked.

I shook off the images of violence and savagery that crowded at the edges of my mind. "I'll get him," I said. I left the gardeners shuffling uncomfortably and went back inside to find my uncle, my slippers leaving wet footprints on the floor.

I hated having to disturb Jack with anything tonight. The events at Liberty Park, along with the shocking and painful revelation that Jack was actually my father's assumed-dead brother, had left the city in chaos and had naturally left the gentry uneasy. There was so much work to be done and tonight was a new beginning. He needed to focus and prepare as much as possible.

And, if I admitted it to myself, there was another reason I felt reluctant to tell him about the mysterious discovery. Something had been different about him in the past four weeks, a fanaticism that nestled inside his rumbling words. It made me wary, but we were so close to achieving all that we'd worked for, so close to actual change, that I felt reluctant to give the small anxieties in my mind any credence.

Jack was in my father's study when I found him. He was reading, as he often did these days, having been deprived of access to books when he lived in the Rootless ghetto. He snapped the book shut when he saw me. "Madeline. How are the preparations for the dinner coming along?"

For a moment, his resemblance to Father was overwhelming, and something tightened in my chest. "There's something on the patio you need to see," I said.

He got to his feet, leaving his cane leaning against the desk. We walked back through the ballroom, where servants rolled tables laden with fresh flowers and empty silver platters in from the kitchen elevator. Savory scents and sweet smells wafted up from downstairs, and already Crawford, the butler, was laying out bottles of wine from the cellar. The sun was dipping low outside. I would have to go upstairs soon to change and have Elinor fix my hair.

Jack opened the doors and we both stepped back outside, me wishing that I would have thought to get a cloak and him showing no sign that he even noticed the cold. The creases in his face deepened as his eyes lit upon the blood, and they grew deeper and deeper as he interviewed the gardeners, listening to the same answers I had heard not five minutes ago.

"Should we alert the constables?" I asked when he finished.

He stared at the western horizon, where oranges and pinks and purples mingled together and glanced off the sparkling snow. "The guests will be here in a couple of hours. And we're not even sure that a crime has been committed."

"But surely the police could identify it as blood for certain? And maybe there's somebody in the city who's been hurt and the constables are looking for any possible leads, and—"

Jack held up a hand. "I'm not ignoring this, Madeline. But we have important work to do here tonight and I don't want it interrupted by something that's probably inconsequential."

"They could come and take a couple of pictures, maybe a

sample and then leave," I insisted. "In and out before the party even starts."

Jack met my gaze, determined gray eyes on determined gray eyes, and I managed to keep the eye contact until he finally exhaled and shrugged. "Fine. We'll call the constables. But I will make it clear that they need to be quick. My people will not take kindly to seeing the police roaming the estate, not after all the violence of the past year."

"I understand," I said. "And thank you."

He nodded at me. "Finish clearing everything else," he told the men. "But save the patio until after the constables have looked at it." He looked at me one last time before leaving. One by one, the men filed off the patio, grabbing their shovels and picks.

I stood there for a minute longer, my breath steaming, absorbed by the bloody snow. It seemed like a portent, like a warning out of a fairy tale, but for what? Things couldn't be better right now. The Rootless and the gentry would meet tonight, converse and mingle and actually learn about each other. My father had been removed from power. And David— my cheeks warmed as I thought of Captain David Dana and his bright blue eyes and sharp smile.

And I had David. Things were good.

I went upstairs, where I found Morgana curled into a silver ball on my bed. I rubbed behind her ears for a moment, glad to see her alive and clearly unharmed, and then started to change for dinner.

Elinor had already laid out my gown, a flowing chiffon of mint green with a wide sash and a short train. I wanted something understated, something that wouldn't seem too opulent to the Rootless, but also something that wouldn't seem cheap or boring to the gentry, who already didn't trust me after what happened in Liberty Park. I wanted to show them that I was still a Landry, that I still had a foot in their world, and that trying to help the Rootless didn't negate any of that.

As Elinor pinned up my hair, sliding antique hairpins into the mass of waves with almost unnerving focus, I watched the blue lights of the constables' cars flash across the windows. I wondered what they would make of the stain, and if they would try to analyze the blood or search for someone who was missing or hurt, and if they could find any other clues as to who did it.

I tried to shake the worries and fears out of my thoughts, but they clung to me like wet leaves, cold and unwelcome. What if someone were truly hurt? What if they were still hurting?

Stop, I told myself. I was overreacting, on edge from the violent events this winter. Jack seemed to think it was nothing, and if that wasn't the case, then the constables would be able to help. I had to focus on making tonight a success.

With a murmured *thanks* to Elinor, I rose from my vanity and went downstairs. The evening was beginning, whether I was ready for it or not.

TWO

Jack and I stood in the foyer to welcome the guests, my gown affording very little protection from the gusts of freezing air that circled through the house whenever the front doors opened. The Rootless contingent was the first to arrive, and I felt some dismay at their small number—less than twenty in all.

"So few," I murmured to Jack as they filed in through the door, looking uncomfortable and wary. "Did we invite more?"

"I invited them all," Jack said. He licked his lips as he looked down at the floor. "I am sure the reasons for refusal are varied."

There was something he wasn't saying. Rather than ask, I waited—a tactic I'd learned from my father.

"Many of them feel that we should not move forward with a formalized agreement with the gentry," Jack finally said, and his quiet voice made it plain that this was a difficult admission for him. "Only a handful see the wisdom in working together. Some have even gone as far as to suggest that I've had a gentry agenda all along, being both a Landry and a son of the Uprisen."

The Uprisen was the small influential group within the gentry that set legal policy and government agendas behind the scenes; only the oldest and wealthiest families counted themselves members. My ancestor Jacob Landry had been the founder of the Uprisen, and my entire life I'd been groomed to take a seat at the table with the other eleven families. So had Jack—before he'd faked his own death and forged a new place for himself among the Rootless.

"Things were easier when my identity was unknown," he said.

"I can imagine."

The group finished coming in, and we greeted them, me signaling to the servants to circulate around the guests with hors d'oeuvres and small flutes of champagne, which the Rootless seemed reluctant to take. Instead, they clustered together at the far end of the foyer, looking to Jack for reassurance.

A scowling man with slouching shoulders and darting eyes hung near the back. I was surprised to see him: Smith, the angry revolutionary who had once yanked me through a window by my hair. Jack had helped the other Rootless find gentry-style clothes, tuxedos for the men and gowns for the women, but Smith had refused. He still defiantly wore his Rootless clothes, patched brown pants and a tattered gray shirt.

He, of all the Rootless, was the most resistant to working with the gentry. Why had he even come?

Eyeing Smith, I moved across the marble floor to speak with the Rootless, to encourage them to make themselves at home. Most of them smiled at me, most of them shook my hand and thanked me for standing up for them in Liberty Park, but not him. He moved right past me as if I didn't even exist.

"I thought there was going to be dinner," Smith said to Jack, glancing around the foyer with barely contained revulsion.

"It's traditional for guests to mill in the foyer before dinner starts," Jack said pleasantly. "It gives a chance for conversation." What Jack didn't mention was that he didn't want anybody to see the constables packing up their things and leaving the patio. Better to keep the guests safely ensconced until he was certain that they had gone.

Smith walked closer, but he didn't bother lowering his voice. "You're turning into one of them," he said. "Why are we even here? Alexander Landry is driven out and you have control. Can't you force the Uprisen to change?"

"Not without a fight," I broke in. "If you push them, there will be more violence, maybe even war—"

"A war that we would win," Smith said over me.

"—And that war would only hurt your own people and your own cause," I continued.

"She's right," Jack said. "After all, without Alexander to lead them, the gentry may feel it's in their best interest to negotiate. We have our proposals, our demands. We will ask for the gentry to switch to a safer power source—wind or solar—and they will see the irrefutable logic in that." His voice did not ring with confidence, and Smith's curling lip indicated that he noticed this.

"At the very least," Jack amended, "we try this first."

I turned to Jack. I didn't like the way he said *try this first*, as if this attempt at diplomacy was something to be scratched off a list, a perfunctory task to attempt before moving on to the real solution. And I worried that for people like Smith, the real solution would always be one of rubble and ashes.

Of blood.

But before I could say anything else, he stepped close to Jack and said, "The time for negotiation was two centuries ago. I don't want their money or their handouts. I want a world where the gentry are no more. Now, do you have the spine to see a plan through or not?"

"Smith, now's not the time."

"No, it wouldn't be. Not in front of your new friends," Smith snarled.

He stalked off and Jack cleared his throat. "He can be a little hotheaded," he said mildly.

"A little?"

The door opened once more and I turned, hoping to see David, and only barely masking my disappointment when I saw it wasn't him. The Wilder family looked faintly uncomfortable with the Rootless nearby, but when Jack stuck out his hand, Mr. Wilder shook it, only hesitating a moment. I beamed at him. The stigma against touching the skin of a Rootless person was so strong that I'm embarrassed to say it had once prevented me from helping a very sick girl. If someone as important as Clarence Wilder was willing to shake hands with the leader of the Rootless, that was a very good sign.

Mr. Wilder looked up and met Jack's gaze as he shook hands. "Thank you for inviting us," he said. His gaze slid over Jack and me, and I knew he was remembering the countless times he'd shaken hands with my father, the times he'd kissed my mother's cheek and patted my head. Landry Park without my parents—especially my father—was still a strange thing to the gentry. It was still a strange thing to me.

"It's good to see you again, Clarence." Jack's familiarity was surprising to me, but it shouldn't be—after all, he'd been the heir to Landry Park once, and men like Mr. Wilder used to be his peers.

Philip, the Wilders' son and heir, gave me a tight hug. He smelled like fresh laundry with just a whiff of Scotch. Although I'm not a demonstrative person, I hugged him back. We'd spent a lot of time together over the last year when our fathers had taught us how to run our estates, and I liked to imagine that we were friends.

"Where's your sister?" I asked him. Marianne wasn't the type to miss a party.

"She's coming later, but she's probably still off with Mark Everly. We were both planning on going over to his house this morning, but I ended up staying home instead—he's got a cold and I wasn't interested in catching it."

"So he won't be here tonight?"

"Marianne will have to come alone; what a hardship." He rolled his eyes, but his voice softened when he added, "We're expecting an engagement any day now. Speaking of missing guests, where's Captain Dana? And Miss Westoff?"

"Cara is upstairs with my cousin Ewan. They'll be down any moment. And Captain Dana will be here shortly." *I hope*.

Philip straightened his cuffs, silver links gleaming against the white fabric, the fabric striking against his dark skin. "So, the idea is that we're supposed to mingle with these people?"

"The idea is to find common ground," I said. "They're the same as us. They just don't want to live in fear or pain any longer. I think we can all relate."

Philip's mouth quirked. "I guess. But what do I even talk about with them?"

"Use your natural charm. There are two girls our age over there."

"Now *that* is common ground." He winked at me and then whisked a couple of champagne flutes off a silver tray, walking over and presenting them to the young Rootless women. They accepted with giggles.

When Jane Osbourne came in, I didn't wait for her to walk

over to greet me. I met her right at the door, unable to keep a smile from my face. Jane's mother was one of the Uprisen, and Jane and I had been close friends since we were girls. She was one of the few sensible people I could number among my acquaintances, and she and I had spent many dances and dinners in quiet conversation while the others socialized and drank. She gave me a warm hug and looked around the room.

"I can't believe you managed to get Rootless and gentry together in the same room." Her genial expression flickered as she caught sight of Philip charming the Rootless girls.

"I asked him to be a gentry ambassador," I said, recognizing that look. Philip was a bit of a flirt, but he was talking to those girls at my behest, so I felt partly responsible for Jane's discomfort.

"Oh, of course," Jane said, equanimity restored in an instant. "I'm glad to see that at least a few of the guests are off to a friendly start."

"Please, help yourself to some drinks and food. I'm on greeting duty."

Jane nodded, her dark curls bouncing gracefully against her long neck. *Philip better notice what he's missing*, I thought as she walked off with her parents. I liked him, but Jane was undoubtedly the best girl in this city.

More gentry arrived, but still no David. I discreetly pulled my tablet out of my deep dress pocket and checked to see if he'd called or messaged. He hadn't.

READ THE ROMANTIC, DYSTOPIAN DUET!